Love on a Limb

A GREAT EXPECTATIONS LOVE STORY

The Graykens, Book 1

LAURIE LEWIS

WILLOWSPORT PRESS

Love *on a* Limb

A GREAT EXPECTIONS LOVE STORY
The Graykens, Book 1

By Laurie Lewis

Copyright ©2017 by Laurie Lewis
ISBN-13: 978-0-9972041-6-2
Published 2017 by Willowsport Press,
an imprint of JATA Inc.
Mount Airy, MD 21771
Cover design by Keslie Houser
www.laurielclewis.com

FOREWORD

Readers so embraced Matt and Mikaela's story, and were so convincing in their requests for sequels, and in their suggestions for those sequels, that I decided to build off Matt's company name—Great Expectations—and create a series of romances and love stories about the Graykens, and the people whose dreams they help bring to life.

LOVE ON A LIMB is book one and will be followed by part two of Matt and Mikaela's story in the fall of 2018. Here's a bit about the story behind their story, Love on a Limb.

The tension in romance comes from the struggle to overcome the obstacles separating people. Death is arguably the greatest obstacle, or it should, at least, make the top ten list. *Love on a Limb* is the story of two good people in the crucible of an extraordinary medical trial—leukemia—and how that experi-ence changed them and their ability to maintain promises made to one another.

I wanted to add some interesting twists on this age-old struggle between life and death and love and faith. Some of the most exquisite elements in the story were inspired by real life stories. I think they'll completely capture your heart, make you laugh, and send you to the tissue box a few times.

I was interviewing a dear friend named Michelle—a WWII survivor of the German bombing campaigns and occu-pation of France—for an upcoming novel, The Letter Carrier,(2019). Michelle's daughter, Beatrice, came to the interviewsand proved to be an incredible research help and translator of old documents. It was a strange, small-world moment. I told her I was currently working on *Love on a Limb,* about a couple's battle with leukemia, when Beatrice shared that she had fought a battle with leukemia when her son was diag-nosed. Like her mother's telling of WWII stories, this brave lady shared her own medical war stories about her battle to save her son's life. She taught me about cow shares, AHCC, and so many details. I hope I was able to capture what she taught me—the courage, joy, strength, creativity, and tenacity love brings to such a fight.

Other sweet elements in *Love on a Limb* were inspired by two friends who shared a great love story. When the husband found out he was dying, he arranged to have flowers sent to his wife on their anniversary for the rest of her life. I tweaked that idea, and turned it into Mikaela's plan to inspire Matt, and Matt's plan for Mikaela. I hope you love these little details as much as I do.   Laurie Lewis

For Tom, whose love
always pulls me back in.

1

The sheer audaciousness of the mission Matthew Murray Grayken was about to embark upon exceeded the thrill of riding Chile's white-water roller coaster—The Terminator—and loomed more soul-satisfying than skydiving over Dubai's man-made archipelago, Palm Jumeirah.

Matt Grayken was about to ask a total stranger to marry him.

He pulled the pocket square from his Brooks Brothers jacket and wiped his sweaty palms, staining the unforgiving silk. It, and the nerve-soaked suit would need to go to the cleaners now. He pulled his phone out to add that task to his packed schedule, then stopped, chagrined, and put the device away. The task could wait.

The cause of the day's mission amplified the ever-present lump in his throat. He returned his focus to the woman with the nametag that read Mikaela Compton. She was the embodiment of compassion that served those on the other end of the room. Her peace washed over him again as it always did when he watched her from afar. He loved the way she leaned in when speaking to someone, beginning and ending each encounter with a caring smile and a touch. Compassion beamed from brown eyes that crinkled when she turned a sober moment to laughter, as she did nearly every minute as she joked with patients and cheered their progress at each station.

From the first day that chance allowed him to see her, only recalling her soft brown eyes, that smile, and those gentle hands could calm him as he lie awake, shivering from night sweats, staring at the ceiling. In order to see her, he moved all his future appointments to the last slot when it was easier to linger, soaking up more of her optimism and hope. And then he decided to shoot for the moon and propose to her, a total stranger.

Matt waited for her to check on the patient nearest to him, and then he cleared his throat and said, "May I ask you a question?"

She moved to him with a dancer's grace, her brown hair bouncing within a tousled lump atop her head, as if she had gathered it while turning a somersault. Somehow the way the stray pieces fell seemed elegant, perfect, stylish around her delicate, unadorned face. He waited for it, and then it came, the caring lean-in followed by a gentle hand on his shoulder and that smile that warmed his chills away.

"I'm not your oncologist's nurse, but I'll try."

Matt imagined what it would be like to hold her close, to fill his arms with her comfort, and then he realized how long he'd paused, soaking in the humanity she offered in a place of plastic and poison.

He lowered his voice to a whisper. "Actually, I . . . uh . . . I have a . . . uh . . . a proposition for you."

He cringed. His smooth, well-practiced proposal fled from his mind leaving that crude string of words in its place. He waited for her to slap him or, worse, to turn on her heel and leave.

"A proposition?" A momentary show of skepticism erupted into a sunburst of pleasure that illuminated her face. She placed her hands on her hips, tipped her head askew, and offered him a wondering scowl. "You're the third one today, and I have to warn you, you're up against some tough competition." She pointed down the row of chemo stations to a bald older man and his smiling wife, who were intently listening to the exchange. "Mr. and Mrs. Davenport keep me stocked in fresh vegetables from their garden on the chance I'll let them adopt me. Isn't that right?" The Davenports supported her claim enthusiastically.

"And Mr. Fitzhugh whistles, 'I Love You Truly' to me every appointment, and calls me his best girl."

A rail-thin arm raised and waved to her. Nurse Compton shot the man a smile and turned back to Matt with a playful shrug. "What can I say? They've set the bar pretty high." She gave Matt's shoulders a pat, followed by another of her thousand-watt smiles, dismissing with grace and caring what he assumed was another of a hundred daily come-ons.

She turned to go, and Matt reached for her hand, brushing his fingers over her skin. She turned, as if sensing something different in this exchange which likewise restored feelings long dormant in Matt. "Dinner then?" he asked.

Their eyes locked as she studied him, weighing the invitation. "It's not allowed. Nurses can't date patients."

He was prepared for this response. "The administrators agreed to bend the rules . . . for a substantial donation. But I know you have a class at six, so we could go after—"

She jerked her hand back. "How'd you—"

Guilt flooded Matt at being the cause of the sun's eclipse. He knew she was different. This was not a woman who would enjoy being scoped out and studied. He wanted to kick himself. "I'm sorry . . . I . . . I overheard you telling the other nurses."

The tension in her face and shoulders eased, but did not disperse. From behind her he heard two of the other nurses whistling a tune he couldn't immediately identify. It clearly had meaning for Nurse Compton. She shot a scathing glance over her shoulder at them, but the volume only increased, and her scolding slipped into a smile before stiffening again, giving Matt's hope renewed footing.

"What are they whistling?" He chuckled as her face burned with embarrassment.

"WDM, Baby!" cheered a nurse with a Jamaican accent.

Matt's hands spread wide in surrender as he pled with the sheepish nurse. "Oh, come on. You've got to tell me now."

Nurse Compton capitulated after one last glance back at the encouraging twosome. "Well-Dressed Man." When nothing registered on his face, she added. "By ZZ-Top? Surely you've heard it before." Her head bobbled back and forth as she sang an off-key rendition of "'*Cause every girl crazy 'bout a sharp-dressed man?*"

Matt leaned back and tipped a salute to Nurse Compton's backup singers. "Thank you, ladies." He returned his attention to the only one whose opinion of him mattered and found her twisting a loose lock of hair. "It appears I have their vote. What do you say?"

A slow nod began. "Are you sure you're up to it? After treatment, food is the last thing on most of our patients' minds."

"I could do something light."

"All right. Something quick. Before class. I know a place down the block—Meriwether's. I'll meet you there at five."

It wasn't the romantic dinner he'd hoped for, but Matt nodded and said, "Perfect. I'll get us a table."

The moisture from the harbor added to Maryland's already oppressive August humidity that left everyone sweat soaked and limp after a few minutes outdoors. His limited tolerance for hot weather was further diminished since his treatments had begun, rendering the adventurer an AC-loving indoor dweller who spent less and less time outdoors.

Four blocks from Prospect's campus, Meriwether's was Baltimore's food equivalent of a NYC subway station. Their staff of short-order cooks slaved away over a visible twenty-foot grill serving a constant stream of pre-pay call-ahead clients zooming in and out for their pink-and-brown-bagged sandwich orders. The girl at the register tagged Matt's deer-in-the-headlights shock and awe and shouted over the din, "Carry-out or dine-in?"

"In!" he shouted back, following her finger-point to the rear where the narrow hall broke into a chic little dining room where music played in the rock-concert decibel range. It was decorated like a walk-in version of their take-out bags.

He grabbed two paper menus, found a small table near a corner, and hailed the waitress. After a few minutes of perusing sandwich listings named after musicians, he looked up and found Nurse Compton leaning against the door jam, covering her mouth as she laughed. Her chin dropped and came back up apologetically. She wriggled her finger his way, beckoning him, and he gladly followed.

"Sorry. I really didn't think you'd show."

"So, this was a test?" She shrugged, and he tried his best to read her lips.

"You sounded like a potential chainsaw murderer back at the clinic. I figured you could've picked up another murder victim in here if that was your intention. Instead, you stayed. I also ran your wild claim by my administrator."

She tilted her head to the side. "It checks out, but I'm not sure if that makes me feel better or more leery. As far as the administration is concerned, all your donation bought you is the right to make your case to me. Whatever happens from there is up to me, and any agreement we come to must remain on a need-to-know basis with the hospital. So, you've got my attention. Would you like to go somewhere a little quieter?"

His shoulders slumped in gratitude. "Please!"

Two doors down sat a rustic Italian bistro. The owner greeted Mikaela by name. As she led the couple to a table, Mikaela said, "We won't need menus, Carmen. Just two bowls of Wedding Soup with extra spinach and meatballs, please."

"Got it," said the middle-aged woman who gave Matt an approving glance that he caught and that Mikaela brushed away with a wide-eyed glance.

Once they were seated in a quiet corner and gave their drink orders, the nervousness began again. Matt toyed with the salt shaker. "Thanks for coming."

"Let's begin at the beginning. I suppose we should formally introduce ourselves." She extended her hand. "I'm Mikaela Compton."

He wanted to tell her that he already knew her well, every curve of her face, the little curls at the corners of her mouth, the slim straight shape of her elegant nose. But he opted instead to simply say, "Lovely to meet you, Mikaela. Matt Grayken."

"Nice to meet you, Matt. Do I detect a bit of an Irish accent?"

Matt felt his own cheeks warm. "We emigrated here when I was three, when my folks moved their import/export business here. You'd enjoy my parents. They still have very prominent brogues. Mine generally only returns when I'm nervous." He smiled.

"You? Nervous?" She closed her eyes and shook her head. "I don't think this is your first pick-up, cowboy."

Her candor disarmed him. For all her sweetness, there was also a strength there that added to her complexity. "Seriously, I can't tell you the last time I asked a woman out."

"Oh, I see," she said, wagging a finger his way. "They ask you." She shook her head as if incredulous. "Of course, they do. Curly dark hair. Killer eyes."

"And don't forget, I'm a WDM."

He enjoyed how easily she blushed. His gaze dropped to the table top. "There's a difference between asking an attractive woman to accompany you to a social function and going out on a date just for the fun of it. Hmm . . . Yep. Sadly, it's been a while."

"I can relate."

"I figured as much." And when she seemed offended by his response, he quickly countered with, "I didn't mean you wouldn't have a string of willing suitors, it's just that . . . when you care for ailing parents, work full-time, and go to school, it doesn't leave much time for a social life."

The explanation made things worse as the stalker alert returned to her face.

"You probably don't realize how much you reveal about yourself to your patients. I've listened. It's what made me want to meet you."

Mikaela leaned back into the booth and crossed her arms over her chest as one brown eyebrow rose. Matt rushed in to calm the rising storm. "Let me explain."

He was grateful their order arrived in time for him to gather his thoughts. When Carmen left, he slipped the straw from its case and began stirring his Coke. "A patient's wife looked especially tired one day. You pulled her aside near my chair and explained that you understood how demanding being a caregiver was because you were the surprise baby born to older parents who you cared for until they passed."

Her expression went limp, and her hands dropped into her lap. "I didn't know anyone else heard me."

Matt leaned in. "Don't be embarrassed. It's refreshing to find that level of selfless caring in someone, especially someone so bright and beautiful and young."

Her head dipped slightly. "Thank you."

"You're already an RN, so I assume the classes are for your bachelors in nursing, or beyond. Are you leaning towards medical school?"

She smiled and nervously folded the wrapper to her straw. "Yes, med school was the dream. Still is, but I moved into nursing to help keep my family afloat when my parents took ill. I still need to work full-time, so I can only take a few classes per semester." A melancholy smile crossed her lips. "I'm already twenty-six. At this rate, I'll be seventy when I graduate, and I'll probably just do my residency in the assisted living center where I'll be living."

"Very efficient." They both chuckled, but Matt sensed the worry behind her laughter. He leaned forward and drew a deep breath. "I might be able to help with that." Before her defenses moved back into place, he abruptly added, "As you probably guessed, I'm dying, and I'd like you to consider marrying me."

A panorama of humor and perplexity moved in waves across her face, settling into shock. "Are you serious?"

"Dead serious." He smiled to lighten the sting, but Mikaela wasn't having it.

"That's not funny." She pulled her napkin from her lap and threw it on the table as if preparing to leave. Matt placed his hand over hers, his eyes pleading with her to stay.

"Please. Hear me out. Then, if you want to leave, I'll never contact you again."

He found it oddly comforting that she didn't pull her hand back from his for several seconds, and when she did, it was a slow, gentle withdrawal. He moved the dishes to the side and cleared the table between them.

"The ending of a life is never funny, and I shouldn't have treated mine so irreverently. I'm not sure what the appropriate attitude is for such a situation. My impending death was not unexpected. I've been a draining hourglass since my second battle with leukemia. It hit me during college. I didn't put my life on hold, waiting for the next bout of cancer to come. I've done the things I wanted to do—some dangerous, some professionally successful, some soul satisfying." He closed his eyes and shook his head. "I have great parents, but their first inclination will be to pull me from the Prospect Cancer Treatment Center and drag me across the earth to see every traditional doctor who has a new theory on treatment. I've made my choice. I like Prospect's approach, and I don't want to be a medical vagabond again."

"Do they even know you're sick again?"

"Not yet. I'll tell them in time to make some final memories together."

Opposition to his plan was evident in her pinched lips and furrowed brows.

"If you don't want to turn to your parents, then what of friends? Extended family?"

"Choosing a caregiver from extended family would be a slap to my parents. So would turning to a friend. Besides, the last thing I want is to feel like a burden to someone."

"And there's no one else? No special someone you'd want to share these last months with?"

"Is that as pitiful as it sounds?"

She looked away. "It's . . . sad."

"If you were in my place, who would you turn to?"

Mikaela's expression was filled with rebuttals that were never given voice. Resignation washed over her. "I don't know. I really don't know." Her hand pressed over her mouth.

"I have seven brothers, but they're married with kids. I guess I'm as alone as you."

Matt took her hand, realizing he had planted a new worry in her already-burdened heart. "You're not alone, Mikaela. You are well loved by so many people. I'm sure any one of them would be there for you. But for me, the question is more about who I'm comfortable being so vulnerable with. I just didn't make time, or perhaps I never wanted to be that vulnerable with anyone before." He blew out a rush of air and shook his head. "What I most want in my life right now is someone to wake up to in the morning, share meals with, and count on when I need help. I want to spend my last days in the company of someone who can laugh at my lousy jokes, keep me well as long as possible, ease my pain when it comes, and still make my days meaningful and joyful." His eyes never left hers. "As soon as I saw you I thought 'now there's a woman I would enjoy seeing every morning, breaking bread with, and talking about the news or the weather.' Plus, you're a great nurse. You're everything I need right now."

He looked at her, studying her response to his confessions, and found sadness there.

Mikaela swallowed hard, and leaned forward. "So why marry me? Why not just hire me?"

"Because I don't want to be the pitiful soul with only an attorney, billing hourly, as his voice. I want a wife with the legal power to speak for me when I can't speak for myself and the personal connection no one else will challenge."

"Like your parents when they come to take control of your care."

"As well-intentioned as they'd be, yes. And I trust you."

"You'd be pitting me against them."

She leaned back, but he was impressed that she wasn't discounting everything he had said. "No. I would make my wishes clear. You would just enforce them when I no longer can." He leaned farther forward, to close the distance between them, and looked straight into her eyes. "I know you're alone, and I know money's an issue. I can fix that. I have a lovely home that will be yours when I'm gone. And I'll pay off your debts and provide tuition to medical school. You'll be a doctor, Mikaela."

She stirred her soup silently until her head came back up, refusal written in her expression. "But we're strangers."

"You're not a stranger to me. I've watched you serve your patients. I feel I understand you better than I understand people I've known for years." He sat back against the booth and relaxed. "As for me, let's take a little time to get comfortable with one another. I'm actually a pretty funny guy on topics other than death." He raised his eyebrows, offering her his most dazzling smile. "I love to dance. In fact, I've been told I'm not bad. And I can provide references to prove I'm a man of good moral character. I have a Sunday School certificate from fifth-grade to prove it."

Mikaela dipped her head, but her shoulders wriggled, and he knew she was laughing.

"Eat," she said, pointing to his bowl. She likewise dipped her spoon as a thoughtful silence settled in between them.

Matt breathed in deeply and closed his eyes. "This feels good on my stomach. See, you already know what I need."

Mikaela pointed back to the soup. "More eating."

They continued on with small talk about the restaurant and its owners, who had become her go-to between work and class. Matt's eating slowed and he sat back.

"How far are you into treatment?" Mikaela asked.

"I've almost completed this round of immunotherapy. What happens next will depend on the results of the next tests. Maybe chemo. Maybe radiation."

"And always nutrition." Her head dipped toward his bowl and he took a final spoonful.

"See, you're good for me. You have a kindness about you that gives me peace. When I die, I'd like to be in my own home, feeling those things. Not fearful in some sterile room. That's just not how I want to go."

Her mouth fell slightly open, and she nodded. "I understand that. I would feel the same way." Her eyebrows rose as if in preparation she were preparing to discuss something delicate. "So how exactly do you see this *marriage?*"

"Whatever you want it to be. A quiet legal ceremony before a justice of the peace or a church wedding with bells and a big reception. It's your wedding. It's your call."

"What if you get another remission?" Her voice trailed off.

"Now that would be the best outcome of all. We could

place a clause in our agreement that unless our arrangement was so amiable that we each agree to continue, you could leave without the divorce or our financial terms being contested. Unfortunately, my doctors don't give me reason to think that's going to be necessary."

She slipped her hand back again and sat upright with her elbows on the table. "You've spelled out the financial terms, and the wedding plans. So far, this is just a lucrative long-term nursing job with companion care, but what are your expectations for—" her voice lowered to a whisper, "—*the marriage?*"

Of course, he knew this delicate issue would arise, but it was the most painful part of the equation. "I hope we'll be great companions, enjoying friendship, respect, humor. But that's not what you're asking, is it?" He played with his spoon as he gathered the right words. "You want to know if a dying man would play on your sympathies to lure you into his bedroom?"

She didn't flinch. "The thought crossed my mind."

Try as he might to remain even, he knew his disappointment showed on his face. "Fair enough. No, Mikaela, I am not asking for a full marriage in that way, nor am I looking to fall in love. I want to avoid that, as much to protect me as to protect you."

"I don't understand."

"I don't want to grieve for anyone else as I pass, nor do I want to leave someone else grieving for me."

"So just friendship and companionship?"

"Yes, but neither is a small thing. I'm embarrassed to admit that I find myself feeling a little anxious. I would be a bit possessive of your time and company."

"Would I need to quit my job?"

"Not at first. I intend to work a while longer. When I quit, I'd like you to do the same. That's when I'll need you the most."

Mikaela nodded quietly as she stared down at the table. Matt couldn't read her expression, and his heart clutched.

"So what do you think?"

She looked up, tilted her head to the side, and studied his face. "I'm up for a second date."

2

Their second meeting led to a third and into September. Mikaela didn't mention her budding, albeit terminal, relationship to her brothers who continuously noted her penchant for strays and lost causes. They were married. They didn't understand how fully her parents had filled every empty moment of her life not dedicated to work and school. But her parents were gone now, and Mikaela hadn't found a personal connection to fill the emotional gaps and holes that remained when she finally crossed her doorway at the end of the day.

Matt, and thoughts of him, filled every empty nook and cranny with humor and kindness. She grew in his light, and he frequently told her that he benefited from time with her. Was the pleasure of his company worth the self-inflicted pain of knowing she would likely watch him die? That was the question. She had handled loss before, stunning loss and the agonizing anticipation of it, and she knew she would not have forfeited joy just to spare herself sorrow.

She pulled her shoes on and scanned her lonely living space. Apartment life denied her the right to bring home anymore stranded kittens or puppies, and the gifted carnival-prize beta fish had finally succumbed. She was as alone as she had ever been, and perhaps that made her reckless enough to welcome a dying friend into her heart with eyes wide open. She knew they were living a dream of denial, but their individual loneliness was diminished by having someone fill the empty hours, and for that even temporary joy, she proceeded.

They spent their time together simply, with strolling conversations in the gardens on Prospect's Baltimore medical campus, or in Baltimore's harbor area where they asked one another questions as they watched the autumn tourists, and boaters enjoying the end of the season. The game was tit for tat. Mikaela asked a question of Matt, and he responded by turning the light of introspection on her as they became comfortable with each other. The questions were generally fluff, delaying further discussion of the ultimate reason they had found each other.

"Favorite music?" asked Mikaela as a yellow leaf fluttered to the ground.

"Favorite music . . . well . . . my parents taught me to appreciate and love classical." One corner of Matt's mouth curved upward into thoughtful smile. "But when I'm feeling deeply introspective, I turn to classic folksy rock—Cat

Stevens, Crosby, Stills, Nash, and Young. The smooth older stuff."

"And what constitutes deep introspection?"

Matt rubbed the back of his neck and smiled sheepishly. "Mostly self-pity."

The answer put a temporary chill on their game. Matt guided their walk to an ice cream vendor where he broke the conversational ice by supplying frozen treats.

"Where do you live?" asked Mikaela as she licked her single-dip cone.

"I have a brownstone in Georgetown. Very Feng Shui. Or Spartan, depending on how you look at vacant, undecorated rooms."

Mikaela's shoulders rose as a single giggle escaped. Her five foot eight inches softly collided against his toned six feet, like a physical rimshot in response to his joke. He absorbed her assault with a smile, and she couldn't help but notice how well they meshed.

"Your turn."

"Where do I live?"

He nodded and licked a drip on his cone.

"I have a tiny studio apartment over a consignment shop on Pratt. It's perfect for me right now. I'm hardly ever there, it takes about three minutes to clean, and my landlord, who owns the shop below, gives me great bargains on things I need."

"Very efficient for a busy life."

Mikaela noticed how their steps just naturally fell into sync.

"Tell me about your family."

Matt cleared a lick of ice cream from his lips and began. "My father's people have been in the rye whiskey business for generations, and my father noticed that most of them died young from overindulging in their own goods. He and my mother were fortyish, childless, and unhappy. My father knew he was heading down the same destructive path that took his father and his grandfather, so he had an epiphany of sorts. He granted my mother's long wish to adopt a child."

"You're adopted?"

"Yes, when I was still an infant. Then my father asked his siblings to buy him out, and we moved to New York. My parents bought a small import/export business which they built into a conglomerate of over thirty-five companies."

Mikaela focused on her cone and shivered as she considered how different their worlds were. "You're a conglomerate owner's son."

"And a principal in my own venture," he added defensively. "I moved to the D.C. area and built Great Expectations. We create high adventure experiences for clients."

"Sounds pricey."

"What is a dream come true worth? Clients name it, and we do our best to make it happen exactly as they want—travel, food, accommodations, and the most exclusive, exotic locations on earth. We've sent families on safaris, round-the-world cruises, Arctic adventures to see polar bears and seals, you name it. Now you know what my family and I do. Tell me about yours."

She looked down and shook her head. "My family is nothing like yours."

Matt stopped and squared himself to her. "It made you who you are, so it must have been pretty spectacular."

She smiled up at him, awed by how adept he was at making her feel his equal. She wriggled up ramrod straight and sniffed comically before breaking into cockney accented. "I suppose we were in our own way." They laughed and continued their stroll. "We were a large working-class family. Seven sons, all named after presidents."

"Republican or Democrat?"

"Mostly historical. George, Thomas, James, John, Abe, Franklin, and Dwight."

"And if you had been a boy?"

She gave him a comically indignant glare. "Ronald, of course."

"Very patriotic."

"Thank you."

"And then . . . surprise!" He laughed and raised his hands in the air.

"Exactly. I arrived after a twelve-year gap, the little princess, but most of my brothers were gone into the military before I was old enough to really know them. My father was a sailor before he went to work in the shipyard. Asbestos exposure likely killed him, but he wasn't one to hire attorneys and sue people. He said he made his choices and accepted the risk. Mom was a homemaker with a weak heart."

"And you stayed behind to take care of them."

Her mouth pressed into a thin line. "I don't regret a minute of it. I always felt very loved. My brothers are spread across the world, so I don't see them often, but we have a family text group, and we shoot each other stupid messages and photos from time to time. And I know they'd race to be with me if I ever needed them."

Matt tossed his partially eaten cone in a trash can. "Then I declare you the wealthier of our pair."

"Growing up as an only child, did you ever miss having no brothers and sisters?"

"Not that I recall. Probably because I have some of the finest chums a person could ask for. My best friend Daniel Lebed and I have been together since grade school, and the rest have been with me since my prep school years. They are like brothers to me."

Mikaela recognized the look of disguised pain that crossed Matt's face. "Are you getting sick from your treatment?"

He smiled reassuringly. "You owe me a question. Are you trying to wiggle out?"

She didn't press the issue. "Nope," she replied with spunk. "Lay it on me." Matt shook his head at her, and she wondered if he found her funny or crass. "I had all brothers, remember."

"I understand. Tell me about them. After growing up in a

large family, was it sad to watch them each head off and leave you behind?"

"A little, I suppose, but I always had my parents, and most of the time, one brother or another seemed to be passing through on leave. And there were certain advantages to being the last and late child. The budget loosened up, and I inherited my brothers' clunker at sixteen."

"Aha! You sold out for a car."

"I confess that I did." She laughed and offered up another question. "If you could be anywhere . . . right now . . . where would you like to be?"

Matt slowed his pace to a stop and turned her way. "Just where I am, Mikaela."

His voice was as soft as air and she breathed his words in. "Me too," she answered.

The moment demanded a response all its own, a touch, or an embrace, but Mikaela resumed their previous pace and Matt followed footstep for footstep as the silence grew awkward once more.

Matt provided a respite. "I've travelled a lot. Were you asking about physical places I've been?"

"Yes," she replied with relief. "Is there a city you adore? Or something you long to revisit?"

"There is wonder and beauty everywhere, but I'm most content when the sky is above me and the wind is on my face."

"Which explains your company."

"Exactly. I once spent three months alone on a mountain

range with nothing more than a sheet of canvas to call home. It was the most meaningful experience of my life."

"Really? Why?"

"I think everyone should have a period in their life devoid of things. That's when you really come to know yourself. Who you are, what matters most, and who is of ultimate importance to you."

"Is that what you found on that mountain?"

"Uh huh."

His smile seemed pained as he checked his watch, as if he had touched on a topic too personal to pursue.

"I should head back to Rockville. I have work waiting for me at the office."

Mikaela placed her hand on his arm, the first touch they had shared since the stilted hug that began the day's encounter. "I have one other question before you go."

She saw worry pull at his mouth. He nodded and said, "Ask me anything."

"You said something the first day, about how you wanted to avoid falling in love, as much to protect me as to protect you. It sounded a little ominous. What did you mean by that?"

Matt placed a finger across his mouth and dropped his gaze to the sidewalk. Without saying a word, he turned, and upon finding a bench, he cupped Mikaela's elbow in his hand and led her to it, motioning for her to sit. He joined her, but when she turned to face him, Matt leaned forward, his arms on his knees, with his gaze set on the ground.

"I was in college when I had my last cancer recurrence. Staring down death in the prime of a young man's life is a strange experience. It made me self-destructive. I figured I was living on borrowed time, as if life was a finite thing . . ." the next words came out with forced deliberateness, "and I intended to spend every minute fully and die on my own terms." He turned to face her. "I was selfish, Mikaela. I did what I wanted without thought of the consequences to myself or others. I clubbed and partied and hurt people, more people than I probably know, and worst of all, I quite literally broke my mother's heart."

He drew a deep breath. "I woke up one day in a lavish hotel room with people whose names I didn't know in a city I couldn't remember, feeling so empty that living at all seemed worthless. I walked out of that room with nothing but my wallet and the clothes on my back. I hired a bicycle cab, and when the driver asked, "Where to?' I emptied my wallet into his hands and said, 'Somewhere peaceful,' and I fell asleep. When I awoke, I was at his home, a hovel of a cottage at the foot of the mountain, with him urging me to follow him up a trail. At the top was a piece of canvas stretched across four poles, and the most humbling view of God's earth I had ever seen."

Mikaela held her breath, anxious for him to continue.

"The man's children brought me food and a jug of fresh water each morning. Some days I hiked the trails. On others I watched the family far below me as they worked and played and took care of one another. Mostly I just sat there and thought, and remembered wonderful moments with my parents. At the end of three months, I had an indescribable hunger to get home, but I was too late. When I called my father, he told me how inconsolable my mother had been with worry for me, and then one night, she'd had a small stroke."

Mikaela gasped. "Oh, Matt. I'm so sorry."

"The flight home was the longest, most agonizing of my life, and then seeing her face twisted, her body so weak, and to know I was, at least in some part, the cause?" His head hung down and then lifted. He looked into Mikaela's eyes. "I told her how sorry I was. That I wished I could trade places with her, and take her pain and afflictions away. She smiled and told me that I now understood what it really meant to love someone, to care more about them than you do for yourself."

He closed his eyes and shook his head. "She slowly improved, and I finally understood a few critical lessons about love."

Mikaela could barely eke out the words, "Such as?"

"That the greatest pain isn't your own, but that which comes from watching someone you love suffer. I finally recognized that my parents' grief and pain over my illness was at least as great as, and probably deeper than, my own because they were powerless to help me. And I realized that love isn't all romance and rainbows. There's an excruciating vulnerability and responsibility that comes with love. I don't want to leave this life grieving for someone else I'm losing, nor do I want one more person to grieve that way for me.

That's why I want to keep things light. Friendly. Nothing more."

"Aren't you shutting your parents out again?"

"We said all a family can say after Mom's stroke. I don't want them to grieve for months. I'll stay in touch and tell them in time to share some moments together."

Mikaela struggled to camouflage her emotions and push the words past the lump in her throat. "Thank you for helping me understand. You're a good man, Matthew Grayken."

The words seemed to give him no comfort. "A man asking way too much of you."

She placed her hand on his arm. "I have a few conditions of my own. Since this is primarily a long-term care arrangement, I don't want your house or your fortune. I'll move into your home, and I'll send you a contract with a standard daily rate for home care. Not a penny more, okay?"

Wide-eyed, he nodded.

"I'll cancel classes for this sem—"

"I don't want you to do that."

She placed her hand on his shoulder and leaned in to emphasize the next words. "You're in for the fight of your life. Besides your immunotherapy, I'm going to make some other changes to your diet and lifestyle. I'm making you my priority, and *you* need to make you *your* priority. Agreed?"

"One hundred percent. Will you also marry me and be my legal voice?"

This knife sliced deep into her core. Here was a good

man whose humor and kindness filled the hollow ache within her, but their marriage would be like a sandcastle at low tide. She would pour her heart into it, making its short lifespan as beautiful as she could, and then it would be washed away by death. Instead of hope and joy, depleting time and sorrow loomed for them. Could she keep her emotions compartmentalized? Healthcare worker/patient? Could she actually bear such an arrangement? Her mind swirled, trying to imagine living within the same walls with Matthew Grayken. Would life be better . . . would *she* be better for having shared this wrenching experience with him? More importantly, could she survive losing him at the end?

Pleading crinkled the corners of his eyes as he watched her wrestle. She saw how deeply he needed her. Only her. It was humbling to know he believed she alone could be his comfort and peace. She placed her hands back in her lap and drew a deep breath.

"Yes. I'll marry you."

3

The wedding was set three days out, per Mikaela's request, and at the courthouse, a neutral place without ties to either bride or groom, per Matt's suggestion. The normal radiance of Mikaela's smile seemed dim as they walked side-by-side along the bustling lunch crowd enjoying a warm autumn day at Baltimore's Inner Harbor. Matt sensed she was having reservations about the arrangement. Fatigue plagued him, so he placed a hand on Mikaela's back and guided her to the concrete steps that overlooked the waterfront. Once they were seated, the discomfort between them increased as they stared separately at the boats moving across the water.

"I've been lying awake the past two nights trying to put myself in your shoes. Trying to fathom how I've altered every dream you've ever had about your wedding day, and about falling in love. You'll have all those things someday, but I've changed that trajectory and sent you off on a detour. I'm fully aware of your sacrifice, and I want you to know I'll understand if you can't go through with the marriage. I'd be grateful if you'd just agree to be my nurse."

Her head turned his way, and he thought he saw a momentary panic sweep across her face.

"Then who would be your voice?"

His gaze dropped to the sidewalk where a pebble lay. He picked it up and tossed it into the water. "Maybe I've worried too much about what I want. Maybe I'm falling back into old, selfish patterns." He looked at her. "I don't want to regress. I hope to meet my Maker as a better man."

"I haven't changed my mind, I just . . . I don't want this marriage to feel like a business proposition. You spoke about friendship, and respect, and kindness. From what I've seen, that's more than a lot of married couples have, so I can accept those terms, and I respect the need to protect us from becoming romantically entangled, but how will we appear in public on our wedding day and beyond? Especially as your health fades. As two caring people? As employer and faithful nurse? As gold digger and sugar daddy?"

Matt worked hard to suppress a laugh, then quickly quelled it when he saw how serious the matter was to Mikaela.

"Can we at least make this wedding feel legitimate? Like a real wedding?"

He leaned close and smiled. "It is a real wedding."

"You know what I mean." She blushed. "My friends think

you swept me off my feet. That we're crazy in love." Her speech sped up as she went on. "Could you play the part of the doting groom that day? What do we do at the end of the ceremony? Slap each other on the back? I don't want to dodge curious glances from people who notice something odd about our union, and I don't want to spend the rest of my life explaining 'us' to people who question my motivation and character behind my back. What are the rules here?"

The pitch in her voice rose, almost childlike, and Matt's throat tightened. Instinctively, his arm reached across her shoulders, pulling her to him. His head guided hers into the crook of his neck. He felt her shake beside him. "As I see it, there's no me going forward. There's you and there's us. I want us to be happy and, most importantly, that means I want you to be happy. I'll kiss you on our wedding day, and you'll be the dearest person to me the rest of my life. That's my promise to you."

He reached into his pocket and withdrew a ring box. "I should have given this to you the day you agreed to marry me." He opened the box, revealing a white gold band with a satellite-sized diamond that sparkled like a disco ball in the sun.

"I can't—"

She yanked her hand back against her, but Matt caught it and held it gently in one hand while the other brought her chin up to meet his gaze. "I plan to be a lot of trouble, and this is my apology in advance." She didn't return his smile. "Real marriage? Real engagement ring. Okay?"

Mikaela's hand shook as he slipped the ring on. He inter-twined his fingers in hers and pulled her close, whispering in her ear. "I won't forget who needs who in this relationship, Mikaela. You are my anchor. I intend to hold on to these hands, in public and at home, and my arms are open anytime you need to be held."

He felt her body relax in his arms, then she asked, "Should I take your name?"

"I'd be honored if you did, but I won't be offended if you don't."

He felt her shake from within his embrace. As he buried his face in her hair, he breathed her in, secretly breaking the fundamental term of his own agreement. He chose Mikaela because he had fallen in love with her weeks before. It had happened before they shared a word, before her eyes met his, as her heart brought comfort to others like him—those sick and frightened and in need of hope. His own fear disap-peared in her, leaving only remorse. He regretted his fate, wishing he had met her sooner, but he knew he wouldn't have noticed her simple beauty, valued her goodness, or been worthy of it then. Perhaps his illness had made him a better man. A man worthy of Mikaela. He hoped so.

Lost in the moment, neither of them realized that the people gathering around them had witnessed him place the ring on her hand. Scattered applause drew their notice, and when they lifted their heads to see the cause, they found a semicircle of smiling, eye-wiping people celebrating their engagement. Annoyed at the public glare on their private moment, he was nevertheless grateful for the intrusion that broke his love spell, hurtling him back to practicality. To reason.

He stood and raised Mikaela to her feet. After an awkward bow, acknowledging the crowd's kindness, he looked at Mikaela and said, "I'm taking the rest of the day off. Besides the license, what do we need to make this wedding perfect?"

Mikaela's eyes widened. "Flowers. You have your WDM suit, but I guess I should get a dress. And who will stand with us? The courthouse staff or do we need witnesses?"

"Your call."

"I'd like Eliza and Martine to be there if that's all right."

"Of course. I'll call my friend Daniel to be my best man. What else? A meal for after the ceremony?" He saw how his enthusiasm over the plans restored joy to her eyes.

"Oh, yes! But what? Elegant or fun?"

"Bride's choice."

She squeezed his hand. "Fun. Definitely fun. And I know a great place."

"I knew you would."

She hugged him tight. "Thank you." And then her smile faded again. "What about your parents?"

"What about your brothers?"

"They have families and they're scattered across four states and three continents. Believe me, under the circumstances, it'll be better to get their forgiveness than to ask for their blessing. But you're an only child. You have to tell your parents."

She had raised his greatest concern. The issue that could derail all his plans. He pulled Mikaela close, held her hand with the ring prominently displayed in front, and took a selfie of the two of them. Seconds after sending the photo and a short text to his parents, the phone rang. He took a deep breath and answered the call privately to protect Mikaela in the event his parents were less than congratulatory.

"Hello, Mother. Is Da also there?" His lips trembled when he heard the happiness in her voice, knowing the sorrow he had not yet revealed. "Her name is Mikaela Compton, and yes, we're getting married." He tightened his hold on Mikaela, whose face was ashen with concern. "In two days. We've been dating for . . . a little while now." He smiled sheepishly at Mikaela over the gross exaggeration of their relationship's history. "Her parents have both passed away. I know you haven't met her, but I assure you that you'll love her."

His parents voiced the very concerns Mikaela feared, and he released her hand and walked several steps away while getting grilled about the hasty wedding, Mikaela's intentions, corporate rumors, and his health. Matt quickly cut his parents off and turned his back to Mikaela. "Yes, you've heard correctly. I've already turned a great deal of my day-to-day tasks over to capable department heads. I haven't had a creative thought in months, Mother. Da, you know I think best outside the office. If I travel, I want Mikaela to go with me, and I want to do it properly. We're standing before a judge in Baltimore. We'd love to have you if you can come, but we understand that it's short notice." He listened on as his mother's panic quieted and she began offering advice and instructions. When he saw the toll the exchange was taking on Mikaela, he shot to the point with his parents. "I'll speak to Mikaela about that and get back to you. Yes. Love you too. Goodbye."

Mikaela paced in a tight circle, muttering "I knew it," a hundred times. She confronted Matt. "They hate me already. What did you agree to tell me?"

"It doesn't matter."

"Yes, it does. They're your parents. For better or for worse, they're going to be part of my life too."

Matt sighed long and low, his reserves nearly spent. All he wanted was peace. "They see this as a practice wedding to keep things proper between us if we travel together. They want to throw a big, 'real' church wedding at Christmas, and they want us to visit as soon as possible."

"A practice wedding . . ." she muttered. Matt could see the earlier magic of the day vaporizing before them. He placed his hands on Mikaela's shoulders and looked into her eyes. "I don't care what they or anyone else thinks or says. This marriage is the only one I will ever know. It may not be the marriage we could have enjoyed under different circumstances, but you are the only woman I will ever take as my wife. This is as real as it gets for me, Mikaela."

He wanted to burn that message into her heart, to protect

his brave savior against all comers, including his own parents. He closed his eyes against the sting there, and when he opened them, he found himself within a breath of Mikaela. "Are we okay?"

She smiled up at him. "We're okay."

Matt knew *he* actually wasn't. A thousand horses' hooves hammered against his chest as logic and nature battled for control. Six inches. It was the current distance from his hungry mouth to hers. The irreconcilable distance between boundaries and abandon. Six lousy inches between a full life with a potentially agonizing goodbye or a tepid skid into eternity. And then he remembered the promised kiss at the end of the ceremony. How would he get through that?

4

Mikaela stood in front of the mirror bright and early Thursday morning, dressed in her off-the-rack bridal dress purchased two days earlier. After securing the lace veil's headband into her bun, she surveyed her reflection. She had fallen in love with the third dress she tried on. More romantic than sexy, it suited a courthouse wedding. Delicate lace skimmed over the comfortable underskirt which hugged her slender frame. Narrow sleeves provided some warmth if the air turned cooler, while the fluted bottom swished along the floor with a playfulness befitting a future garden party. She gave her short lace veil a gentle tug until it fell just below her eyes with a touch of flirty mystery she loved.

She had no personal frame of reference for the specifics of what a bride should feel on her wedding day, but an undeniable quiver of excitement, mingled with fear, quickened her heart. Not fear of Matthew Grayken, but that her childlike prayer for a miracle might be denied.

She looked at the clock. Matthew would arrive soon. She became giddy at the thought, and she quickly rechecked her list of traditional wedding items. The something old was the pearl earrings and necklace set from her brother Michael on her sixteenth birthday. Her dress and veil filled the something new. The three blue peonies tucked into the bouquet of white calla lilies delivered that morning would be the something blue, and the borrowed item was a very personal treasure— her mother's favorite book of Shelley's poems Mikaela always kept tucked in her purse to keep her mother near. Mikaela didn't know the history behind the wedding traditions, but she knew if anyone needed all the good luck and help they could get, it was her.

She sat in her favorite chair and scanned her tiny apartment. A truck had already moved the few things she was taking to Matt's house. To *her* new home, a place she hadn't found time to see. Matt insisted they keep the lease on her apartment until they were certain the arrangement would work. If it did, they would fill the first few getting-to-know-you weeks purchasing everything else that would be needed to transform it from a Spartan bachelor pad to a welcoming home/hospice.

She thought of her parents, as she had so many times this week. Years ago she'd accepted that she would be alone on this day. No mother to give her advice. No father to walk her down the aisle. She always expected her brothers to be there,

giving her away, or as groomsmen. They and their overprotec-
tive-from-afar mentalities would never accept her arrangement with Matt, but she believed her caring parents would
have given her their blessing, and in her heart, she believed
they were with her in spirit.

The doorbell buzzed, and chills coursed along her spine.
Matt's cheery voice called to her through the speaker. "Mrs.
Matthew Grayken's car is here."

Mikaela stood and held onto the arm of the chair, uncer-
tain her quaking legs would hold her. Her trek to the speaker
pad evidently exceeded the time Matt expected because a
second buzz sounded followed by a nervous, "Mikaela? Are
you there?"

She found his reliance on her heartwarming. She pressed
the speaker button and replied. "I'm sorry. There is no Mrs.
Grayken here, but a future Mrs. Grayken is present." She
heard his sigh of relief through the speaker.

"Buzz me up?"

Barely six seconds passed before Matt was at her door.
The moment felt dreamlike as she opened the door and saw
Matt there, looking like a magazine-cover model, and yet he
seemed to melt when he first saw her. His square shoulders
lowered in sync with his jaw. She read sadness on his face,
not pride or attraction or excitement. Then the sadness slowly
shifted into awe. Moments passed before he whispered, "You
. . . look like an angel."

Mikaela felt as awkward as she had at her sixth-grade
dance. "Thank you. You look very handsome, Matt."

"WDM," he quipped before coughing to clear his throat. Mikaela also found it hard to breathe, as if the air was thick with the invisible dust from the draining sands of their time.

He picked up her suitcase, and she grabbed her purse and bouquet.

"Thank you for doing this, Mikaela. I—"

Mikaela's finger pressed to his lips. "I wouldn't do it if I didn't want to."

"Thank you." A half-smile tugged at his mouth. "Shall we?"

A white luxury car with sparkling white interior sat at the curb with a black-capped chauffeur manning the open, rear-hinged door. Mikaela's mouth gaped at the sight of what looked like a vehicle from a sci-fi movie. The chauffeur hurried to take the bags from Matt, who then escorted Mikaela to the back seat. Her feet sank into the thick wool carpet, and the buttery leather seats felt like a hug.

Matt slid in on the other side and closed the window between the driver and them. "I couldn't arrange a carriage quickly enough, but how's this?"

"Perfect," she gushed as she ran her fingers over the leather and wood trim. "What kind of car is it?"

"Let me dazzle you a little first." He pushed a button and two twelve-inch TV screens rose from the front seatbacks. Another button caused a mini-fridge to pop open from the side door where two bottles of Fre Chardonnay were stored with fluted glasses and a small cheese and fruit box.

"It's non-alcoholic. See? I'm following doctor's orders."

"Very good," she gushed. "I'm proud of you."

Music played, and the seats reclined and began buzzing, delivering a Shiatzu massage. Best of all, the interior went dark as the roof lit up with a fiber-optics-provided starlit sky at ten a.m. Mikaela was overwhelmingly impressed.

"Is this your car?"

"You mean *our* car?"

"Is it?" she exclaimed.

He laughed. "No. It's a rented Rolls Royce. Just for today. We own a silver Jaguar and a black Range Rover. That's as ostentatious as I get."

"And a red 2014 Honda Civic. Fully paid for."

"Then we are set."

The wonder of the car and Matt's efforts to make the day special were not lost on Mikaela. Awkwardness still crept in during lapses in conversation when the two relative strangers began another round of their question-and-answer game. They were in the middle of the second round when they pulled up in front of the courthouse.

Mikaela looked for Eliza and Martine but she didn't see them. A man with auburn hair was standing outside. Mikaela assumed he was Matt's college friend, Daniel, when he raced down the stairs to greet the car.

The window rolled down, and Daniel leaned in on Mikaela's side. His glance moved from Mikaela to Matt, and back again. He then reached an arm across Mikaela to grab Matt's hand in some secret handshake that ended in a finger wriggling retreat.

"Matt-the-maniac is back! Best joke ever, man! When do the rest of the guys show up?" He stood back and gave Mikaela a long look. "I will say this for you, my friend, when you punk someone, you do it with class."

Mikaela wanted to simultaneously smack the guy and run away. She felt her body fold inward while Matt exited the car without responding. Daniel cut the chauffeur off and opened Mikaela's door, extending a hand her way. She stayed seated, waiting for the ground to open up and swallow her, or for her hammering heart to simply decide to stop beating.

Salvation came when Matt positioned himself mere microns from his friend's face and snarled, "Shut up, Daniel."

Cowed, Daniel backed up a step. "I'm just messing with you, Bro."

"Not today. Not on our wedding day. Got it?"

"Whoa!" His face went slack, and he stepped back. "I thought this was a prank. You're seriously getting married? At the courthouse? Right now?"

Mikaela offered no comment as Matt took her hand and helped her from the car, wrapping a protective arm around her. "You don't need to be here unless you can be civil."

Daniel became instantly contrite as he straightened his tie. "My apologies, Matt." He turned his attention to Mikaela. "I-I-I was out of line. Please forgive me." He offered his hand and pulled Mikaela into a hug. "Matt's the first of our little group to marry, and admittedly, the circumstances of the ceremony took me by surprise."

Matt shot him another scathing look before leading Mikaela up the steps.

She felt less like a bride than a curiosity, a specimen to be stared at and gawked over. Matt seemed to understand that her will to proceed had deteriorated. He stopped her outside the main entrance of the courthouse and leaned close, pressing his forehead to hers.

"I didn't answer the last question in our game. Greatest fear, remember?" He barreled on without waiting for her to answer. "My parents took me to Disneyland when I was seven. I was determined to take on the newest ride in the park —The Tower of Terror. After spending a few hundred dollars to buy our admissions, we wasted half the day waiting in line for that one ride. My father tried to lure me away by describing all the other venues and shows we could be enjoying, but I was committed to my decision until the last hundred yards or so, when I heard the screams of the current riders and saw the sheer terror on the face of a kid ahead of me. I looked for a way out and found 'the chicken door,' the last escape for people whose fears got the best of them. This is that door for you, Mikaela. I think you're amazingly brave for getting this far, and I'll understand if you want to turn and escape now."

His words gave her an out, but his expression begged her to stay. Mikaela didn't want to take the chicken door. She had given this hasty marriage a great deal of thought, and she knew she wanted time with this man. Mikaela looked at him and smiled. "Just hold my hand and don't let go, okay?"

She felt his large hand wrap over hers with a gentle squeeze. "Just like I promised." The joy radiating from his face chased the chill from her heart like the first rays of morning on autumn frost. He opened the door and her life changed forever.

Martine and Eliza were waiting inside the lobby. They had expressed their concerns about the wedding multiple times over the past few days, but they set their worries aside amidst compliments and hugs, restoring more of the day's diminished excitement. Mikaela witnessed Matt's natural goodness as he greeted the women. He'd seen them only from across a room, but he treated them as dear friends. For a moment, she wished she had trusted in her brothers' love for her and Matt's way with people, and invited them as well. Her mind began running forward to family occasions, and then, as always, the clutch of Matt's prognosis pulled her back.

Besides the couple entering the judge's chambers, no one else was in the lobby. Matt held her hand as they approached the clerk who smiled as if she knew a secret. She directed the little party to another room down the hall. Matt wore the same secretive smile, and Mikaela's heart rate sped up as she tensed in anticipation. When the door opened, all she saw were flowers! Stands and stands of glorious sprays lined the room, and at the front was a man Mikaela recognized from the evening news.

Matt kept his hand in the small of her back as he led her

forward. "Mikaela, this is my good friend, Senator Burton. He'll be officiating today. John, this is Mikaela."

Mikaela offered her hand to the senator as her mind swirled over the seriousness Matt placed on this quick court-house wedding. The flowers were magnificent, but his commitment to her was on full display in his stern defense of their marriage to Daniel, his gentle acknowledgement of what he was asking from her, his offer to release her from their agreement, and having the union solemnized by a senator. She knew time alone would not define the exquisite adventure on which they were about to embark. Her attention returned to the extraordinary man standing beside her, gazing down upon her. Martine and Eliza were sniffing, and even Daniel seemed transformed by the reverence of the moment.

"Are we ready to begin?" asked the senator.

Matt raised his eyebrows, deferring the answer to Mikaela.

"Yes," she whispered, and the prepared reading began.

She heard little. Matt centered her with his eyes, his hands never leaving hers. His attention was fully consumed in her to the point that Daniel had to nudge him when the time came for Matt to make his vow. Mikaela held her breath, weighing everything about his vow—the pitch, the volume, the conviction it reflected. Mikaela began to shiver when, in place of the simple yes she expected, Matt unexpectedly recited a verse from one of her favorite poems—*Love's Philosophy*:

The Fountains mingle with the Rivers
And the Rivers with the Oceans,
The winds of Heaven mix forever
With a sweet emotion;
Nothing in the world is single;
All things by a law divine
In one spirit meet and mingle.
Why not I with thine? –

"Yes, Mikaela, I take you as my wife."

Her lips trembled. She wondered if he knew that *Love's Philosophy* was the poem her mother recited to her father as he lay in his sickbed years ago, and the words Mikaela read at each of her parents' funerals. In a moment, he had summoned her parents and brought them to her wedding.

Mikaela leaned forward and muttered. "How could you have known what that poem means to me?"

Matt dabbed at her tears with his pocket square as he answered. "I noticed you always carry that little book of Percy Shelley poetry in your purse. *Love's Philosophy* seemed most appropriate for today."

"It's my favorite."

The senator smiled and nodded her way. "Mikaela, do you have something you'd like to share with Matt?"

She hadn't prepared anything, but without hesitation, the second verse came as naturally to her as breathing, and she squeezed Matt's hands and began:

See the mountains kiss high Heaven
And the waves clasp one another;
No sister-flower would be forgiven
If it disdained its brother,
And the sunlight clasps the earth
And the moonbeams kiss the sea:
What is all this sweet work worth
If thou kiss not me?

Wedding bands were exchanged, but before the senator pronounced them husband and wife, Matt moved to the kiss, quickly deflecting any mention of death and parting. He took Mikaela's arms and pulled her near, sliding his hands around her to keep her close, and then he kissed her, but not simply with his lips. She felt as if they were merging into one being as his fingertips pressed into her back, connecting her to him. His heart pounded against hers as warmth and passion fired. And then he pulled back, his expression becoming haunted, fearful, hungry, and then quickly shifting to a smile that felt staged.

He had defined the rigid terms of their passionless marriage of friendship, but the heat in their promised wedding kiss left Mikaela shaken and confused. She turned and found Martine and Eliza crying as they swept her up.

Martine took her by the arms and stared straight into her eyes. "I had my doubts when you told me you were marrying him. I wondered what kind of marriage this was, but after that kiss?" She gave three swoon-worthy sighs and fanned herself. "Congratulations, Mikaela. I'm so happy for you."

Mikaela had barely recovered from Martine's analysis when red-eyed Daniel swept her up in a hug. "Mikaela, I hope to someday find what you two have."

Mikaela wasn't sure what they had.

"We need a picture," said Daniel as his arm waved, indicating that he wanted them to move together and pose by one of the floral arrangements.

She complied, but she noticed that Matt seemed distressed. Before others noticed the change in him, she took his hands and looked into his face. "Daniel wants to take a wedding photo."

"Oh. All right." His eyes crinkled with concern. "Are you okay?"

Mikaela thought back to the kiss, wondering if something had changed in their arrangement. "Perfectly okay. Are you?"

Relief flooded over him. "Best day of my life."

"We're going to be good together." She said it as much to assure herself as him.

His face brightened. "Yes. Yes, we are. Lead on to our great new life."

A limo was waiting outside to drive the little group to The Capitol Grille in D.C. for lunch. At three o'clock, Matt tipped the server and sent the guests back to Baltimore in the limo while the Rolls pulled up for them. Mikaela's knees began to shake. They were at the point of no return. The great unknown. The moment they moved from a wedding to a marriage, and Mikaela had no idea what lay ahead for them. Matt looked as pale as she felt, and their combined nervousness caused her to shrink into the seat.

Matt pulled three silver packages from a storage compartment. They were wrapped in purple ribbons and tagged one, two, and three.

"Open number one," he said, placing them in her lap.

Her shaking fingers struggled to untie the bow, but after a moment the first box opened, revealing a velvet jewelry box. When she lifted the lid, she found a diamond and sapphire necklace and matching earrings, with a note that read:

They cannot make more beautiful that which is already perfect, but they can be a reminder that you are, and will always be, my treasure.

Always,

Matt

She froze, unable to speak or respond as tears filled her eyes. "Thank you. You couldn't have said anything more perfectly wonderful, but . . . you didn't have to do this."

Matt tipped her chin to turn her face his way. "This is a real marriage, and in a real marriage, the husband gets to give his wife a wedding present."

Two tears traced down her cheeks. "But . . . I didn't . . . I don't have—"

Matt's own eyes shone. "You've surrendered your entire life to me. There is no greater gift than that. No matter what I ever do for you, or give to you, I'll always be in your debt. Now, turn around and let me fasten it. You might enjoy wearing it tonight."

"Tonight? What else do you have planned?" she asked as she turned to receive the necklace.

Matt smiled, enjoying her excitement. "Uh, uh uh . . . you'll have to wait and see." He carefully removed her pearls and placed them in the velvet box. As soon as the clasp on the necklace was secured, Mikaela used her phone's mirror app to see how she looked in the necklace. Her lips began to tremble again.

Panic filled Matt's voice. "I can take it back if you don't like it."

Mikaela grabbed his hands. "I love it. Who wouldn't? It's the most beautiful thing I've ever seen. I'm just realizing how different our worlds are. I've never had an occasion to wear something like this. What if I don't fit into your world? What if I embarrass you?"

"Oh, Mikaela." He turned her and pulled her to his chest as his arms encircled her. His cheek rested against hers as he said, "I have one character trait upon which you can always rely. When I speak, I always say what I mean. I never lie or color the truth, so hear me now. I assure you, any man would count himself blessed to have you in his life. Our situation places us in a rather elite club. Time is more precious when it's so limited. Relationships are also more precious, but you knew that long before I did. Neither of us may fit in my world anymore because that world is out of sync with real life, just as I was before we met. You are true north to me. My way home."

They said nothing more as they listened to music, enjoying the ride to whatever undisclosed place Matt had chosen. When the car finally stopped, they were at a hangar at Dulles International Airport, where a private jet sat on the tarmac. Mikaela felt as if she were in a fairytale. Matt held his hand out to her, his were shaky as she felt.

"Never? Not even commercially?"

She shook her head.

"I want to enjoy a hundred firsts with you, beginning today."

"Do I dare ask where we're going?" She looked down at her dress. "I'm still in my wedding dress."

"That dress is perfect for what I have planned."

The Gulfstream jet was like a flying Rolls, and Mikaela's awe continued as she turned her head this way and that, looking in every nook and cranny.

"This flight is a gift from my parents. This is their corporate jet."

She mentally linked his parents to the jet and panicked. "Your parents own a jet." She shook her head as she allowed the notion to sink in. "A *jet*, Matt. I'm sorry, but this boggles my mind. What do I serve them when they come to dinner?"

The question obviously amused him. "The in-law special."

She rolled her eyes at him. "I'm serious. How do I talk to people like them?"

"Like they're people who already love you, because they are."

She wrapped her arms around him. "This day is nothing I expected. Thank you for making it magical."

"The magic isn't over, so I suggest we each lie back and get a nap before we land. We have about an hour gate to gate."

Matthew pulled blankets from a closet and handed her one as she slid into the window seat. He took the aisle beside her and buckled in. He was fast asleep in moments, but Mikaela didn't want to miss a moment of the adventure as they flew along the Atlantic coast. He was still sound asleep when they landed, and she felt ashamed that in her exuberance she had missed the signs of his fatigue. She took his pulse which was steady, but his coloring was more pale than normal. She shook him gently as the plane landed and taxied to a hangar.

"You're not feeling well, are you?"

Disoriented at first, he shook off her concerns and insisted he was just a little tired.

"You said you always speak the truth. How are you feeling?"

Annoyance registered on his face. "I'm . . . a little tired, but otherwise fine. None of my plans are strenuous. Please, open the second box."

Determined to keep closer tabs on him, Mikaela opened the box and found a tiny toy helicopter. She looked out the window to a pad where a helicopter was revving its engines.

Her eyes widened with excitement. "That's for us?"

He nodded and smiled over her enthusiasm. The next hour was spent viewing the magnificence of New York City from the air. After landing, Matt had her open her third gift, two private box tickets to a sold-out Broadway show.

"You've spent a fortune on this day."

"It's only a day, a fraction of what I would have loved to have planned."

Mikaela noticed the circles under his eyes and his attempt to disguise a yawn as a cough. "You're exhausted."

He offered a sheepish smile. "I can sleep in tomorrow."

"Matt, this day has been like a dream, and I feel like a princess. You absolutely exceeded every fantasy I had about my wedding day, but I know you have treatment tomorrow afternoon, and I think it's time to go home."

Matt sat forward and pointed to the waiting limo with a shaky hand. "We'll ride through the city, spend two hours in comfortable seats watching a stellar show, have dinner at Le Bernardin, then we'll fly home right afterwards. I promise. I can do this."

Mikaela placed her hand on his forehead and was relieved that it was cool to the touch. "I know you can." She offered her first married half-truth. "But I don't want to push you too hard. Do it for me. Let's head back to D.C. so you can introduce me to my new home."

Surrender showed on his face, but Matt offered no argument. He placed a call to the pilot with the change in their itinerary. The plane door was open and waiting for them when they arrived at the hangar.

Mikaela didn't know what Matt was thinking or feeling as the plane took off, whether he was frustrated that she nixed the remainder of his carefully made plans, or grateful to abandon the charade of health. He didn't say, and Mikaela didn't ask, but a solemn quiet hung in the air on the way home, as if the helium had been expelled from their denial-filled day, leaving weighty reality in its place.

Matt was sick. Very sick. They could run away from that truth for a few hours here and there, but short of a miracle, there was no escape. So Mikaela set her sights on a miracle.

5

The Georgetown house was an elegant two-story brownstone townhome on Potomac Street near the pulse of the city's social center. Built in 1900, it had four beautiful fireplaces and gorgeous cherry floors. Everything else about the house was sterile and white. Except for the giant black theater-style sofa that faced an equally obtrusive black, seventy-two-inch flat screen TV.

"The maid came through the other day to get the house ready for you." He gave Mikaela a walking tour through the open kitchen, dining room, and living area. "The fridge is pretty empty. We'll need to go shopping." He moved to a door to the right of the staircase that led to a second sterile, white story that smelled of fresh paint. "I turned the downstairs den into my room. It seemed more practical." He quickly opened the door revealing another tidy space painted in that recurring white palette. The small room was dwarfed by a king size bed decorated in teal and brown.

"I had the movers place your things upstairs in the master."

Mikaela noted how slowly Matt climbed the stairs. She assumed this was the practicality that convinced him to move to the main floor. He smiled proudly as he moved to the last room down the hall and opened the six-panel door. The room had been freshly painted a soft gray with cheery yellow trim. Her double bed with her adjustable mattress, and other personal items, barely filled a corner of the space.

"Check out the master bath. I hope it'll be your sanctuary."

The soft gray and yellow décor continued in the bathroom, where it met a slate floor and gray and white tile. The spa shower and white porcelain Jacuzzi featured a dozen massage jets.

Mikaela sighed. "It's beautiful, but I feel terrible about taking your room. I don't need all this space."

"I want you to feel comfortable and happy here. I confess that I might come borrow that massaging shower from time to time."

"Anytime."

Matt surveyed the space. "I haven't done much with the place since I bought it last year. I never noticed how much it looked like a hotel until the other day."

"The paint is fresh. When did you find time to do all this?

The flowers, the senator, all of today's surprises, and the house?"

He wriggled his eyebrows over two very tired eyes. "It took some doing to make it all happen in three days,"—he leaned into the door jam and smiled her way—"but it made me the happiest I've been in a long time."

"No wonder you're exhausted." She stood away from him, her hands extended. When he took them she said, "Thank you for this, and for everything. I feel very welcome here, Mr. Grayken."

Their eyes met and held, but he didn't return the implied invitation for him to acknowledge Mikaela as his wife. She stepped closer, slowly. Matt leaned in, his lips parting, and then he stopped. A low sigh escaped those ready lips, and he closed his eyes and dropped her hands, ending the moment.

Mikaela felt the friend barrier go up like an iron curtain, rejecting any offer of further closeness. The difference in mood between the passionate wedding kiss and this rejection caused a shock to her heart, as if Matt had placed theoretical defib paddles on her chest and yelled, "Clear!"

He backed up and said, "Swimming calms me. I . . . uh, leave for the pool around six before heading to the office. I don't suppose we'll see each other in the morning."

She stared at him, but her mind was elsewhere, on the conversation where he laid out the contractual terms of their "marriage" which he appeared prepared to keep.

"Will we, Mikaela?"

"Will we what?" she snapped back, bringing her hands immediately to her face in contrition. "I'm sorry. I'm tired."

Sorrow drew his features downward. "I understand. I share your . . . fatigue."

Mikaela dropped her gaze to the floor.

"What if I take the train to Baltimore for my treatment? We could drive back to Union Station together in your car, pick up my car, and then go grocery shopping. Or vice versa. There's a farmer's market down the block."

"All right."

"Good. Then I'll say goodnight and see you tomorrow at the center. Good night, Mikaela."

"Good night." She watched his haunted eyes fix on her until the door closed and clicked. She ran to the bed and fell backward onto it. Despite the wedding kiss, Matthew Grayken was, as he said, a man of his word, holding true to the terms he'd outlined.

She was definitely going to need that fancy shower. And lots of cold water.

Matt left Mikaela's room and went to his own. Soon thereafter, he heard noises in the kitchen. Neither he nor Mikaela seemed able to sleep. He hated himself for creating a situation more painful than his aloneness, placing the woman his heart yearned for within arm's reach, and then holding her at bay. Four months ago, before the confirmation of the AML's return, an army couldn't have kept him from a woman who looked at him the way Mikaela did. And now, a promise could.

He awoke the next morning and found a note from Mikaela on the island:

I inventoried the contents of our cupboards. We're going into battle mode. That means we're going to boost your immune system by only eating whole foods in as natural a state as possible. Yes. Take the train up and I'll drive home so we can shop. Today is your last chance to eat junk. From then on, you'll only eat food I clear. Got it?"

Mikaela

He smiled at the reference to *our* cupboards. She was in this for the count. Clearly frustrated with him, but in this fight.

He wrote her a note in return.

I'm ready and willing to follow all orders. See you at sixteen hundred hours.

Btw, can't tell you how good it is to have you in the trenches with me.

Matt

6

M att skipped the pool and went directly to his office. Leaving early for treatment made it hard to keep up with work. He needed the head start on the day, but that wasn't the only reason he skipped his swim. It terrified him to admit that swimming now left him weaker instead of stronger. Mikaela's note made him feel hopeful enough to let go of the old routine and prepare for the battle plan she described. He was absolutely grateful to have her in his corner for this fight. The fight of his life.

He knew the time was coming that he would have to walk away from work. Such an admission would have once terrified him, but leaving work now felt less like a surrender and more like part of that strategy Mikaela mentioned. He would hand the reins over and leave the company today if it meant he could win this fight, but there were so many others whose needs he had to consider, people who were counting on the company to stay solvent so they could pay their mortgages and launch their children's futures. It was for them that Matt carried on.

He was amazed that company revenues were holding, and even growing, in some markets, even though he was delegating more of his responsibilities to his VPs so he could attend treatment. They in turn handed off more of their day-to-day work to department heads. As a result, the office rumor mill was churning with wild speculation about his absences and early exits. He made no effort to explain his daily departures, even to his senior staff, knowing one of them would inadvertently leak the information to his parents, milliseconds after they were apprised.

He took great pride in the fact that six-year-old Great Expectations was considered an extremely employee-friendly company. He instituted some additional perks as compensation for the staff's increased load—catered lunches, flexible start and end times on Fridays, and bonuses for exceptional work. Mikaela's battle strategy had given him another idea to address the company's need for growth while his absences increased.

He called the company VPs in and told them he had placed a dozen of their exceptional summer interns on the payroll. Some squawked about the move. Matt knew they were already on edge. He looked around the table at the men and women who had helped him build Great Expectations into a successful international venture. He owed them some stability.

"I know I've been away quite a bit lately, and I've heard the rumors being whispered by the staff. Without going into great detail, I'll confess that there have been some changes in my life recently. You may find a Mrs. Grayken popping into the office sometime soon."

"You're engaged!" cheered Stuart, the VP of Sales.

Matt pulled on his chin to contain his smile. "Actually, I got married yesterday."

Cheers erupted around the table as people leapt up to congratulate Matt.

"I'm so happy for you! I have to tell you, we were worried about you," said Georgia, the VP of Marketing.

Stuart nearly shook Matt's arm off. "My wife has been looking at new cars, but I told her to hold off because, frankly, Matt, we were afraid the company was going under."

Ben, the forty-two-year-old CFO seemed less relieved than the rest of the team. "Does this mean you'll be back in the office full time again?"

When all were seated once again, Matt stood at the head of the conference table and said, "I know I've shifted some of my responsibilities to you, and I apologize for any undue burden that's caused you, but I don't want you to worry anymore about the company or about your futures. The answer to Ben's question is . . . no." He heard the executives take a collective breath. "But I realize that we can't continue managing things in the same way. Some changes are needed. In fact, that's why I hired those young millennial interns. I'm not that much older than they are in years, but we corporate stiffs who worry about the bottom line need their fresh eyes and input to capture the emerging younger market. I've set them up in the small conference room. I told them to think of it as their 'War Room,' and told them they have two months to get into battle mode. I want them to think outside the box. To brainstorm new marketing campaigns and ways to capture their peers. If we decide that their ideas have merit and are worthy of being implemented, they'll each get a $5000 bonus. If those ideas advance the company, every employee will see an increase in their revenue sharing. It's a win-win, people."

A low murmur filled the room.

"I'm also preparing to restructure the executive board. I may step back as president and serve as CEO."

Ten worried sets of eyes shot left and right as each member assessed what the others were thinking. Ben was the first to give their cumulative concerns a voice.

"What's really going on, Matt?"

"Other needs and possibilities have captured my attention. In order to pursue them and keep Great Expectations on target, I'll need one of you to step up and serve as acting president. If that opportunity intrigues any of you, please see me privately after this meeting."

He hadn't expected to make this announcement so soon, but he felt as if an elephant had been lifted from his shoulders. He led the executive board to the War Room where they spent an hour with the interns, listening as ideas flew around the table. Their response was what he'd hoped for—

positive enthusiasm—and even his execs seemed energized by the exchange.

He normally felt guilty on days he clocked out early, but not so this day. He drove to Union Station and picked up the Acela Express to Penn Station, anxious to see Mikaela and tell her how he had instituted a battle plan of his own. He knew her feelings were still raw, but her note seemed forgiving, as if she too realized it would take time to arrive at a comfortable place where they could be partners and friends. Or so he hoped.

He argued the point during the cab ride to Prospect's Medical Campus. To his surprise, Mikaela was waiting outside for him. The very sight of her cheered him, until he exited the taxi and saw her red-rimmed eyes and her hands in constant motion.

"I wanted to catch you before I leave. I'll be back in an hour," she said.

"Leave? Where are you going? What's wrong? You look like you've been crying."

He reached for her hands, but she pulled them back and clasped them together. "I'm heading to Lexington Market to get some organic produce. I'll be back. Just go get your treatment."

The light turned and she speed-walked away across the halted traffic and away from Matt without a glance back. He wondered if she really would return.

The pumpkins and paper leaves in fall colors did not

lesson the sober mood in the IV infusion room as all eyes turned to him. Martine checked him in and got him settled.

"Are you my nurse today?"

"No. I wanted a minute with you. What did you do to Mikaela?"

"I-I-I didn't do anything."

"Um hmmm," she said with a roll of her eyes as she rolled up his shirt sleeve. "She's been a mess all day."

The report bit into his heart. "We're not your typical newlywed couple, Martine. We've got some hard things on our plate."

"Um hmmm . . . I didn't want to like you. But then I saw that kiss, and I said, 'He really loves her.' And then I saw her come in here today, one day after that happy kiss, all closed mouth and sadder than I ever saw her before, even when her momma died, and I said to myself, 'Martine, you were right about that man. He's going to wring the life right out of that sweet girl.'"

He felt his heart slam to a stop. Mikaela was in pain, and he was the cause. "Hurting her is the last thing I'd ever want to do. Her happiness means every-thing to me."

"Then fix it." And then she walked away.

The patients' glances and whispers burned into him, adding new misery to a treatment that now seemed pointless. Living with Mikaela made her miserable, and living without her would be agony. He watched the immunotherapy drug drip into his arm in a two-beat pattern, providing a musical score for his self-recrimination—*self-ish, stu-pid, pet-ty, thought-less*.

Mikaela arrived at six-thirty. She seemed calmer, more settled as she came over to his seat. "Ready to go home?"

The Jekyll/Hyde moment caught Matt off guard, and even more unsettling was the fact that she was out the door again before he'd collected his things. He was breathless by the time he caught up to her in the hallway. "I'm not moving another step until you tell me what's going on!"

She spun and raised her hands to quiet him. "Please be civil. I have to work here."

"I will yell and scream and kick, if that's what it takes to get an honest answer from you."

"All right. All right." She hushed him with her hands again. "Just get in my car, and then we'll talk, okay?"

Matt's feet felt leaden as he followed Mikaela through Prospect's parking garage. She turned the key, but before she put the car into gear, Matt placed his hand on the gear shift and said. "This isn't going to work, is it?"

She turned to him, her tears welling. "I was okay this morning, then Martine announced that we were married over the weekend, and every patient wanted me to tell them *our story*, how we met, how you proposed. I tried dodging the details, but the story followed me all day long until the patients in your appointment hour started trickling in, people who knew you were in treatment. Their comments became medical instead of romantic. Half the people hoped we'd reenact the wedding kiss for them. The other half turned into grief counselors." The tears spilled over. "I just couldn't take it. I had to get out of there before you arrived."

Matt lifted his hand from the gear shift, rolled down his window, and leaned his elbow on the ledge. His head fell into his hand. "Drive, please. I need some air."

Mikaela headed into the street and picked up the ramp to the highway. The traffic sounds and the wind filled the painful silence between them, but the chill remained as Mikaela pulled into the alley that led to the garage.

Matt noticed his car was missing when the garage door lifted. He groaned as his head dropped back against the seat. "I forgot to remind you to drop me off at Union Station. I left my car there when I took the train this morning."

Mikaela braked with a jolt, adding her own groan of frustration. "Can we pick it up in the morning?" As if answering her own question, she pulled in and put the car in park. "On the way back, maybe we could pick up a table for the kitchen."

Matt looked at her, his mouth agape, afraid to breathe. "You want to buy a *table*?"

"We need a table," she answered matter-of-factly, punctuating the comment with a push of a button and the pop of the trunk, which opened automatically.

"We?" Matt's heart slingshot between sorrow, elation, and utter confusion. He understood the analogy of walking on eggshells, and he didn't care for the feeling. Irritated, he yanked at his tie until it hung low and loose beneath his collar, then he turned to challenge Mikaela. "An hour ago, I thought you were moving out, and now you want to buy a table?"

"I never said anything about moving out. There's a big difference between having a hard day and quitting. The two concepts are totally unrelated." She opened her car door and moved to the trunk with Matt matching her step for step.

Mikaela reached for the bags, but Matt jutted his arm forward, petitioning her to stop. "Back at the hospital, you said you couldn't take it. That you had to get away."

"And I did. I went shopping. See?" She snatched her two grocery bags, then she set them down and leaned against the car. "All right. Some things definitely need to change between us. I don't want to navigate our odd relationship in public where people know so much about your health and our story. I'd like you to change your appointment time to the morning when I'm not in the infusion room."

"All right. If that's what you need."

"Thank you. You set the boundaries and I agreed to them. No romance. No falling in love. I get it. Then we both need to stick to the rules. Be warm, be kind, be amiable, be respectful, but no more blurring the lines. Like that kiss that made me think you wanted more than friendship from me."

"You asked me to kiss you at the wedding. To be a doting groom."

"That was more than a ceremonial wedding kiss, and you know it."

He felt his face drain and then flush. He was guilty as charged on the kiss, with no easy alibi.

"You can't pull me close to comfort me then push me away." Her hands waved before her like a barrier. "I don't have much experience with dating, and our situation is confusing enough without crossing signals. Just be my friend, okay?"

He wanted to mention a few crossed signals coming from her direction too, but he held his tongue and said, "Okay. I'm sorry."

"We'll figure it out. It's only day two."

7

Mikaela had Matt set the groceries on the island before he slipped into his room to change out of his suit. She began organizing the organic produce, essential oils, and powdered elements along the counter near the sink. Then she pulled the recipe from her purse. After locating the blender, she threw berries, spinach, milk, and ice in and hit "start." As the ingredients whirred and grinded, she followed the recipe, adding tiny amounts of several powdered items along with drops of two oils in brown bottles.

When Matt reappeared, he was dressed in sweats and a zipper-front hoodie. He looked at the beige mixture and gave a weak smile. "What's that? Dinner?" Distaste registered on his face. "You're the boss."

"Consider it a non-alcoholic, vitamin-packed aperitif."

"Is that part of my new nutritional plan?"

"Yep." Mikaela poured the sludge into two glasses. "This is Prospect's proprietary, immunity-packed super shake."

"How did you get the recipe if it's proprietary?"

She curled her lips inward and gave him an innocent look. "The head nutritionist is a friend. I sweet-talked him into giving it to me."

She handed a glass to Matt, who took a reluctant sip. "Hmmm . . . not bad."

"See, big baby?"

"So, elaborate on how one sweet-talks a nutritionist."

Mikaela noticed the return of his generally undetectable brogue, and knew he was a little bothered by this topic. "We dated for a very short while. After my mother passed."

"A short while, like one date?"

"Two . . . maybe three dates." She took a sip from her own shake, eyeing him over the rim of her glass. "I broke things off. We weren't a good fit."

Matt took another sip as Mikaela began pulling the ingredients for dinner from the bags. "Can I help?"

She noticed that he suddenly was the lost guest in his own kitchen. "That'd be nice." She gave him a forgiving smile and pointed to the knife block she had sent from her apartment. "There's a cutting board in that cupboard beside you. You could slice the pepper and onion while I stir-fry the chicken."

Matt pulled out a knife and asked, "Is this new?"

"It's mine." She caught herself, remembering how they had laughed about their joint ownership of three vehicles the previous evening, and now they were back to calling things "hers" and "his" again. She rephrased her answer. "I mean it's one of the things I had shipped from my apartment."

"It's great. And this cutting board is . . . also . . . great. Very . . . orange."

"Would you prefer a less orange one?" she quipped back.

"No. Orange is . . . nice . . . and . . . bright . . . and cheerful." He chopped the pepper and started on the onion as he nonchalantly asked, "Did he ask you out after?"

"Did who ask me out after what?"

"Your nutritionist friend. Did he ask you out after you broke things off?"

"A scandalous number of times." Guilt bit at her for weaponizing a reply that could have been a simple yes. She had to remind herself that Matt was not like her brothers. He was refined and unaccustomed to sarcasm served with a side of exaggeration. In a more contrite voice, she explained. "It never would have worked. He's a true Dead-Head. He and Jerry Garcia meet up every weekend in a cloud of smoke, if you know what I mean."

"Ohhh. Gotcha." Matt's laugh was hearty and filled with relief.

It pained Mikaela to see how stilted their banter had become. "Drink, drink, drink your smoothie."

"Yes, ma'am." He downed a large gulp.

"Besides, I told him I'm off the market." She smiled and wriggled the fingers of her left hand, showcasing her rings. "They're the best defense a girl could ever have."

Matt barely smiled. "Does he know you married a patient?" He slammed the knife through the onion. "A man who can barely lick a double dip ice cream cone let alone a rival?"

Mikaela took a step toward Matt and caught herself. It would be a breach of the blasted "agreement," the very list of rules she had accused Matt of violating an hour earlier. The contract was contrary to every instinct in her. She felt like a mime with her tied hands, denied the ability to comfort—her natural means of expression.

"First of all, it's 2017 in America. Secondly, I was raised with seven brothers, soldiers who taught their baby sister how to take care of herself, so despite the gentlemanly intent of your nineteenth-century sensibilities, I don't need a security detail to handle Griffin's or any other guy's uninvited attention. Thirdly, give it time, Matt. We're just getting started."

Matt set the knife down. "I'm not normally a chauvinist. I'm just reacting badly to the changes I feel inside. Everything the doctors do to me makes me weaker. I don't see how this sludge is going to make me strong."

The defeat creeping back into his voice drained her optimism. She tried to regroup and get him to rally. "The immunotherapy treatments strip the cancer cells of their ability to hide from your immune system. Now we're going to amp up your immune system so it's as strong as possible for the fight."

"I'm sorry." Matt leaned over the island, then stood and took a generous swallow. "Thank you for researching all this."

"You're welcome. Boosting your nutrition is only part of the plan. We're also going to eliminate anything that might lower your immune system, like mercury from certain kinds of fish and smoke from cigarettes. And the doctors have other treatments lined up if this round of immunotherapy doesn't work. Do your parents smoke?"

"Not anymore."

"Good." Mikaela tore her lettuce. "We need to visit them, you know."

Matt eyed her curiously.

"I'd like to ask them about your childhood illnesses and get any info they have on your birth parents."

Matt shook his head. "There's nothing. It was a closed, private adoption through an agency. Our attorney tried to find my birth mother when the leukemia first appeared, but it's like she dropped off the earth. She may have died. Supposedly, her poor health was the reason she gave me up."

"Maybe there are other siblings. There had to have been documents."

"Oh, there are. They just offer no helpful information."

Mikaela felt a door slam shut on one hopeful option.

"They froze some of my bone marrow before starting chemo when I was a child. That restored my health until college. Umbilical stem cells gave me a second remission, but my red blood cell count is too low for that option to work this time. I'd need the marrow of a close relative, and there isn't one. If a bone marrow transplant is your battle plan, let it go now, Mikaela. You might as well quit now and move home."

She dropped the sack of fruit and turned on Matt. "Why did you say that? I thought this was my home now."

Hurt showed on Matt's face. "You said you didn't want the house."

"A house is not a home. A home is people, and memories —" her voice broke, "—and little things a family collects together to make it theirs." She picked up the fruit and opened the fridge door, leaning against it as she cried. Matt stepped toward her and then backed off.

"Do you want me here? Do you want this to be *our* home?"

He stepped away and fell back against the island. "Of course, I do."

"Then stop accepting the inevitability of your death."

8

Saturday morning, Mikaela rose early and unpacked the last of her things—a trunk of clothes, a few more kitchen tools she loved, a dozen of her favorite books, family photos she placed in her room, a few colorful family knickknacks, and two chenille blanket throws that she laid on the sofa. She stood back, pleased by how the splashes of color already made the house seem homier.

Eight o'clock passed without a sign of Matt. She curled up on the sofa under the crimson blanket, scrolling through her phone. Outside the window, she heard a cardinal singing from an evergreen bough.

About a half-hour later, a door squeaked behind her and she bolted to her feet with a start, her book in prime throwing position. Matt's hands came up in his defense.

"I'm sorry I startled you." His smile showed no trace of sorrow.

"How long have you been standing there?"

"Not long. A minute maybe. I liked seeing you there. You looked . . ."

Mikaela's hands flew to her hair, which hung in tangle waves down her back. "A mess?"

"No. Comfortable. Like you were home."

She didn't know why the comment caused her to blush. She hurriedly folded the blanket and moved to the kitchen. "Did you know a cardinal lives in the shrub by the window?"

"Maybe we should hang a bird feeder out there."

Anxious for tasks to fill their first full day alone, she pulled a notepad and pen from a drawer and replied, "I'll add it to our to-do list."

Matt's eyes widened. "I . . . used to keep my chargers in that drawer."

"I moved them," she replied as she jotted "buy a bird-feeder" on the short list of errands. "They're in the end table drawer. I hope you don't mind, but I need a place to keep medicine logs, menus, shopping lists. This drawer seemed perfect."

"No . . . I . . . don't mind," he replied as he pulled drawers, searching for the errant cords. "I'm glad you're making yourself at home. The pillows, the blankets. They're nice." He leaned against the counter. "Did you move anything else? Just so I know . . ."

She watched his reaction as she explained, "There was a stack of files and old catalogues on the counter. I thought the blender should go there since we're going to need it twice a day." Mikaela noted that his eyes remained wider than normal and he nodded like a bobblehead.

"And the files and catalogues?"

She repressed a smile over the challenge these simple adjustments posed to the former bachelor. "Since you're using the den as your bedroom, I moved them to a shelf in the stereo cabinet."

"Perfect," he replied, though he showed no sign that the idea seemed perfect to him, or even acceptable for that matter. "And if I wanted to boil an egg, would I find the pots and pans where I expect them?"

"Yes. And I'm pleased to report that the fridge and stove will be staying in their proper places as well."

He stifled a laugh that came out as a snort. "Okay, okay. I'm not as good at change as I thought I'd be. And here you are, completely upended. Just draw me a map and I'll adjust."

After breakfast, they drove to Union Station and picked up Matt's car. After dropping Mikaela's car off, they took the Range Rover to go table shopping. Matt was so moved by the joy she found in sharing that small adventure that they spent the rest of the afternoon in the crisp late September air, strolling Georgetown's curio shops, buying art prints and kitchen gadgets.

Mikaela pulled him into a Christmas shop bedecked with lights and steeped in the scent of balsam. Like radar, she zoned in on the trees laden with Christmas ornaments, some elegant, some merely for fun. She moved from tree to tree, swooning over one decoration after another. Matt used a variety of excuses to leave the store and wait for her down the street, but she clamped her hand over his arm and dragged him to a regally-bedecked twelve-foot tree that mocked his fear of spending Christmas in a pine box.

Mikaela dangled several whimsical ornaments before Matt's eyes, swooning over each one before selecting a few. The more her enthusiasm bubbled, the harder he found it to breathe. He wondered if he'd live long enough to see the blasted baubles adorn a tree.

"You don't love them."

"Get whatever you like." He heard the irritation in his voice and tried to mask it with a half-smile.

"Do you think these are gaudy? You probably grew up with an elegant tree?"

"Isn't it a little early to be thinking about Christmas?" He batted a clay cupcake dangling from a silver cord. "If you need to do this now, why not just buy a matched set of gold balls?"

"Because these are memories." Mikaela's eyes brightened like the twinkle lights on the tree.

For the first time, he noticed what ornaments dangled from her left hand—a bride and groom, a heart, a plane, a helicopter, a taxi, the New York City skyline, and a tacky-looking crab ornament with "Baltimore" painted across it—mementos of the short time they'd already spent together. A chill coursed through him as he realized the marital sentiment she was expressing.

Her other hand held an assortment of ornaments representing places they'd never been and things they'd never done. Mikaela had selected three balls painted with D.C. scenes—the White House, the Washington Monument, and the Capitol. These were easy destinations mere blocks from the house. The other ornaments were completely random—a picnic table with tiny dishes and food set upon it, a movie theater ticket made from clay, a canoe, a bowling pin set, and a golden star.

He cocked his head sideways and drank in her slightly crooked smile, the gold flecks in her eyes, the whimsical mop of hair that flopped to the left. "But we've never—"

"But we will! We'll make a list and do these things together."

Her enthusiasm gave him the courage to likewise suspend medical reality and join in her denial. He found a pair of red lips and a puppy ornament. "What do you think? First kiss? And I think we should get a dog."

"Uhhh. . . Okay on the lips, but we should discuss the matter before actually purchasing a living thing." She held up a boat ornament and a pair of pot-bellied old timers seated in front of a TV.

Matt eyed them as a knot grew in his throat. "You and me in fifty years?"

"Eighty. No way I'm letting you look like that in fifty."

He caught the sheen in her eyes, the denied tear she wiped away when grousing about catching a speck of glitter in her lashes, but he knew that they were living on wishes and dreams.

Exhausted by the day's outing, Matt retreated to his room to rest, comforted by the sounds of Mikaela humming mere feet away. He felt certain he could smell her cologne wafting through the door. He soon realized the scent had found its way to his shirt sleeve as he brushed her arm in the store. He pressed the scent against his nose and breathed Mikaela in as he fell asleep.

Some time later, while fighting to pull out of the fog and awaken, he heard the bang of pots in the kitchen and happy tones drifting from the stereo. After a while, the banging stopped and the oven door closed with a slam. He wondered what healthy casserole Mikaela was baking. Her voice neared his door. He assumed she was in the living room singing a duet with the guitar player on her CD. Matt sat on the edge of the bed and listened to the perky lyrics about a man whose reason for coming home was the woman waiting for him there. The tune was happy, as were the lyrics, but they harrowed his heart, leaving him melancholy and depressed.

He selected Handel's Water Music from his phone's music list and placed the phone in the speaker cradle. The order and symmetry of the music failed to calm him this day as it usually did. He cranked the volume up a bit, lay down, and closed his eyes, but peace still did not come.

Another song from Mikaela's CD filtered through the closed door. The folksy love song's mellow tones and haunting lyrics taunted Matt like a siren song, conjuring longings he tried to dispel, hitting him deep in his gut. He turned off Handel and let the mellow tones slice into him, bleeding out his fear and loss. He filled his arms with a pillow, clutching it close, catching Mikaela's scent as he inventoried his losses. Overwhelmed, his body hunched over into a ball of grief. His anger and sorrow, inadequacy and fear released in a guttural wail, muffled by the pillow.

Then he remembered he was not alone.

The stereo's volume decreased, followed by a rap at his door, and Mikaela's worried voice. "Matt? Matt? Are you okay?"

He considered not answering and allowing her to think he was having a bad dream, but then he heard her footsteps retreating from the door, the slide of a kitchen drawer, and her anxious return. He recognized the scraping sound at the doorknob as she used the trick he taught her in case of an emergency—sticking a paring knife in the doorknob's hole and twisting it to unlock the door.

In a panic, he grumbled, "I'm fine. I'm fine." But he was too late. The door opened, and Mikaela stood in the doorway, staring at him as he stood before his disheveled bed, still clutching the pillow to his chest. He glanced in the mirror and caught his reflection—his downturned mouth, narrowed brows, hunched shoulders, and eyes half-closed in self-pity.

He wanted her, and he wanted her gone, knowing that every day would be the same. A long goodbye. An enduring musk-scented agony. She would never know him. Not the man he was. She would only know this weak, sniveling, fearful creature transformed by cancer. He hated who he'd become and hated having her see him this way.

He saw her mouth drop. He rushed past her and through the door into the chill. Too weak to run, he took long strides to place as much distance between himself and the house of pain as he could until he arrived at a gated school yard. He managed enough energy to jump the fence, finding rest on a swing. His feet moved him back and forth as he stared ahead at his brief future. He could chase Mikaela away and live quietly and alone, but he knew distance wouldn't help now. He was past the point of no return. She was in his thoughts, in his heart, in him. He would hurt if she left and hurt if she stayed, because he already loved her.

He reconsidered the terms of the agreement, assessing the harm in telling her how he felt.

Because the closer we become, the deeper the pain becomes at goodbye.

He twisted the swing and let it go. The motion matched the twisting in his heart. Mikaela was likely angry at him, and rightly so. Instead of facing things honestly and telling her the truth, he had run.

Out of pride.

And he'd hurt Mikaela.

He thought back to the morning at the Christmas shop and to the ornaments she'd purchased. Memories from their infant marriage. She was attempting to make something beautiful from the limitations he had placed upon her. She was honoring the spirit of their union, but he could not say the same. Instead, he had been a callous friend. A thoughtless husband.

Acknowledging his marriage straightened his thinking and gave him a renewed sense of duty and purpose. They were in the middle of their first marital squabble. The normalcy of it felt foolishly sweet, and he considered what husbands do in such a situation. He remembered passing a florist on the street. He'd never noticed it before. Perhaps because he'd had no one to buy flowers for. But he did now, and he wasn't going to waste this exquisite opportunity.

The sign said the shop closed at seven on Saturdays. Matt slipped in with mere minutes to spare and looked at the arrangements on display. Roses were the only flowers he had ever sent, and even a romantic dolt like him knew this was not the time for roses.

He saw a potted plant moving along the wall as if under its own power, and then he saw the source of its locomotion. A broad-chested man with a Marine insignia on his arm was seated in a wheelchair, carrying the plant.

"Can I help you?" he called out.

"Kudos to you for maneuvering around in here with your chair," said Matt.

"I'm very careful," the man answered, with a broad smile. "I've laid out the room to accommodate these wheels. No big deal. Whad'ya need?" He set the plant on the floor.

"Flowers for my wife. Something that says, *I'm sorry.*" Matt felt a sense of privilege in uttering those phrases.

"Ohhh, well . . . flowers have a language all their own. Purple hyacinths are a good apology flower, as is asphodel. White poppies are the flower of sorrow, but they also offer consolation."

"What flower says I'm sorry I was a jerk?"

"Whoa . . ." The proprietor chuckled. "You're going to need a large bouquet of all three."

Matt extended his hand. "By the way, my name is Matt. I live up the street. I think you and I might be seeing a lot of one another."

"Good to meet you, Matt. I'm Gino. Newlywed?"

The question warmed Matt's heart. He dipped his head and smiled. "Yes. Very newly wed. As in two days ago."

"And you already need apology flowers? Ouch."

"I'll take the mega bouquet, but I left the house without my wallet. Would you bill me?"

"I saw you walk past here an hour ago looking like you'd lost your best friend. I'd say you're worth the risk." Gino rolled into the refrigerated room where the blossoms were stored. "Last customer, ten minutes before closing on Saturday after my help has left?" He blew out a long breath and shook his head. "I'll have to get creative."

Matt's curiosity grew as Gino pulled purple hyacinths,

white poppies, yellow asphodels, and assorted greens. "Mind if I ask you a question?"

"Like what's a Marine doing selling posies?"

Matt blushed. "I take it you get that question a lot."

Gino smiled and moved the flowers and greens to a low table in the back. "My father owned a landscaping business when I was a kid. I worked for him on weekends and in the summers mowing grass and planting so many flowers that the thought of a desert and guns sounded like heaven. Don't get me wrong. I'm proud of my service, and I loved my team, but while I was lying in a hospital in Germany, considering what life was going to look like as a paraplegic, flowers suddenly seemed pretty nice. So here I am."

Matt contemplated everything Gino said as he watched another man, reduced by the cruelty of fate, making the most of what was left him. Gino carefully placed each stem until the arrangement was perfect and glorious, then he wrapped the arrangement in a plastic bag to protect it from the evening air. The price tag was lofty, but Matt didn't care. He left the shop feeling like Santa Claus.

The spring in his step diminished as he reached the darkened house. It was only eight o'clock, hours past Mikaela's planned dinner hour, but not late enough for her to have turned in. Fear raked across his heart at the thought that she'd left him. That he'd driven her away.

He took the eight steps in twos, his heart racing as he reached the door and rushed inside. After flipping the lights on, he set the flowers on the island where he found a note waiting for him. His hands shook as he opened and read it.

I waited for almost an hour and then I headed out to the street to look for you. Am I a nurse dealing with a difficult patient, or am I a wife dealing with a disgruntled husband? Why won't you talk to me?

Drink your sludge. It's in the fridge along with the burned casserole.

Mikaela

His guilt was nearly as intense as his relief, which was nearly palpable, leaving him as weak as a new foal and happier than he believed he could ever be since his diagnosis. The flowers, as beautiful as they were, seemed a pedestrian, anemic offering against the chaos he'd brought into Mikaela's life. He searched his limited knowledge base on Mikaela's likes and interests for some grand gesture to show her he was trying.

He still knew so little about her. They had spent but a few hours together simply talking, except for the twenty questions kind of conversations they'd shared on their walks. Her kindness and courage were her hallmarks, but he also knew she was conversely a rough-and-tumble tomboy with a romantic side that embraced the world with childlike enthusiasm. She was a woman-child, a lover of Shelley's poems and old movies from Hollywood's glamour days. A woman of faith, she was inclined to notice a cardinal's song. And then he recalled how she ogled the beautiful gowns in a Georgetown dress shop's window.

Matt remembered a piece of mail he had tossed in a drawer weeks earlier. He pulled it out, checked the dates, and got an idea. He found a piece of blank cardstock, pulled up a card-making app on his computer, and set about designing an apology he hoped would earn him forgiveness and make Mikaela swoon.

9

Mikaela awoke as exhausted and drained as she was when she finally fell into bed the previous night after searching the neighborhood for Matt. She had heard him come in but resisted the urge to head downstairs. Instead, she sat on the edge of the bed, hoping he would come to her. He did not, and she did not sleep for hours.

It was her first weekend in Georgetown, where she was still a relative stranger, but during their shopping stroll she noticed an old stone church whose beautiful Greek architecture drew her eye. She had no idea what denomination met there, but she was too far from Baltimore to make the service in her familiar congregation. More than a sermon, she needed the strength and support of being in the company of others petitioning God for something dear.

She made her way to the kitchen to prepare Matt's healing smoothie and extra for herself.

The flowers caught her attention first. They looked like a small Garden of Eden, a massive arrangement more suited to a fancy hotel's lobby than a kitchen island. She winced and shook her head until she saw the homemade card. The cover featured a graphic of a sad puppy sitting in a pee-puddle, with a face that pled for forgiveness. The humor and sentiment performed the magical alchemy, transforming distance and discomfort back into warmth.

The message hit every point she needed to hear.

Mikaela, what can I say? I was a jerk. A proud, selfish, frightened jerk, who recognizes that he has an angel trying to help him. I'm so sorry.

I'll try not to keep everything bottled up inside me anymore. I'm not a big "talker," but I'll try to do better if you'll promise to forgive me if I regress and break for the door again.

I hope you're still willing to make memories with me. I'd like to start by making a special one with you. Open the green envelope. I hope you say yes. Don't panic. We'll go shopping.

Matt

Everything about the green envelope seemed elegant and intriguing. The bright green paper was thick with a sheen that glistened. Mikaela lifted it and ran her finger over the embossed address which read, *Mr. Matthew Murray Grayken.* She turned it over. An embossed crest was pressed into the flap that had already been carefully opened. She lifted the flap and found a large ivory invitation with an embossed green border peeking out from inside. The invitation was written in a raised cursive font that read:

The Pleasure of Your Company is Requested
at an Evening of Art and Music,
in Recognition of the Irish Embassy's Observance of
Lá Saoire i mí Dheireadh Fómhair,
Monday Evening, October 30, 2017,
7:00 p.m. Formal attire.

An embassy gala! Matt's offer to take her shopping now made sense. She had nothing to wear to such an occasion, and that thought filled her with both excitement and dread. Neither did she know what to expect at such an event or how to talk to the people who attended such an affair.

Her initial intrigue shifted to panic and then to something more mellow and tender as she withdrew and read the smaller RSVP card. Matt had written *Mrs. Mikaela Grayken* as his guest. She wondered what was going through his mind when he wrote out her married name for the first time. Did it comfort or torture him?

His haunted expression from the previous evening returned to her. She had replayed the scene a dozen times, wondering what had caused Matt such pain, and then she understood.

The music.

"When I'm feeling deeply introspective, I turn to classic folksy rock—Cat Stevens; Crosby, Stills, Nash & Young. The smooth, older stuff."
"And what constitutes deep introspection?"
"Mostly self-pity."

She cringed as the words and tunes of those mellow love ballads she had played reverberated through her mind. They were filled with emotional lyrics about lost love and forever love, all wrapped in poignant melodies created to pull at the soul. She felt that tug last night as her thoughts drifted to Matt in the other room. She was sure he felt it too, and those feelings caused him to flee.

Remorse washed over her. She faced the fact that despite her arguments to the contrary, she was still hoping to make the marriage more than Matt intended. He had clearly laid out rules, which she had accepted and even doubled down on.

And yet, in her core, she believed he also wanted more from their union. But what did she know? She had so little experience with men and relationships. What if his attentiveness was simply Irish courtesy, or the manner of men raised in a world of wealth? She accused him of blurring the lines, but she knew had also taken a big eraser to their agreement, and caused Matt the very pain he had asked her to help him avoid.

His mother's lesson to Matt now had deeper meaning for her:

I now understood what it really meant to love someone, to care more about them than you do for yourself.

She had put her wants ahead of Matt's, and still, he had returned kindness.

The invitation to the gala burned her heart. Her cheeks flushed red, and she placed her hands there to cool them as she stared down at the card. To accept, she needed only to check the "will attend" option. She couldn't do it. Instead, she left Matt a brief reply on his card—

I'm sorry too for violating your privacy. Thank you so much for the invitation. The gala sounds divine. Heading to church. Can we talk this afternoon? And what is Lá Saoire i mí Dheireadh Fómhair?

She set the note where Matt would certainly see it, and she left the house. The trees were beginning to put on their jewel tones. After a brief respite of two cool days, Indian summer returned with warmth and beauty. The brisk, five-minute walk to the church got her heart pumping, while her mind raced with the things she wanted to say to Matt.

She arrived twenty minutes early for the service. The familiar smell of polish-soaked aged wood instantly made her feel at home. She settled into a pew, listened to the organ prelude, and studied the beautiful stained-glass windows. The Biblical stories of trial and love, told through the perfect placement of carefully cut glass, felt particularly tender to her now.

The ancient organist looked down at her and smiled several times as she played. Her music provided a soothing backdrop for Mikaela's continued prayer for a miracle for Matt. When the service ended, Mikaela remembered little from the sermon, but she took away renewed peace and strength she knew she'd need in the coming weeks.

Mikaela slipped into the house to discover the source of the delicious aroma of sautéed onions and sausage drifting through the open dining room window. She studied him, enjoying the pleasure he appeared to be getting from his labor. Matt was standing at the stove with his back to her, stirring something in a pan. The towel slung over his shoulder gave him the impressive look of a practiced chef. Mikaela grinned at the scene, then caught her breath when she noticed his jeans and button-front shirt both looked a size too big now, a worrisome sign that he was losing needed weight.

Her eyes drifted to other changes that had happened during her absence. A white tablecloth edged in garishly sequined green clovers, gold coins, and leprechauns, covered their new table where two place settings were arranged. Celtic music played in the background. It was clear Matt had gone to a great deal of trouble, and she wanted to give him the entrance his preparations deserved. She slipped outside again and entered with a bang of the door.

"What smells so delicious?" she asked as she entered.

A hopeful smile graced Matt's face. He delivered his reply in a thick Irish brogue that caused pure joy to bubble within Mikaela.

"I read your note, and felt you needed a good Irish orientation." His answer concluded with a little bow.

Mikaela clapped and laughed, and fell against the island that separated them.

"So, what's in the pan?"

Again, his brogue was on full display. "Bangers and mash."

"Bangers and mash?"

"Bangers are sausages. When they get too hot they sort of pop, and give off a wee little bang. I found a few in the freezer and thought I'd treat you to one of the Emerald Isle's finest delights."

"Ahh. . . I see. And mash?" Her interest caused Matt's smile to widen. He pointed to the steaming pan. "I see. Mash is mashed potatoes."

"Aye! I know sausages and mashed potatoes aren't on the nutrition plan, but I had such a hankering for them today that I hoped you wouldn't mind if I was bad this one day."

She felt a sting begin in the corners of her eyes, so she diverted to humor by trying out her own poorly executed brogue. "I think it's a grand plan."

"Please be seated, milady."

She sat and fingered the sparkly tablecloth. "You didn't tell me I inherited this through marriage."

"That'd be my lucky poker cloth."

Mikaela chortled. "Now you sound like a pirate."

"Arrr . . . Another of my many charming personalities. With your permission, I'll drop the performance before my throat gets hoarse." Matt set a bowl of mashed potatoes covered in browned sausages and onions with a sea of gravy atop the whole mix. "Dig in. I'm anxious to see what you think."

The weight of his expectation hung over her first forkful. She was delighted she could honestly give him a two-thumbs-up assessment as gravy dribbled down her chin.

"So, you like it?"

She winced. "Too much, I'm afraid. Is this one of your mother's dishes?"

"Weekly fare when I was a child. She rarely cooks now except on holidays, so I was forced to learn to make it myself."

Matt dug in, and Mikaela was pleased at his appetite. She was worried about the excess shirt fabric in his shoulders. "I think we should revive your mother's once-a-week tradition."

"You do?"

"Just drink a glass of sludge before dinner. I, on the other hand, might have to run a few laps around the neighborhood to work this off. So, what is La Soar Me Dread Fomhair?"

It was Matt's turn to laugh. "*Lá Saoire i mí Dheireadh Fómhair?*" (It sounded lyrical when he said it in Irish.) "It's the last Monday in October, when banks and government offices close to give families a long holiday. Lots of artsy things are planned—sports and marathons and the like."

"I don't suppose they'll be eating bangers and mash at the gala."

"No. It's quite the posh affair. Most of the invitees either work for some government, a large business, or industry. I haven't gone in a few years. I'm not one for working a room, but the music is lovely and the food divine. And it'll give us a chance to take a twirl on the dance floor and show off my moves. That is if you'd do me the honor."

Mikaela chuckled and nodded. "I'd love to."

"Then I'll be the luckiest man in the room."

"You're still stuck in your Irish persona, you know."

"I must be channeling my da."

"We should plan a date to see them."

He set his fork down and held Mikaela's gaze. "And we will, once we get things settled betwixt us." His voice changed back to the serious tone Mikaela recognized. She missed his playful side immediately.

"It was the music, wasn't it?" she asked.

His eyes closed, and his head dipped, assuring Mikaela that she was right.

"I admit it stirred the very longing I was trying to avoid, but that's my problem, not yours."

"I won't play that CD when you're home."

He reached for her hand and then pulled back. "It's bigger than that. There's no use denying there's an attraction between us." He shook his head and his eyes rolled. Mikaela understood the pained pull he was expressing. "Honestly, I've never felt that kind of hurt before. The closest thing to it was seeing my mother in the hospital. But why should I be surprised? What man wouldn't be attracted to you?"

Mikaela held her breath.

"These few minutes together today leave me more convinced than ever of the rightness of our plan. We can be close. Have fun. Make each other happy. As friends. But we need to be honest and tell each other when we hurt. I don't know about you, but I think we can do this. I think we could bring each other a lot of joy if we're honest with each other and hold to the plan, because pain is all that exists when we cross that line."

A lump formed in her throat. It was too big to speak past so she nodded her agreement and masked her sorrow by returning to her food.

"I'll mail our RSVP today." He pushed his plate away and leaned his elbows on the table. "I have another idea. Do you have any vacation time coming to you?"

"Two weeks, and a week of personal time."

"Can you take it right away?"

"I can take my personal time immediately and put in for the vacation break. Why?"

"I'm giving my board notice Monday that I'm going on sabbatical beginning the following week. I've already prepared them. I'll finish up this round of treatment on Wednesday and do my labs. There'll be a break while the doctors plan the next course of treatment. I thought we could start in on that list of memories of yours. I have a few I'd like us to make as well."

The news brightened her mood. "I'd like that very much."

"Great. Then it's settled. One more week of the daily grind and then we follow wherever those Christmas trinkets you bought lead us."

10

They easily filled every minute of the next week with work and errands. Matt relinquished all household control to Mikaela, who spent the first two evenings shopping for accessories to warm their home's white interior. Muted accents and pops of crimson, black, and teal, made the sterile space inviting.

Matt's last treatment occurred on Wednesday, with critical labs to follow the next day. The pair marked the occasion by looking forward to the Embassy gala. They walked downtown to side-by-side formal shops to purchase a suitable ball gown for Mikaela and to have Matt measured for a new tux that fit his diminishing frame. Matt handed Mikaela a credit card in her married name before they left the house.

"Hold on," said Mikaela, who held the credit card with the same distaste deserved by a slice of green bologna. "Adding me to your accounts was supposed to be a formality.

For emergencies. I told you I plan to pay my own way. Like roomies."

Whatever resistance she had to the idea of actually using the quickly melted in the warmth of Matt's plea. "I know, but please let me buy you a dress. Please."

She reluctantly slid the card into her wallet, feeling grateful for it when she saw the price tag tucked discreetly into the dress worn by the mannequin in the window.

"Matt!" Her volume was barely more than a whisper, but her eyes screamed panic. "This dress is seven thousand dollars."

He smiled. "It's okay. We'll live on sludge and bangers." He smiled and signaled to the attendant who hurried to where they were standing. "Something smashing, please. For the Irish Embassy Gala."

The woman nodded. "She's in good hands, sir."

"See you in an hour?" he said to Mikaela, offering her a reassuring wink.

Mikaela nodded nervously, and he slipped away and into the menswear store.

The attendant sized Mikaela up. "Let's get you into a fitting room and measure you."

Minutes later, five decadently expensive gowns were brought for her to try on, but Mikaela asked to try on the dress she had seen in the store window first—a black satin Zac Roselle design. It was among the simplest in appearance, with a fitted bodice, jewel neckline, and cap sleeves all in satin. Its one adornment was a broad, flat bow sewn over the entire bodice. It further accentuated her slim waist. The skirt skimmed over her narrow hips, falling into wide, loose folds around her feet. It was the most elegant thing she had ever seen.

"Shall we try on another?" asked the attendant. "Or is this the one?"

Mikaela twirled on the pedestal and watched the skirt billow like a flower "This is definitely the one."

The attendant nodded her approval. "Would you like me to send for your husband, so he can see?"

"No, no, no, please. I'd prefer to surprise him."

"Very well. I'll box it for you while you select your accessories."

Mikaela was out of the store having purchased shoes, gloves, a wrap, hose, and proper support garments, all before Matt was dressed.

His brows wrinkled. "Couldn't you find anything?"

Mikaela masked her excitement as pleasant satisfaction. "I did, kind sir. It's all being delivered. Thank you for spoiling me. How about you?"

"The tux needs to be altered. I hope they won't need to do it again in four weeks."

Mikaela had the same concern. "We'll have to make bangers and mash twice a week from now until then."

Matt offered her a smile that belied the worry evident in his face, so Mikaela changed the topic. "I saw a florist up the block. I'd like to pick up a few mums for the flower bed."

Matt held up his arms. "We can only carry four back to the house."

"Four will be perfect."

Gino recognized Matt and rolled to the door. "This is either your wife, or you're going to need another apology bouquet."

Matt returned the joke with a brief chuckle and placed his hand in the small of Mikaela's back, guiding her forward. His touch burned straight through to her heart.

"This is Mikaela. Mikaela, Gino created the bouquet on our island."

She extended her hand to Gino. "It's beautiful. Thank you."

"Very nice to meet you. Don't thank me. I've seen some despondent beaus in here, but your husband was the saddest newlywed I've ever seen. All he wanted was to be forgiven, and after meeting you, it's easy to see why."

Mikaela blushed and said, "Thank you." She also felt Matt's hand linger on her back.

"So, what can I get for you folks today?"

"Just mums," said Mikaela, who wondered if the astute florist could sense the awkwardness between the couple of supposed lovers.

"All I have left are large ones. They're twenty-five each or two for forty-five."

Matt peeled off a one-hundred-dollar bill and handed it to the florist. "We'll take four. Thanks, Gino," said Matt as he hefted two pots and turned for the door.

"Mikaela, whatever he did, forgive the poor guy. He's a wreck when you're upset with him." He laughed and wheeled over to the register as a soft smile crept its way to Mikaela's lips. She was not the only one who thought Matt's feelings had deepened. Gino saw it too.

Matt could barely draw enough breath to speak as they each walked two heavy mums home along the lamplit street. His arms were so spent from the errand that he dropped the mums rather than setting them down on the stoop when they arrived.

Mikaela spared him from having to explain his fatigue by saying, "We've had quite a day. I think I'm too tired to even watch TV tonight. How about you?"

"I'm ready to turn in too."

They entered the house and each fell back against the kitchen wall and closed their eyes.

"Today marks the last day of treatment. Tomorrow is lab day. I'm excited to see your results."

"It's also our one-week anniversary. We made it seven days. So, what do you think?"

Mikaela opened her eyes and studied each feature of his handsome profile, weighing his goodness and the joy he'd brought her against the challenges their circumstances presented. She easily concluded that happiness won, hands down. "Best week of my life."

Matt turned to her, his face a study in chiseled awe. "Really?"

"Really." She still felt as shy as an adolescent when they talked this way. "How shall we celebrate?"

"I celebrate every day I wake up and you're still here."

***

Mikaela rigged it so Matt would open the door and walk straight into a bouquet of five helium balloons Thursday morning. The initial sleepy-eyed shock gave way to childlike pleasure and on to guilt. "How did you pull this off?"

"I bought a little helium tank at the party store. Everything is better with balloons."

His mouth pinched into a pouty frown. "I'm sorry. I didn't get you anything."

Mikaela jutted a mug of sludge out to him to restrain her arms from delivering the hug she was dying to give him. "You've given me an adventure, a home, a best friend, and a seven thousand-dollar evening gown. I think you've got the anniversary covered. But these are to mark the end of treatment."

"For this round."

"Details. And your labs are being drawn today."

He bit his lip. "Yep."

"I've been praying for you, and I feel very good about how you're doing. The news is going to be great!"

"You think so?" He held his hope out like a bag of fruit he was waiting to weigh on a scale called Mikaela.

"I do." The peace that filled his eyes was worth over-promising. "How about I pick up a couple of crab cakes tonight for a special dinner."

Matt turned her way. Uh-oh was written on his face.

"Thursday night is standing poker night with the guys. I missed last week because of the wedding . . . not that poker compares in any way to the wedding."

"With Daniel?"

"And a few other of our chums who migrated to the capitol area."

Mikaela leaned her head back and laughed. "You're very adorable when you're guilty."

"I'm sorry, Mikaela. I could cancel . . . or you could come."

"No. Go. I'm glad you're seeing your friends. Are you taking your lucky tablecloth to the game?"

"No way. Bad protocol. A man never takes his flag into another man's castle."

"Well, I wish you luck." She pinched the hem of her peach-colored uniform's tunic and offered a little curtsy. "I hope you win a big old pot o' gold."

Matt gave her a raised eyebrow glance and returned her Irish brogue. "Oh, we don't play for money, lassie. We gamble for much higher stakes."

"Oh, do ya now? And what might they be?"

Matt's voice turned ominous. "I could tell you, but . . . well . . . I do play with two of the government's finest, in which case, I might have to kill you."

"I'll pass, thank you. See you tonight then?"

"If you're still up at eleven."

"In that case, I'll see you in the morning. I'd better finish getting dressed for work."

She walked three steps, and then Matt sent this question her way. "So, you're saying you really think the labs are going to be good?"

Her answer was based on the faith she'd poured into every prayer and wish she'd offered since she'd met Matt, knowing that her future hinged on this answer as well. "Yes." She shifted to a cheerier topic. "Two more work days until we begin our adventure."

"It'll just be a new destination on the adventure we've already begun."

11

M att thought of himself as an Aladdin-like man who needed to choose his words carefully before approaching the Giver for his grand wish. Aladdin rubbed a lamp and summoned a genie. Matt submitted his body to the lab techs, closed his eyes, and asked God, "Please give me more time with Mikaela."

He left the lab relieved that, good or bad, things were out of his hands. Either the therapy and sludge and medications and dietary plan had worked or they hadn't. He would know in a week.

The peace he felt over his looming vacation magnified the toll the past twelve weeks had taken on him. The gnawing guilt of not pulling his normal weight and of letting his employees and stockholders down, had been multiplied by the stress of racing to treatments. The physical aftermath of being pumped with abnormal levels of bio-engineered agents hadn't helped either. But today, the thought of owning his own time energized him. He pushed buttons on his Range Rover's stereo until he found a station playing classic rock with a hard-driving backbeat that matched the wild abandon in his heart.

When he entered the building, whispers and silent head nods followed him. One of the new hires shot a pistol point and a wink his way, while a secretary slapped him a high-five. Matt slipped into Ben's office and found him unusually jovial. Suspicious, he asked, "What's going on around here? Did someone slip a little of Dr. Benson's nitrous oxide into the ventilation system? There's an inordinate amount of giddiness in the office today."

Ben gave Matt an uncharacteristic hug and back pat. "We're all just so happy for you."

Matt leaned away and weighed the comment. "Because?" he asked slowly.

"Because of your marriage. It's been good for you, Matt. We all think so."

"Thank you."

"You're welcome. Does this mean you're staying on as president?"

"I'm here to address that very issue. Assemble all the VP's in the conference room in thirty minutes, please."

As Ben left to gather the leadership team, Matt entered his office to gather his thoughts. If his lab test results weren't promising, he'd bow out for the sake of the company. If they looked good, he'd consult with Mikaela about their futures, whatever they'd be, and decide about his position. When he entered the conference room, his VPs all wore the same giddy expression he saw on the other employees. His message changed that quickly.

"Thank you for your support of my marriage. It means a great deal to me. As you know, I leave for vacation tomorrow. In ten days, when I return, you'll have my decision on whether or not I'm stepping down as president. Please use this week and a half to draft your vision for the future of the company. I'll review your plans when I return."

Ben hung back after the other VPs left. "I know something more is going on, Matt. I respect your privacy and won't press you for details or ask you to change your mind, but you are Great Expectations. This is your baby. Always has been."

Matt squared himself to Ben and placed his hands on his friend's shoulders. "Those solo days are past. Over two hundred families count on this company for their security now. It's their baby too. The future is wide open and full of opportunities. We just need someone with vision at the helm. Don't think you're being disloyal by applying to replace me. I'm rooting for you."

"If you choose me, I'll make you proud."

"I know. See you in ten days."

Matt's throat grew tight as he exited the building and the company he built. He knew his days here could be very limited. It was another loss cancer might have dealt him. As he drove out of the parking garage, he passed Stuart's faded orange Nissan that the CFO held off replacing until he knew the company was stable. Rows of employees' cars stood as stark reminders that his health and the lab results affected more lives than his. He thought of Mikaela. And then he prayed again.

Rush-hour traffic was already backing up, so Matt chose a more scenic route that carried him past a hardware storefront aflame with mums and pumpkins. He stopped in to buy a potting trowel, so Mikaela could plant the mums they purchased, and ended up buying a ten-foot pre-lit Christmas tree from a stack of boxes being readied for a future display. The box was so large, Matt had to open the convertible top to fit it in, and so he headed down the road, top down, wind blowing, base and drums pounding, all the way home.

Joy engulfed him as he considered Mikaela's reaction to his surprise. Like the employees at his office, he wished he had someone to join in his high jinx, someone to share his secret and to simply high-five. This tree was his token of hope, a sign that he was planning to be here in December, to spend Christmas with his wife.

He wrestled the heavy box out of the car and into the garage, hiding it beneath the tarp he used to cover his small, token wood pile. The exercise left him sweat-soaked and wobbly, but his happiness continued to prevail as he left for the poker game at Daniel's place.

He was twenty minutes late and fully expecting to get razzed for both his sopping appearance and the ultimate group betrayal—marriage—but he was still completely unprepared for the sight that greeted him as he opened the door.

Each of his six poker friends were dressed in orange prison jumpsuits, with one leg manacled and chained to an "iron ball."

The teasing continued unabated throughout the first hour of the game. Pizzas arrived, and the chips and cards were pushed to the center of the table while everyone ate. Six pairs of eyes settled back on Matt.

"So . . ." asked Nelson Woodruff, an investment banker. "How's it feel to be off the market?"

Matt sat back, prepared for this question. "I highly recommend it. You should try it yourself."

Gunther Gnudsen piped in. "I hear your wife is a real looker." His brows wriggled and his eyes half closed. "It must be nice."

Matt thought of Mikaela and what the guys were implying by their sophomoric eye-wriggling and joking. Mikaela deserved better, and though he wasn't a husband in the way they assumed, marriage to Mikaela had taught him enough on the subject of love and respect to school his irreverent friends on the matter.

"It is nice," began Matt. "It's wonderful, actually. You guys think you know about passion and romance? I'll tell you what's romantic. To feel your heart rate increase just because your wife smiled at you from across the room. Or to watch that same woman, who's smarter and more capable than most of your corporate associates, get up a half-hour early to make you a special breakfast because she's worried about you. And passion? Imagine feeling your body electrified from simply holding her hand or from the privilege of putting your hand on her back and knowing she's with you. She's on my mind all the time. The things I want to tell her. Or silly things I want to buy her. I drove by a hardware store on the way home, saw a mum, and wanted to buy her a shovel. I ended up buying a Christmas tree too." He raised his face to the ceiling and laughed aloud, "And right now, for the life of me, I can't imagine what I'm doing here, with pizza and you lugs, when I could be home doing something as simply wonderful as talking to Mikaela." He stood and packed his chips. "There's a big difference between sex and love, my friends. One is instinct. The other is . . . well . . . I hope you grow up and find out."

He walked to the door and smiled back at the group. "I love you guys, but marriage beats poker, hands down."

The truth of his words was manifested in the urgency he felt to see Mikaela. He couldn't wait to give her the potting trowel and let her know thoughts of her and their home and even their mums stayed with him when they were apart. He wished he had set the Christmas tree up and surprised her. Right now, all he wanted was to get home and see her curled up on the sofa under the red blanket, with her bun flopping to one side and a smile for him at the ready.

He parked and hurried inside, but Mikaela wasn't on the sofa. She was lying on the floor, her feet scraping and kicking while her body lay buried beneath ten-feet of artificial evergreen boughs. Grunts and sighs echoed from the dark recesses of the tree, and then it burst into light as a cheer broke loose.

She crawled out and found Matt smiling down at her. "Rats. I wanted to surprise you."

"Oh, you did. How did you get that in here? I could hardly drag it into the corner of the garage."

She stood, her bun dangling off the back of her head with more hairs yanked out than were still in. Two red lines marred her cheeks after meeting boughs more personally than she had intended. The pull to draw her into his arms caused his entire body to ache. He was glad her attention was still on the tree, straightening a branch here, fluffing a bough there, so she wouldn't see the want in his eyes. He sat in the over-stuffed chair and swallowed past the lump in his throat to say, "It's still September. We haven't even bought a pumpkin yet, but our tree is up."

"We're progressive!" She laughed and turned to him with her arms spread wide before stopping, pulling them back, and crossing them over her torso. She took a step toward the tree and pointed to the heart ornament, which was hung near the bride and groom, plane, helicopter, taxi, New York City skyline, crab, and lips, commemorating their time together.

He pulled the trowel from the bag he held. "I suppose this is too big to hang."

Mikaela's mouth opened with surprise. "You remembered the mums." She took the trowel and held it against her heart. "I think anything is possible in this house."

12

The employees were eerily quiet on Friday. Matt figured his impending vacation and possible departure from the president's seat had everyone in a dither. The lunch he ordered for the entire staff loosened things up so he could wind up pressing needs and leave the office with a smile instead of guilt.

The subject of guilt prompted him to phone his parents. He'd been dodging their calls by sending short texts, delaying the inevitable introduction of Mikaela until she and he were ready to deflect questions he was not yet prepared to address. He knew the time for a family dinner had finally come.

He called his mother and spent twenty minutes reassuring her that he was happy, that he had no regrets about the marriage, and that Mikaela was indeed the best thing that had ever happened to him. When he heard the tone of her voice return to its normal timbre, he knew she finally believed him, and they moved on to making plans. Now he just had to tell Mikaela.

She was waiting for him when he arrived home. "I didn't expect you for another hour."

She walked over and offered him a taste from the spoon she was using to stir something on the stove. "The center was slow today, so they let me off early. What do you think about the sauce?"

"It's good. What is it?"

Matt knew he had failed a critical husband quiz when Mikaela's neck slumped, landing her chin near her chest. "A protein-amped cheese sauce to go over the chicken, but if you can't tell it's cheese, then I've messed something up." She returned to the stove.

Matt tried to sound nonchalant as he said, "I called my mother today."

Mikaela spun around.

"I told her we were taking the week off from work. She invited us to come up and spend next weekend with them in the city."

Her brows narrowed with concern. "The whole weekend?"

"You're not happy."

"It's not that." She fell against the island. "I'm looking forward to meeting them."

"Then what?"

"It's just a long first visit, especially when we're keeping secrets from them."

"I know. I'm working on honest answers that will deflect any questions about my health."

Mikaela returned to her sauce. Matt was certain his health status wasn't the only secret she was referring to. Her uncharacteristic quiet continued into the evening as they planted the mums and watched a crime drama on TV. Citing their busy next day, Mikaela suggested they each turn in early. She seemed better in the morning as they packed a picnic lunch and headed into D.C.

She rented Segway motorized transports for their tour of the city. The scooters were as great an attraction as the monuments and grand buildings they dodged other humans to see, and by day's end, they had visited all the sites on their ornament list and a few they hadn't planned to see.

On Sunday morning, Matt was dressed in his suit, waiting for Mikaela when she descended the stairs.

She stopped before reaching the landing and cocked her head to the side, studying him.

He pursed his lips and smiled. "I thought I'd go with you."

She slowly descended the last two steps. "To church?"

"You'll find that my religious attendance is not as uncommon an occurrence as last month's total eclipse."

She giggled. "I'm sorry. Forgive me."

"So, will you allow me to share your pew?" He crooked his arm and turned it her way. Mikaela hesitated for a moment and then glanced his way. He assumed she was verifying that this contact was approved by the FDA, Social

Services, or other official entity. He entreated her with a little elbow wiggle, and she slipped her arm through.

The punishing hurricanes barreling through the tropics and along the southern coast had pushed head winds north. They whipped Mikaela's long hair as she and Matt walked to the stone chapel, but Matt noticed that whatever hair-tidying she did involved only her left hand, while her right arm remained solidly linked with his.

He struggled through the unfamiliar hymns during the service. Mikaela sang full throated, albeit slightly off pitch. He also noticed how she spent most of the service with her eyes closed. Matt studied the shifting expressions on her face, as if she was responding to an important conversation. The sincerity of her prayers humbled him, leaving his arms prickled at the weight she placed in her communication with God. Perhaps for him.

The last-row berth made them one of the first out of the chapel. They paused for a moment on the stoop of the old church, breathing in the scent of wood smoke trailing from a local home's fireplace.

Matt closed his eyes and smiled. "I've always loved fall."

Mikaela linked her arm around his and they strolled on.

Day by day, the pair saw local sights people travel across the globe to see. They marked items off their list, and hung corresponding ornaments on their tree. By Wednesday night, they were each embarrassed to tell the other they were exhausted and ready for a break. Matt was up first the next morning. He checked the daily activity list taped to the fridge and sighed as he steeled himself to keep the promise he'd made to fill the week with memories. To his surprise, a different page awaited him.

WEDNESDAY
  1. Sleep in
  2. Long hot showers
  3. Massages
  4. Afternoon naps
  5. A Mystery Outing

He gladly returned to bed and was pulling the covers up over his chin when his phone rang. It was his oncologist. He considered not answering, but he knew they'd try again, likely when Mikaela was near. He took the call.

"Good morning, Dr. Gorman."

"Good morning, Matt. I have the results of your lab work. I'd like to discuss them with you."

Matt intensely scrutinized the doctor's every word and vocal inflection, to determine whether the coming news was positive or not. All he could read was his own fear, and he made a decision.

"Mikaela and I are on vacation this week, and if it's all the same to you, I'd rather wait until Monday to know."

"I understand. Enjoy your vacation. Just check in with me on Monday."

The call ended, but Matt's worry and analysis continued. He ended up skipping item one and heading straight to the shower to ease the tension creeping into tender muscles and joints. He thought he saw bruising and felt pain where there had previously been none. When he rubbed the steam off the mirror, his hair seemed thinner, and the circles under his eyes seemed more purple and pronounced than before. His hands shook and his stomach roiled, sending him to the toilet where he heaved, but nothing came up. Exhausted and weakened, he sat on the floor and closed the lid, using it as a pillow. He eventually dragged himself to bed and fell back asleep, awakening an hour later, well after Mikaela was up and dressed.

"Good morning, sleepyhead. Looks like someone else needed a quiet day too."

"Why do you say that?" he stepped forward, suddenly needing to lean on the island. "Do I look run-down?"

"About the same as me. Being a tourist is hard work." She peeled the schedule off the fridge and held it up like a poster. "I'm worn out too. Do you mind if we just relax today?"

"You too? Honestly?"

"Honestly. These first seven weeks of marriage have been busy and—"

"—stressful?"

She scowled. "I was going to say complicated. I love the idea of spending time together, and making memories, but they don't all have to involve crowded venues and navigating around thousands of people, do they?"

Matt slumped over the island and rolled his head back and forth over the cold granite. "Thank you. I thought I was falling apart."

"No more than me, but you'd better get showered. We have massages at noon. Doesn't that sound yummy?"

She pushed a glass of prepared sludge his way, and with those few words of optimism and perspective, Matt felt healed.

He returned for another, more relaxed shower, marveling over Mikaela's innate ability to know what he needed. Whether she truly was as exhausted as he was, she relieved his worry and sense of despair without his needing to confess them aloud. To him, that was love. The best kind.

Massages were followed by a few hands of rummy and an old movie on TV.

"What's tonight's mystery surprise?" asked Matt as he stretched and yawned.

Mikaela checked her watch. "I think it's time to show you." She stood and extended her hands his way. His reached out, and she pulled him to a stand, landing him within inches of her musky scent. He felt as weak as he had in the morning and yet for completely different reasons.

Mikaela didn't allow the moment to linger, as if she too remembered that similar previous moments had ended poorly. Instead, she turned on her heel and grabbed her purse, snagging her keys from the kitchen hook as she headed to the hall closet where a blanket roll and shopping bag awaited. She pulled a small cooler from the fridge. "Follow me," she said with a mischievous jingle of the keys, and Matt gladly did.

"We have about a ninety-minute ride west. Why don't

you choose a station to entertain us?"

Matt chose a peppy oldies country station with twangy tunes. Even the syrupy, sappy love ballads caused no emotional distress as the pair yodeled and crooned for the forty minutes required to break out of the city traffic and onto Route 270, where, gratefully, traffic was moving.

Mikaela turned the radio off and asked Matt to pull an envelope from her purse. "I jotted down some more questions, and I think it's my turn to start the asking."

Matt settled back into his seat. "Okay. Do you need this list?"

"Nope. It's for you. I've memorized the questions."

"Very well, smart girl. Fire away."

"Question one, what did you do growing up that got you into trouble?"

Matt gave the question some thought, and then a memory came to mind, causing him to laugh. "I poked holes in all the tins of peaches and sucked the juice out. It never occurred to me that it would have been better to have actually eaten the peaches since they were ruined anyway. Plus, I was destined to get caught when my mother saw the hole in the can."

"You little devil. See? There's one drawback to being an only child. You're always at the top of the suspect list."

"So true. Now one for you. What was the first thing you bought with your own money?"

Mikaela began laughing immediately. "I saw a magazine photo of J Lo wearing thigh-high lace-up boots. I wanted them so badly that I saved all my babysitting money for months and ordered them online, but when they arrived my mother wouldn't let me wear them. She said I looked like a wanton woman."

"A wanton woman . . . Who's the devil now?"

Mikaela pinched her eyebrows close. "Hmmm . . . "I think we need more music." Mikaela clicked the radio back on and smiled.

When they reached Frederick, Mikaela took the Route 70 exit toward Hagerstown and headed over the mountain. They were now farther west than Matt had traveled in Maryland, and he soaked up the magnificent color show exploding all around.

The sun sank low in the sky as Mikaela took another exit and headed down a few country roads past a sign that read Penn-Mar Park. "We're here."

The remaining foliage masked all but a few narrow sun rays, requiring headlights the remainder of the way until they reached a clearing bathed in soft, yellow light. Mikaela drove past a brightly graffitied rock hill with steps carved into it and parked.

"If you get the cooler, I can get the rest," she called out as they exited the car.

Matt followed her up the hand-hewn steps and to a rock ledge. The shelf looked straight into the cat's eye of the setting sun, which was radiating across the western horizon like an orange laser beam. Below the ledge was a steep drop into one hundred feet of nothingness carpeted by tall jagged rocks and trees, but the sprawling valley between the ledge and the horizon was bathed in an amber glow that spread before them as far as Matt could see.

"Whoa," he said. "What is this place?"

"Don't get too close to the edge if you have vertigo," Mikaela said as she spread two thick blankets over the flat rock base for comfort. She joined him at the cliff. "It's called High Rock. Hang gliders used to launch from that shelf until there were too many accidents. It's illegal to jump from here now."

Between the breeze, and the air-only view before him, Matt almost felt as if he were in flight. "How did you find this?"

"My mom grew up not far from here. My parents used to pack a cooler and bring us here to watch people glide from here. They looked like human butterflies. Do you like the view?"

"It's amazing." He turned to her and smiled. "Thank you for bringing me here, but we should have come earlier. When the sun sets, the view will be gone."

"Just wait. There's another view I think you'll like just as well. The shelf can be dangerous after dusk. It's too easy to fall and slip over. Come sit on the blanket."

She sat and pulled out a flashlight which she set close by. Matt joined her as the sky slipped into a color show all its own. As the sun disappeared and darkness settled, lights appeared from the houses and streets far below, rising to the star-studded horizon until it was hard to tell where earth and sky met.

She opened the cooler and spread bags of snacks and fruit between them and listened to the night music of rustling leaves, crickets, owls, and cicadas. "We can now add the star ornament to our tree."

"I think it's going to be one of my favorites."

"Me too."

They sat in silence for several minutes while a question nagged at Matt's peace. "Mikaela, do you believe in heaven? This place feels like what I imagine it to be."

"I do," she said confidently. "I know life and love don't end here. We go on, somehow, but I'm unsure about the details."

Matt leaned near and asked, "What is heaven like to you?"

"Well, my parents are still very real to me. I talk to them all the time, as if they were on a trip and I was speaking to them on the phone."

"You don't actually *hear* them, do you?"

"No." She shook her head and chuckled. "But I know they . . . that they are aware of me and what I need, because I feel their influence, and I feel their love, every day."

"Maybe that's God."

She shrugged. "Maybe. But I know death isn't nothingness. We go on."

Matt stared off at the light-dotted blanket of sky. "I hold on to that hope."

He reached a hand across the blanket to hers and held it as night sounds played a private symphony for two.

13

"It is hard to slow the heart's race toward hope," Mikaela wrote in her journal, even though she repeatedly warned herself not to read too much into the previous evening's hand hold, and Sunday's arm-in-arm walk. *Be patient. Keep your expectations in check,* she told herself. *Matt's health is as precarious today as it was yesterday.* Everything hinged on the lab results—Matt's health, their happiness, their futures.

But something had changed in her. Faith had turned to hope, and hope to confidence. She prayed with a new surety, believing the joyful effervescence encasing every new minute was a sign that her faith was being answered. That Matt would get better. Those notions brought her comfort as she packed for their flight to New York.

On the ride to the airport, she dared pose the question.

"Have you heard anything from the doctor? Are your lab results in?"

She watched Matt's Adam's apple slide and knew he was preparing to share something unpleasant.

"He called, but I didn't ask for the results. I told him I'd call back on Monday."

The soberness of his reply prickled her arms with worry. She had been prepared to offer bright bride-worthy smiles to her new in-laws. She would now need to camouflage her concern. She stared out the window without commenting, or showing her worry to Matt.

They each busied themselves with snack and magazine purchases until they boarded. Headphones provided sufficient barriers to deflect the topic during flight. They walked off the plane with their carryons, and found an exuberantly waving pair waiting for them just outside the security gate.

Mikaela had seen a photo of the Graykens taken some years earlier, but the people standing at the barrier seemed more likely to be Matt's grandparents than parents. As she drew nearer, the elegant couple's lined faces and gray heads were all that revealed their ages. Matt's father was a strong, towering man with a dapper style. He wore a white cable knit sweater over black trousers. The gray scarf around his neck matched the cap on his head. Matt's mother came to his chin as she stood at his side in heeled boots and a chic sweater set over a brown skirt. Their eyes were bright and welcoming, and they nearly burst past the guard when Matt and Mikaela approached.

"Hello, Mikaela! Welcome to the family!" Matt's mom rattled on with welcomes in a thick brogue as she rushed Mikaela into her arms. "Oh, Donovan. Isn't she lovely?"

Matt was likewise in the arms of his father, who answered, "She is indeed. They make a handsome couple. Imagine how bonnie the grandkids will be."

Mikaela shot Matt a worried glance, and he leaned over and whispered in her ear, "It's his way of saying you're pretty."

She nodded absently and then smiled. "Thank you, Mr. Grayken."

Donovan Grayken stood ramrod straight and drew Mikaela to his side with one strong arm. "Now, there'll be none of that Mr.-and-Mrs. blabber, Mikaela. We're Mum and Da, and we won't hear another word about it."

She felt her shoulders hunch, and she looked to Matt for support. Catherine Grayken came to her rescue. "Don't mind Donnie, Mikaela. We heard your parents had passed, but we know full well you're loved by a passel of brothers. We're a small family-just Donnie and me and Matthew, and while we don't have any intentions of trying to replace your folks, we do hope you'll come to love us and let us love you in return."

"I'd like that very much."

As they made their way to the Graykens' car, the parents' attentions turned to Matt with questions about his weight loss, his graying and thinning hair, and the circles under his eyes. Matt deflected them all by agreeing he needed to work less and sleep more. That sent the conversation back to

Mikaela with guarded requests for her to see that he did all those things. She was exhausted and stressed by the time they reached the Graykens' home.

Their magnificent Battery Park City condo overlooked a pier on the Hudson. Its red brick walls and wood floors gave it a country feel, and it's view of the waterway, with passing barges and boats, suspended the reality that they were actually in a bustling area of arguably the busiest city on the planet.

While the men headed off to the den, Mikaela explored every nook and cranny of the condo's 2500 square feet with Catherine, who explained their history with the home.

"We have a big showplace in Brooklyn Heights. We used it as much for corporate functions as we did for family. After 9/11, this area was struggling, so Donnie and I decided to do our part to rebuild it. We kept the other place as a corporate property and moved here, where we could invest in local businesses to bring life back to this community. It now feels as much like home to us as Ireland. That's what happens when you invest a bit of yourself in a home. You'll see."

"We planted mums."

The juvenile comparison of planting four mums versus rebuilding a community after 9/11 embarrassed Mikaela as soon as the words left her mouth, but Catherine's eyes lit up, and she laid her hand on Mikaela's shoulder with a gentle squeeze. "You understand. I imagine you came from a home with wonderful memories. Thank you for making a real home with our son. You can't know how happy that makes me."

"I'm sorry for the way we rushed off to be married. It seemed romantic at the time."

Catherine's lips pressed into a thin line. "I confess that we were torn. Matt has had a history of occasional impulsiveness, and we feared a hasty marriage meant he hadn't thought things through, but there was something in his voice that convinced us he wasn't simply infatuated. That he was truly in love."

Mikaela's eyes teared, and Catherine's did the same as she took Mikaela's hand. "Ordinarily, you couldn't have kept us from that wedding, but I had just returned from a medical appointment after experiencing some tremors in my hands." She brushed Mikaela's visible concerns away. "I'm quite fine, but we weren't sure, and rather than worry Matt, we decided to trust our instincts and give you two our blessing."

Mikaela wiped at her eyes. "Thank you." She leaned forward as if sharing a secret. "I do love your son. Very much."

Catherine gave Mikaela's hand a squeeze. Her eyes crinkled in the corners as she smiled. "I know. I saw it the moment Donnie overwhelmed you at the airport. I saw how you looked to Matt for your security, and I saw how he came to your rescue. You two are a good match." She patted Mikaela's knee. "And later, Donnie and I want to hear every detail of how you met." With a final pat of Mikaela's knee, she said, "Come. We'll put your things in Matt's old room."

Except for a timeline of photos of Matt, like those scattered around the entire house, there was little of Matt left in the room that had been redecorated as a guest suite. While the two women were alone, Catherine pointed to a photo of a skinny, obviously sick Matt at age six.

"I suppose Matt told you about his brush with cancer."

Mikaela tensed. She wanted information, but she knew the conversation could lead to questions Matt didn't want her to answer. "Yes. Two bouts, right?

Catherine nodded. "When I found out we couldn't have children, we told God we'd accept our fate, and we threw ourselves into Donnie's family business, but the ache for a child never went away. We were both over forty when we decided to adopt, but by then, agencies told us we were too old. We were healthy and in a position to bless some child's life, so Donnie had our attorney seek private opportunities."

This was the topic Mikaela had hoped to discuss. "How did you arrange it?"

"I don't know the details, but the attorney contacted doctors and hospitals in the smaller communities in case women were considering adoption but had not yet contacted an agency."

"Do you know what town or village Matt's birth mother was from?"

"I don't. The attorney tried to locate her when Matt was diagnosed with AML. He needed a bone marrow donor, but the attorney couldn't find her. Not a trace. It was as if the dear faeries who brought her to us came and carried her away." The news disheartened Mikaela, and Catherine seemed affected by Mikaela's response to her joke. She smiled and leaned close, more seriously. "We assumed she used a fake identification during the adoption."

"Matt said stem cells brought him out of the second bout."

"Because we caught it early. Even then, the toll it took on Matthew set him on a wild course. That's why I'm especially delighted that you're a nurse." She patted Mikaela's knee. "You keep a close eye on him for me." She winked. "If he ever does have a recurrence, he'll run from the truth and end up too run down for the doctors to save him. Let us know the minute you're concerned. He'll fight you and he'll fight us, so we'll have to work together to save him. You're our lookout. We know he's in good hands."

Mikaela's insides felt like gelatin. She wondered if Catherine could see the shaking her words had prompted. Matt had done exactly what his mother had predicted, avoided the signs and symptoms for months until the medical options were limited. Hope drained from Mikaela at the same rate her pressures increased. She was caught between her promise to keep Matt's secret and his mother's request for Mikaela to be her informant. She stood, feeling as if she couldn't draw a full breath.

Catherine also rose. "Enough of sad times. Let's go claim our men."

Matt read Mikaela's panicked expression and excused them by saying he wanted to give her a tour of the neighborhood. When they headed into the misty street, Mikaela walked off at a pace Matt couldn't sustain. He called out to her, and she returned and walked straight into his arms. "She asked me to be her ally. To help her save her son."

Matt pushed back, his face grim. "Does she know I'm sick?

Mikaela shook her head and wiped her eyes. "No. She just asked me to be her eyes. She knows you too well. She knew you'd delay and fight treatment until—"

She turned back into his arms, and they stumbled to a bench along the river walk.

"I've placed you in an impossible situation. We'll just get through this weekend—"

In a grief-riddled shout, Mikaela demanded, "Just tell them! They love you. They deserve to know."

"There are only two options if I tell them, Mikaela. They'll want me to follow their wishes exactly like the last time, but I ended up angry with them which nearly destroyed our family. If tell them I'm following my wishes, my last days will be spent with them hurt and angry at me." His hands moved to his head. "I've been over this a thousand times. This is the best solution. We'll be a normal family for as a long as possible, and then I'll tell them. What I need to know is what is best for you?"

Mikaela leaned forward and dropped her face into her hands.

"Mikaela?" he repeated more softly, leaning near and placing a hand on her back.

She revisited the conversation with Catherine.

I do love your son. Very much.

I know. I saw how you looked to Matt for your security, and I saw how he came to your rescue. You two are a good match.

"There is no good answer."

"I know . . . I know . . ."

They wore pasted smiles through dinner at a restaurant down the block. During the requested retelling of selected details from their courtship, they disguised their tears as tenderness. The sleeping situation that should have raised an awkward selection of options was easily remedied by the stress of the day. They shared the bed, back to back, each needing to be alone with their thoughts.

Saturday passed with football on TV, and the shared cooking of Matt's favorite Irish dishes. Donovan recounted moments from Matt's rugby days, including commentary on how that was the real-man's sport. Another night passed with silent hours punctuated by awkward small talk about anything but the increasing emotional distance creeping between Matt and Mikaela. Mikaela spent hours listening to Matt's breathing, wondering if he was doing the same for her, until they both fell asleep.

The parting embraces she gave to the Graykens the next morning were real and filled with love. Catherine slipped a package into her hand. Mikaela opened it and saw a beautiful gold ball embossed with the words "First Christmas—2017. Matthew and Mikaela Grayken."

"The ball is an old antique ornament from our family collection. I had an artist friend paint the words on. Soon, you'll be putting up your own tree. It will make me happy to think we got you started in building your collection."

Mikaela hugged her and held tight, never letting on about the tree and ornaments back home. As they said goodbye and headed for the airport, she almost wished she hadn't met them, because her loyalties were now torn between three people that she loved, and whose wishes were at complete odds with one another's.

14

The Dulles Airport baggage area was packed with people awaiting their luggage. A college sports team and their gear were streaming away from one carousel while what appeared to be an entire tourist group and their baggage was streaming away from another. Matt was grateful they hadn't checked bags. He and Mikaela threaded their way through the crowd and to the pickup zone to wait for their Uber car, which was stuck way down the packed access road.

Matt noticed a tired mother from their flight. She stood by the curb, wrangling a fussy infant and a rambunctious toddler. The father was missing, and Matt assumed he was getting their car, and was likewise stuck in the traffic melee. While the mother rocked the baby and texted on her phone, the toddler placed her stuffed animal in the umbrella stroller and pushed it about.

Cars honked and jockeyed for curb access while security

guards enforced the no-parking rules. A frustrated SUV driver argued with the guard and pointed at the door, insisting his wife was exiting any moment. The guard stomped off, and Matt assumed the next act of the drama would involve a cop and a ticket book.

People pressed in on Mikaela and him as the bulk of the tourist group suddenly poured from the doorway, laden with bags, and jostling for a curb position so they could hail their rides. In the hubbub, the distracted mother and her toddler became separated, and the toddler inched closer to the curb. A roller bag hit another waiting traveler who inched forward into the tiny child. Mikaela gasped as the child fell off the curb and into the street. Matt lunged for the child as the angry SUV driver decided to hit the gas, shooting the vehicle forward and directly at Matt and the child, who had both fallen beneath his view. Mikaela's scream registered in his mind as he cradled the child against him and rolled farther into street, beyond the crush of the SUV's pavement-chewing tires and in front of a braking Jaguar. The Jag's low-profile bumper caught Matt like a plow, tossing him and the child several yards down the road.

Matt was covered in scrapes, welts, and bruises as he lay in the ER. Mikaela attended to him and the child as best she could at the scene, but every minute since the ambulance arrived had been a blur of medical personnel, either attending to him or wheeling him somewhere for tests and scans. The incident accelerated Mikaela's need to be Matt's legal voice, and forced her into a situation for which she has not prepared —needing to explain his medical status to new people. Watching their expressions change from respect for Matt's heroics to shock and then sorrow in response to his diagnosis shook her to the core.

She pushed her way past medical carts and monitors and into the ER cubicle, gluing herself to Matt's side. Besides the nurses and techs hovering near, the EMTs, who attended to him and the child at the scene, stopped by after dropping off another patient.

The male member of the pair scooted over to allow Mikaela to pass. "Hi, Ma'am. Our shift's about to end, but we thought we'd stop by and check on the sleepy gladiator."

The female EMT on the team gave Matt's foot a wiggle and said, "Hey Matt, thought you'd want to know that the little girl is still terrified of you, but she's already on her way home."

Her male counterpart explained, "She says a bad man knocked her down. You beast, you."

Matt half-opened his eyes and laughed.

"Her mom has shown her video proof that you were actually her rescuer, but she's still not buying it."

"Video proof?" asked Mikaela.

"Yep." The woman held up her phone and hit play. "Your husband's a celebrity."

They handed Matt the phone, which was playing a video

of him lunging for the child and disappearing behind the SUV. Mikaela shivered, and Matt winced. He handed the phone back to the EMT.

"Do they identify him in the video?" asked Mikaela.

"No. He's still an anonymous hero, but probably not for long. TV cameras are waiting outside to get an interview."

She wondered if his parents had heard.

One of the men leaned over Matt and patted his shoulder. "What you did out there was a brave thing, man. Get well soon." Each EMT gave him a fist bump and a wave as they left.

Mikaela sat in the chair beside Matt and bit her nail. Matt brushed his bandaged hand past her cheek. "I'm so sorry. I keep complicating your life."

She squeezed one of the few places on his arm that wasn't either bandaged or hosting an IV. "You saved that child's life. I'm proud of you. Just rest now."

His eyes closed and his unencumbered hand reached for hers. "Thank you for everything you did for me tonight. You saved us." His voice slurred slightly, and Mikaela knew the pain meds had kicked in, relaxing his body and scrambling his thoughts. "Seriously, Mikaela," he muttered like a drunk. "I had no idea what an amazing nurse you are. Yelling at people. 'Get back!'" His reenactment of the moment brought a smile to her lips. "You rattled off my vitals and recited my meds and treatments like a doctor. I was so proud of you."

His eyes rolled around and closed again. One of Mikaela's hands held his while the other fingered his dark, tangled curls. She watched the monitors and studied his body's responses while he slept—the rhythm and depth of his breathing, the crinkling of the tiny lines around his eyes, the tension in his lips and brow.

"When can I go home?" he muttered in his sleepy state.

"Not tonight, Superman," Mikaela whispered back as she brushed a wisp of hair from a cut on his badly bruised forehead. "Even if they don't find anything serious, they'll keep you overnight for observation."

He didn't respond, so Mikaela capitalized on the quiet moment and laid her head beside his. "What kind of ornament do we get to mark this adventure?" she thought aloud.

"A bottle of pain meds." He smiled at his own joke, "I love you, Mikaela."

A chill zipped down her arms and back. She lifted her head to see if the words had been spoken consciously, but Matt's eyes remained closed. "Don't leave me. Please, don't ever go."

Mikaela's throat tightened as joy slammed into sorrow. He loved her, but would he say so in the morning? In that moment, it didn't matter. In the deepest part of him, beyond logic and contracts, Matt loved her.

She hovered so near that she could feel the warmth of his breath on her lips. "I love you too, Matthew Grayken, and I'm not going anywhere."

15

Matt awakened with no memory of his confession of love for Mikaela, but with a full awareness of his aches and pains. The leukemia lessened his blood's clotting ability, and as a result, he looked like an eggplant from shoulders to knees. A flood of IV antibiotics were administered to support his weakened immune system which was unable to fight off the many bacterial microbes his open wounds picked up during his skid across the road.

He was more concerned about the loss of his privacy than he was about his aching body. He had been identified as the airport hero, and his parents called in a panic after seeing a replay of his heroics on the morning news. It took nearly every ounce of persuasion he possessed to keep them from taking the Acela train to DC. He prayed that HIPAA laws were as ironclad as he was promised, and that the reporters didn't somehow get word of his leukemia and add it as byline to the story.

The clamor for an interview wreaked havoc as both their phones rang and pinged with requests, but Matt's leukemia brought him one bit of luck. The doctors decided to keep him in the hospital for several days to address the bruising and to continue the IVs. He was relieved that most of the TV media fervor had died down by the day of his release.

It was also the morning his oncologist called.

Mikaela had just hung up from talking to both their offices, clearing their schedules through the week. Matt winced all the way home and as she helped him to the sofa and settled him in a position that hurt the least. Then his phone rang and he visibly shivered when he saw the caller ID. "It's Dr. Gorman."

"The lab results." Mikaela slowly sank into the other end of the sofa.

The phone rang again. Matt answered and said, "Hello."

"Hey, Matt. Dr. Gorman here. How are you feeling? The office staff has been buzzing about you and that little girl you saved, so I understand why you didn't call on Monday."

"Yeah. It's been a little crazy."

"I wanted to discuss your lab results with you before too much time passed . . ."

He braced for bad news, and Mikaela instinctively scooted closer. Matt looked into her eyes, seeking comfort and support, and she answered by placing her hand on his knee.

He broke the conversation. "Excuse me, Dr. Gorman. Would you mind explaining everything to Mikaela?"

He handed her the phone and read the almost imperceptible shifts in her face. He knew the news wasn't good, but something the doctor said caused her eyes to widen. Matt felt encouraged.

"So, what's the verdict?" he asked as she ended the call.

"It's not bad," she answered with a noticeable quiver in her voice. "It's just not as good as we would have liked."

"Am I responding to the immunotherapy?"

She stalled and gave him a tense smile. "Do you want me explain all the numbers and results?"

He shook his head. His heart now ached as badly as his body. "Something he said made you look encouraged. What was that?"

She scooted closer and onto her knees, giving him a smile mixed with a wince. "He suggested that you ought to capitalize on the attention you're getting since Dulles." She inched even closer. "You're a hero. People want to help heroes. Dr. Gorman said you ought to let people know you need a bone marrow donor."

"No." He was unequivocal on this point. "I'm not going to give up my privacy. And then there's the matter of my parents." He shook his head. "Public begging is not an option."

Mikaela sat back and stared at her hands. "Not even to save your life?"

His resolve softened into a plea for her to understand. "I

would have to surrender my life to even *try* to save it. I would lose whatever time I have left. I'm sorry."

Mikaela reached for his arm and set her empty gaze there. "I understand. It's okay. You're right."

He wasn't sure she really did. He laid his hand over hers and waited for her eyes to drift to his. "Please don't be upset with me."

"I'm not, Matt. I . . . I want what's best for you."

"So, what's next? Chemo?"

She gave a slight nod and eased her arm across his shoulder. "As soon as you're ready."

He shivered again, and Mikaela drew the crimson comforter around his shoulders, but the cold ran deep, to places the blanket couldn't warm. Down to his core, where his recently found hope was failing. Going dormant.

He chose Mikaela because he needed her to help him prepare for his eventual death, but her courage and optimism made him believe the immunotherapy and other immunity-boosting efforts could commute the cancer death threat. And now this.

As if she could read his mind, she said, "I've been preparing for this possibility."

Matt finally noticed that she seemed disappointed, but not devastated by the news.

"I've studied how to make chemo easier and more successful. The Japanese have done exhaustive studies on a supplement called AHCC and its effect on toxins and cancer cells. There aren't even that many doctors at Prospect who have an opinion on its usefulness, Dr. Gorman included, but a few others do, and they'd be willing to monitor you if you agreed to try it."

He marveled at how she could restore his faith in a moment. "Whatever you think."

She drew back and looked down at her lap, avoiding his gaze. "I'm not a doctor. I don't . . . can't be responsible for making all these decisions. I'll tell you what I know and think, but it's your life. You have to own the choices."

Matt tipped her chin up and winced from the effort. "I'm sorry. Of course, you're right. Okay, give me something to read. I'll make an informed choice." With those words came renewed confidence that he still had choices and reasons to fight. "What else?"

Mikaela left to grab papers off the printer. She wore a mischievous smile when she returned. Matt loved that smile. It was filled with warmth and fight and hope. She laid a deed in his lap.

"What did you b—" He pinched his brows together. Even that part of his body hurt. "You bought a cow?"

Mikaela sat down with a bounce that jiggled Matt and caused him to groan. She reached to touch him in apology and that made him groan anew, so she rolled her eyes.

"Seriously, Superman?"

"Just call me Captain Grape. And yes, I hurt. Everywhere."

She sat back and laughed.

"Tell me about our cow."

"Our *share* of a cow. We own a third. She lives on an organic farm in Frederick."

"Why?"

"Why what? Why does she live in Frederick, or why is she on an organic farm?"

"Why do we own *any* piece of *any* cow from *any*where?"

"Because raw milk is illegal in most states. Can you believe that?"

"It never crossed my mind."

"Well, add raw milk to your list of research topics so you can make another informed decision. Many scientists believe pasteurization destroys the most important nutritional and immune-boosting properties of milk, and since the only ones who can drink raw milk are those who own their own cow—"

"You bought stock in one."

She comically placed her hands on her hips and argued, "It's called a cow-share."

An involuntary laugh broke from his sober lips. "Of course, it is."

"All right, smarty-pants." She leaned close to deliver what Matt assumed was another comic barrage, but as she drew near their eyes met and understanding passed between them. Understanding that, despite their efforts to make light of their situation, they were alone in a valley and the way out would require a hard, bloody crawl. He saw determination mixed with fear and pure love. It warmed him, as if the hands of her heart had reached into his chest to warm and calm his own trembling heart. Her face hovered near his, becoming almost iridescent from the emotion there. Her expression spoke a language of its own, one Matt translated before she uttered a sound.

"Your plan failed," she whispered. "I know you already love me."

Matt felt the skin of his face prickle as heat rose from deep within him. A sheen of sweat broke across his skin from the stop-and-go battle raging inside. He knew his face took on the same sleepy-eyed glow of unanswered want she showed. He leaned forward, closing the inches between them and whispered back. "I'm afraid you're wrong, Mikaela. I've *always* loved you. From the first day I watched you walk through the clinic." He closed his eyes. "But what does it get us?" He looked down at his bruised body and shook the papers about AHCC and cow shares. "Look at the fight we have ahead."

Mikaela closed the distance and brushed her lips over his. His sensible side told him to push back, but he had no will to send her away again. His battered hands framed her face and pulled her mouth to his. He felt wholly alive for the first time in weeks, not a patient first, but filled with the thoughts and feelings of a man. Of a husband. He tried to raise his arms to wrap her close, but a sharp pain ended the effort as Mikaela pulled back an inch, her smile completely happy and her eyes joyfully bright.

"I love you, Matt." The words were spoken in a whisper, so light and airy that they tickled his lips. "Just finally be mine. Give me these arms to hold on to. This shoulder to lay my head on. This mouth that speaks honesty to me and gives me kisses. These are enough until you're well. Just knowing you love me is enough."

Each word had been followed by a touch that left him weak in the very best way. It took some doing to position their bodies so Mikaela could rest her head upon his chest without causing him pain, but the sensation of her against him was less painful than her absence.

He drank in the heady scent of coconut in her hair, and felt life pump through him with the rise and fall of her breaths. He loved the press of her forehead against his throat and knew in that moment that he had been a prideful fool, squandering precious months on the silly notion that he could bar this woman from fully claiming his heart.

The tree lights' glow softly burned through the first traces of dusk. Small lights brightening a darkening night. He wondered if that was why Mikaela set the tree up early, to remind him that even when they couldn't hold back the darkness, they must hold on to the light.

16

Mikaela awoke first, with proof that it hadn't all been another of her dreams. She was sleeping beside Matt, whose scraped and purplish face was mere inches from her own. For the first morning in her life, her arm was lying across his chest, moving with every breath. The beauty of the moment did not dispel the ever-present worry.

She knew faith wasn't a vending machine where one does a good deed and receives a blessing. The notion violated the very principles of the doctrine—patience, trust, acceptance of God's will—but she admitted, at least to herself, that she had hoped heaven saw Matt's selfless dive to save that child and that God would smile upon this good man and answer their combined prayers. The oncologist's call had been a blow, not to her faith, but to any notion that an easy road ahead was being paved.

She had helped Matt to bed, propping pillows around

him to make him comfortable. Two propped his head and neck, and others were stacked beneath his knees to ease his back. She had lain down beside him to monitor his breathing and make sure the angle of his head didn't obstruct his airway, but the warmth of his body and the draw to just be near him was the reason she stayed. Their new understanding of their union braced her for a lion-worthy fight.

She studied this man, this husband of hers. She loved using the word—husband. Of considering her role as wife. She couldn't deny that she longed for the fire and passion of marriage, but what she knew of marriage and romance had primarily been learned from observing her parents, aging lovers whose romance shifted to gentle kindnesses, soft touches and smiles, shared poems, and in serving one another. Theirs was as devoted and pure a love as she could imagine, and whether she and Matt were blessed to know more in their own union, she felt sure they were mastering the most important aspects of love.

She lay very still, enjoying the clean scent of soap that lingered on his skin and finding a few gray hairs beginning a colony over his ear. She loved the angle of his jaw, the way his brow pinched and relaxed as he slept, the long dark lashes that almost touched his cheek.

Her finger lightly combed through a wave, marveling that she could finally touch him and love him when she wanted. He opened his eyes without a start, as if he fully expected to find her there, drinking him in. He turned his head her way, offering the invitation to a kiss, which she happily accepted.

"I hope you know that I plan to kiss you anytime I want."

He smiled so wide that his eyes crinkled closed. "You have a universal invitation."

She scooted higher up the pillow and brought her lips to his cheek and snuggled close. The tickle initiated another of the smiles she so loved. She sat up on one elbow. "What do you think about me becoming your permanent roommate?"

His body went rigid. "In this room? Or in this bed?"

She bit her thumbnail. "Are you afraid I'll roll over and hurt you?"

Matt slowly slid an arm behind her head and pulled her to his shoulder. "That's not the ache I'm worried about."

She snuggled close. "I just want to be near you. To make sure you're okay during the night. Maybe you'll sleep better knowing I'm close."

He kissed her head but his body remained tense. "Okay. Consider the invitation extended." It sounded more like a willing surrender.

"One more thing," she added nervously. "I'm going to call my brothers and tell them we're married."

His head jerked in her direction. "Are you sure?"

"I've been dodging their calls and missing the family chats. They're going to get worried."

"It's not even seven a.m."

"George is the unofficial head of the family. He's in Bosnia. It's the middle of the day there."

With a final kiss for luck, she sat up and dialed George's

number. On the sixth ring, she prepared to leave a voicemail when George picked up, his voice scolding in a loving way.

"About time you called, Princess."

She switched to the speaker. "I know. I'm sorry."

"What's going on?"

"I'm just checking in. I also wanted to let you know that I've met someone."

"Someone serious?"

She looked at Matt who was hanging on every word. "Yeah," she nodded as if George could see her. "Pretty serious," she answered in a singsong voice.

His voice dropped two full steps on the do-re-mi scale, and Matt's eyes widened. "Like engagement serious?"

"Like . . . eloped serious."

"What the heck, Mickie! Did you call any of the rest of us? Why didn't you call me? I haven't even spoken to this dude! What's this nimrod's name?"

"Mickie?" Matt repeated.

She shot Matt an apologetic frown and switched the speaker off. "His name is Matthew Grayken, and he's as good as they come. Dad would call him a 'keeper.'"

"How did you meet him. Honestly, Mickie. What went through your head?"

"I fell in love. Remember love, George? Check out the YouTube video about the hero who saved a child at Dulles airport. That's my Matt."

George's voice calmed. "Is he good to you? Because I swear, if he isn't I'll—"

"Use him as a martial arts dummy? Yeah. He gets that. And yes. He's wonderful to me."

"Okay, Sis. If you're really happy, then I'm happy for you. When are we going to meet this new brother-in-law?"

"We'll get a plan together soon. Gotta go. Love you."

"Yeah. Love you too, but—"

She clicked the phone off quickly and pressed it against her, awaiting what she expected would be at least six more calls in fairly rapid succession.

Matt's face took on the look of a Shar Pei. "On a scale of one to ten, with ten being great, and one being 'pack your bags and run,' how do you think that went?"

"For George, with our news? We just scored an unequivocal fifteen."

"Hearing that doesn't make me feel much better."

Determined to beat this leukemia, Matt asked for treatment to begin right away. A new central line was scheduled to be inserted in his chest wall on Friday afternoon, in preparation to deliver his first chemo treatment the following Monday. He still had one more responsibility to attend to before admission. He needed to name an acting president in his absence. He arranged for the board to be assembled in the conference room and, once again, his injuries proved useful.

His announcement that he'd decided to take a leave of absence was received without question. Instead, his associates told him how glad they were to hear that he was taking the time he needed to rest and heal. His decision to name Ben acting president was also well received, and as he cleared his desk and left the office that day, he was surprised by how relieved he was to focus all his energies on the treatment ahead and on Mikaela.

Something unexpected had happened in him since his marriage. Mikaela's care and protection became paramount, fully replacing concerns about corporate plans and profits. The marriage of medical convenience had become a love story, where passion had been upstaged by devotion and service. Mikaela deserved more, but she accepted what his battered, sickly body had to give, and now he wanted to be sure she would have someone if the worst should come. He was therefore especially comforted by the plan he had been mulling over for several days. It would require a stable and caring support team, and Matt turned to the sometimes self-involved, but generally best men he knew—Daniel and his other chums.

On the ride home from the office, he called Mikaela who was at work and planning to meet him at Prospect for the catheter installation. Instead of leaving a message and waiting for a call back as he expected, she answered on the third ring.

"Are you still at the office?"

"No. On my way home."

"How'd it go?"

"The board supported my decision to choose Ben, and they told me to go home and heal."

"I already love those people. I still think it's time for me to give notice too."

This was a topic he and Mikaela had discussed at length. "I think you'll go crazy sitting around the house or a hospital every day. Besides, I'll need a good distraction. Bring me stories about all my romantic rivals from the infusion center so I remember to stay on my toes."

"That I can do."

"But you're still coming to the procedure today, right? It's at three." He had been through this maze of catheters and chemo twice before, but this time was just as sobering. Perhaps even more than the others, because this time he knew exactly what he had to lose if the treatment failed.

"Of course. Should we catch dinner at Carmen's place?"

Matt wondered if she'd think he was selfish for asking to spend one of their few nights before chemo in the company of his friends. "I . . . uh . . . actually had another idea. Would you mind if I hosted the guys for poker at our place tonight?"

An obvious pause preceded her rather elongated, "No."

"That sounded very tentative."

"I was just thinking like a wife."

"I do like the sound of those words."

"Me too, but you wouldn't like the choice the wife part of me would make. I'd like to keep you all to myself. Fortunately for you, the nurse in me is taking the lead on this. Clinically speaking, maintaining social activities is good for overall well-being, so I think it's a good idea."

"I thought you could use a diversion too. Why don't you

see if Eliza and Martine are available to go to Carmen's with you?"

"Are you trying to get rid of me?"

"Am I that obvious?" He laughed.

"Completely. Just take care of that lucky tablecloth. I'm already crossing fingers and toes for chemo success. I'm counting on that tablecloth to pull its good luck weight as well."

Matt's smile bubbled into laughter. "Have I told you recently that I'm hopelessly in love with you, Mrs. Grayken?"

"I was thinking the same thing about you, Mr. Grayken." Her voice took on a mellow tone. "I love you so much, Matt."

"Always remember that I loved you first, and forever, Mikaela. See you at three."

The urgency to get his plan in place caused his next call to be to Daniel. Matt hadn't spoken to him or any of the other six jokers since he bailed out of the group's poker game. They had each plied him with apologetic texts which he returned proudly with a beautiful photo of Mikaela snuggled under a blanket with a book. The caption read, "Still married, and life is still grand."

After the Dulles rescue video went viral, they texted again, with a phrase their group pulled from a Walt Whitman poem, immortalized in the movie, *The Dead Poets' Society* —"Oh, Captain, My Captain!" He smiled as he thought of how much he loved his band of merry men.

Daniel picked up on the first ring. "Glad to hear from you, Sport! We wondered if you were willing to host tonight."

"I'm on it. We also need to hold a *Dead Poets' Society* meeting."

He heard Daniel groan. "Come on, Matt. We've already said we were sorry. We get it. We're socially and emotionally stunted professionals who need to grow up. Forgive us already."

"You're forgiven. And I can help you with the emotional and social growth. This is real DPS emergency, Buddy."

The airspace went silent. "Like eleven years ago real?"

"We'll talk tonight, okay? Can you see that all the guys come?"

"I'm on it, Brother."

Matt picked up some poker snacks and dropped them off at home. He saw the notes Mikaela had jotted on some calendar blocks. Today's block had "Catheter insertion. Go Team Grayken!" He flipped the page and read the top of the October calendar page, which now read, "Us versus Cancer." From October second to the twenty-seventh, the length of his first round of treatment, each block was marked with a boxing glove drawn in red, presumably to be colored in after each treatment. It was Mikaela's way of fighting back. He touched the blocks with her messy scrawl and smiled as warmth spread through him.

Happy marks surrounded the block for October thirtieth —the Irish Embassy Gala. He had forgotten. His head fell against the calendar. He wondered if Mikaela had already figured out that the magical evening he had proposed was unlikely at best and most likely DOA.

He took an hour-long nap before heading up route ninety-five for Baltimore. Once the catheter was inserted, he would receive his treatments at a local infusion center to avoid the long daily drive to Baltimore. If fatigue and nausea became too bad, he would need Mikaela to quit her job. He hoped not. He'd like to keep something normal in their crazy lives.

The catheter insertion went as well as having a foreign tube inserted into your body can go. He kept his eyes on Mikaela, who kept her eyes on his chest. He had come to recognize when her nursing persona took over. A cool detachment kept her steady and professional, unfazed by blood or pain or out of control-patients. She began the insertion procedure as his wife—nurturing, supportive, invested—and shifted into nurse Mikaela when the trays were set out, but when his shirt was removed, revealing his still-bruised and now bony chest, a wife's sorrow passed over her face, and Matt knew he was right to make a plan. Just in case.

The news of the DPS meeting summoned a greatly sobered team to Matt's home. Daniel arrived first, looked at Matt and said, "You look like crap," before wrapping his friend up in a long, tearful hug. The doorbell rang in quick succession as Nelson, Gunther, Jacob, Russell, Porter, and Miguel arrived. Matt asked them to sit and explained the situation with his health.

"Mikaela has a big family of brothers, but they're military and scattered everywhere."

"Whatever you or Mikaela need, Matt. You know we're here for you," Gunther said.

Matt expected nothing less from these guys. Gunther Gnudsen, a strapping Swede, was the most aggressive member on their prep school rugby team and a man who also possessed the softest heart of anyone Matt knew. He loved each of these men, chased MBA's and golf balls with most of them during college, bled with some, like Gunther, on the rugby field, and survived his first heartbreak in grade school because of Daniel. They were his brothers.

"I know you guys will be here if I need anything, and I want Mikaela to know that too. I'll also host the next game so you can all meet her and so she can feel comfortable around you."

17

Despite the AHCC, the first week of chemo left Matt more nauseated than he ever remembered being before. Mikaela looked tearful as she left for work each day with Matt's assurance that he was well enough to get himself to treatment. As soon as she was gone, he downed his sludge and counted the minutes until he ran to the bathroom to heave over the commode. No matter how she modified the nutritional drink, or what else he ate, the results were the same. He was down three more pounds the first week.

As planned, the guys showed up Thursday night for poker. Mikaela was less enthusiastic about the clinical benefits of guy-time this week, but she spread the lucky tablecloth over the kitchen table, made snacks, and met the guys graciously at the door. Matt ran the introductions, offering an anecdote about each one and a brief bio on how long they had known each other.

"Mikaela, you met my dear grammar-school friend, Daniel, at our nuptials."

Nelson Tsai spoke up, feigning sorrow. "I want you to know that we were hurt, Matt, deeply hurt, that Daniel was invited and we weren't."

"It was a mistake on my part, Nelson."

"You mean you meant to invite us?"

"No." Matt laughed. "I never should have invited Daniel."

As Daniel lobbed a throw pillow at Matt, the host ducked and continued the introductions. "Mikaela. I'd like you to meet Gunther Gnudsen and Jacob Kieslowski, two prep school rugby brothers who followed me to Yale."

"Who followed who?" Jacob asked.

"Hairsplitting," Matt countered as he turned to Mikaela to explain. "Yale was my idea first, but these two yahoos submitted their applications a day before I did."

Gunther raised his hand. "If it had been a copyright application, we would have won hands down."

Matt shook his head at Mikaela. "Can you tell they're lawyers?" He turned to the last two guys in the group. "Russell Orndorff, Miguel Villanueva and I were study group partners during our MBA programs. Russell's father is a four-star general who managed to get these statisticians jobs crunching numbers for the Defense Department." He leaned close and pretended to whisper. "Don't ask them what they do, or their cell phones will self-destruct and annihilate us all."

Mikaela clapped her hands and bowed to the men.

"Heaven help anyone who taught this bunch. Thank you, gentlemen. Any friend of Matt's is always welcome here." She leaned over and placed a kiss on Matt's cheek. "I'll leave you all to your game. Don't stay up too late, okay?" She was headed for the bedroom when she noticed that each of the men had a similar box with them. Curiosity brought her back to the table. "Matt told me a little about the secret stakes you boys play for. Is that what's in the boxes?"

"You didn't tell her?" asked Daniel.

Matt blushed red and grew wide-eyed. "I was trying not to."

Mikaela marched up to Matt's chair and sat. "Oh, no way I'm leaving until I know."

Gunther shrugged and unlatched his box. With a boyish grin, he pulled out a blister-packed Luke Skywalker figurine and set it on the table.

Mikaela stifled a giggle. "You gamble with *Star Wars* toys?"

"Not toys," Daniel replied, noticeably insulted. "Collectibles. That Luke Skywalker is worth a cool grand."

"Are you kidding me?" Mikaela's mouth gaped open.

Miguel leaned across the table to add his two-cents. "That's nothing. Someone offered me twelve grand for my mint-condition medical droid."

Mikaela looked at Matt. "Why didn't you tell me?"

Matt slumped into one hip and shrugged. "It sounds silly whenever I try to explain it to anyone else. It's just a bit of innocence from our childhoods."

She pulled back on her humor. "It's actually kind of sweet. But how do you bid with Darth Vader?"

"You get the value of your figure in chips, then you put that figure in the pot. At the end of the evening, it's winner take all."

Russell rubbed his hands together as a greedy little smile graced his lips. "Which could be a few thousand dollars' worth of collectibles."

Mikaela stood. "Well, someday little sons and daughters will be very happy to play with your winnings." She looked at Matthew. "You never fail to surprise me." She placed another kiss on his cheek and headed for the bedroom door saying, "Goodnight, gentlemen."

Once the door was shut, Matt dropped into a chair and called an impromptu meeting of the DPS. "Isn't she wonderful?"

Gunther plopped into a chair, glum and wistful. "Now I want a wife."

"First you need to find a girlfriend, Gnudsen," Russell joked.

Jacob looked around the house. "The whole place seems different, Matt. Like a home. I'm happy for you."

"I told you Mikaela was great," Daniel said. "The real question, Matt, is how sick are you?"

His eyebrows wriggled in worry. "We'll know in a few more weeks." He blew out a rush of air. "But thanks for meeting Mikaela and letting her get to know you."

Daniel sat on the arm of Matt's chair. "Like we've all said, we're here for whatever either one of you need. She's in our circle. Just as you are, brother."

———

Nausea plagued the first week of treatment, but neither had the second week gone smoothly. Mikaela tried to be positive when the catheter clogged and had to be reinserted. An infection grew around the insertion point requiring Matt to be hospitalized for three days. Mikaela took the last of her paid leave to be with him. Bruises, proof of Matt's heroics, lingered, and while the color of his bruises shifted from purple to green and then to yellow, the tenderness of the bruised muscles and bones remained. The infection cleared and Matt's release from the hospital was a small victory, but Mikaela knew the chemo drugs were taking a toll on his body, and an even greater toll on his spirit. He was depressed more than he was hopeful.

She came from the bedroom and found him sitting at the counter, cursing shaking fingers that wouldn't or couldn't get the button through the hole of his shirt. The more he tried, the more erratic his motions became until, in frustration, he pounded his fist on the counter.

She watched the agonizing wrestle to get his emotions in check as he set his elbow on the counter and bit his knuckle, pausing there until enough time passed, or enough pain ensued, for his frustration to lessen.

She scuffed her feet as she walked toward him to be sure

he heard her coming. When he turned to her, shame colored his eyes. "How long have you been standing there?"

Her hands cupped the back of his head, bringing it to her shoulder. Her fingers slid around his collar, straightening it and coming to the front where she gently lifted his chin, placing a kiss of hope and understanding on his downturned mouth.

Without a word, she began buttoning the enemy shirt while holding Matt in her eyes.

"Why don't you wear a pullover on bad days?"

He looked away and spoke in a deliberate cadence. "Because I've always worn a button-front shirt on weekdays." Mikaela heard a hitch in his voice. "I'm trying to hold on to some part of my normal life."

Her hands cupped his jawline. "Matt, you need to accept that this isn't a normal time."

"This is Hell."

"No," she said firmly. "This is the best, the most exquisite time either of us have ever known because we are together. But it's also a hard time, and we need to accept whatever makes it easier."

He buried his head against her neck.

"Or you could ask your wife to do the buttons. She works cheap. One kiss per."

He rose from the barstool. "I know you're trying to cheer me up. You've been helpful and kind and, heaven knows, you've been more patient than I deserve, but—" he turned toward her, his mouth twisting as he tapped his fist to his chest—" you can't really know how it feels to spend hours a day with your head aimed over the commode and to be unable to do something as simple as dress yourself."

Mikaela more than heard every word. She felt each one and had lived each one. Before Matt, she had held the hands and cheered the spirits of more sick patients than she could count, but caring for Matt was different. It meant vicarious, agonizing worry and empathy. It caused a level of helplessness Matt had once experienced, but one he had momentarily forgotten. She needed to remind him. She wanted to cry. To lash out. But she had seen marriages split because the caregivers couldn't handle the continual stress and mood swings of their loved ones.

She drew a deep breath and said, "I'm in this in a different, but equally excruciating way. Remember how you felt about your mother's stroke? How you wished you could take her pain? That's me. Sitting here. Every day." She took a long, slow breath. "Don't divide us. Don't pit your pain against mine. And don't try pushing me away. This is us. This is our mutual fight."

She was shaking when she finished. Wanting to be held and wanting to punch him at the same time. He came to her and wrapped his arms around her, telling her he was sorry, over and over until the words became white noise behind their shared tears.

She finally pulled away. "I think it's time for me to quit my job."

Matt nodded and tightened his embrace. "Me too."

Prospect's administrator allowed Mikaela to take her vacation immediately and then agreed to unpaid leave. She and Matt formulated a new plan together, returning to the things that made them happy when they were still emotionally apart. They planned daily activities to keep their minds occupied on things other than the next lab test, and they collected more ornaments for the tree. On Friday, they arranged to have Matt's treatment moved to Baltimore. Afterward, they headed off to a bed and breakfast in Lancaster, Pennsylvania, to rest in the country quiet and enjoy Amish food and culture. They took a buggy ride past pristine, pumpkin-rich farms, and after a long nap, they ate at a restaurant set up like a picnic, with long wooden tables and benches. Strangers sat like family, while bonneted women set bowls and platters of vegetables, fruits, chicken, noodles, and pork before them. Fried funnel cakes, donuts, pies, and ice cream followed, but Matt barely nibbled on anything but bread.

They stopped at the gift shop and bought two ornaments —an etched pewter image of a barn raising and a crocheted lace star that reminded Mikaela of the curtains in the inn.

Matt sat on the edge of the bed, looking out at the farm that stretched beyond the inn's property. He felt Mikaela scoot behind him. Her arms soon wrapped around his shoulders, and her chin rested on his shoulder.

"A strudel for your thoughts."

He crossed his arms over his chest to take her hands and

leaned his head against hers. "I was just thinking how peaceful everything feels here. Simple clothes, simple foods, simple wants. And everything is tied to their faith. It's as if this mortal life is just one experience for them, not *the* experience. They know they came from somewhere near God, and they're going back there when they die, and this life is just a day at school. I don't mean to sound morose or like a quitter, but dying doesn't seem as frightening here."

Mikaela moved beside him. "I like that too. I think our lives and what we do with them matter, but I like your analogy that life is just a day at school."

"Death seems so final when you lose sight of heaven. I've squandered a lot of my life. Instead of hustling to be the best, I wish I had worked harder to *do* my best. To help more people. To make the world better. I doubt God will ask to review a quarterly report."

"You've done a lot of good. You've supported causes and funded programs."

"Maybe, but none of that required anything from me but money I didn't even miss. It didn't stretch me or make me better. I didn't even make an effort to meet the people I helped or to understand their needs."

"It's not too late."

18

Cooler days finally arrived after an unusually warm September. The daily fires in the fireplace provided a cozy place for Matt to rest and rejuvenate as the round of chemo continued. Matt and Mikaela filled their days with short drives into the Virginia or Maryland countryside to enjoy the marvel of autumn and to visit roadside stands aflame with apples, pumpkins, and gourds. On Matt's bad days, Mikaela checked out two copies of a book and they read to one another, or played board games, or watched movies. On his worst days, they napped side by side, and Mikaela cooked to tempt him into eating.

She had all but given up on the Embassy Gala. Matt was too weak for dancing, and the food offered little incentive. Her beautiful gown would either be saved as a celebration dress to be used when he was well, or it would hang as a tangible reminder of what could have been.

She found herself needing time to return upstairs to her private space. She said it was to study, but in truth, she needed a place to cry and to pull herself together before returning to be Matt's rock and shoulder.

He met her at the bottom of the stairs one day, leaning heavily upon the post and looking more green than pale. "What do patients and their spouses do if they can't afford to take off work while they go through this? How do they manage? Pay their bills?"

Mikaela tried to hide her alarm at both his appearance and the question as she descended the stairs quickly to be by his side. "It's hard, Matt. So many of Prospect's patients say that next to dying, their greatest fear is bankruptcy."

"I want to help. What can we do?"

Mikaela helped him to a chair. "Prospect has a financial services department. I'll contact them."

She called and presented the notes from her conversation to Matt. "Your lawyer can empower them to choose recipients and distribute the funds, or he can do it, or we can."

Matt nodded thoughtfully. "First, we need to decide a few things. The what-ifs we've been avoiding."

"I don't want to have this conversation." Mikaela stood, but Matt found her hand and held it, his eyes willing her back with power equal to what she was using to get away. She returned unwillingly. "I feel like you're beginning a long goodbye."

"I promise I'm not. But we need to have this conversation, Mikaela. *I* need to have this conversation. Remember, I'm in the business of making dreams come true. Yours is the dream I most need to assure. I need the peace of knowing that we have a plan, and once these questions are answered, they won't trouble either of us further."

A painful conversation ensued about what they could spare if Matt won his battle, and what Mikaela would need if he didn't. Matt sat on the floor and called his attorney, instructing him to establish an endowment from which cancer patients could receive help with their bills. When that call ended, he called the financial services coordinator back and asked her to choose three young families in the greatest need. He paid their bills outright.

Mikaela curled on the sofa, her knees drawn tight to her chest, watching this very sick man assure that other ailing people—fathers, mothers, children—could live their lives without crushing debt limiting their dreams. When he ended his last call, she moved to the floor by him and laid her arms and head across his lap.

"I'm very proud of you." Her voice cracked on every word. "But please don't give up on yourself. Please don't give up on us."

He combed his fingers through her hair. "I'll never give up. I swear it."

They spent the weekends quietly, with a drive through Alexandria on a Saturday, where they visited a few shops.

Mikaela bought a hand-painted, ceramic angel ornament from an artist on the street. She asked the artist to paint "Matt" along the bottom of the boy angel's robe. She showed it to Matt, and he looked at her with confusion. "Because of what you did for those families. Paying their bills. You were their angel."

Matt insisted they buy a matching girl angel, with "Mikaela" painted along its skirt. "I couldn't do anything without you. You—you are the only angel I see in this pair."

They walked to a street-side café by the Potomac and had a bowl of soup. Mikaela did more stirring than eating as a thought nagged at her.

"The attorney you used to disperse the money to the families . . . is he your attorney or your parents'?"

"He's the lead attorney at Great Expectations. Kind of a cold fish, but very competent. You don't need to worry about the money reaching the people."

"I wasn't worried about that. I was just wondering if he was the same attorney your family used."

"They have a team of lawyers versed in everything from simple contract law to international trade laws."

She tiptoed around the next question, knowing how opposed Matt was to her obsession with finding his birth family. "Did one of them handle your adoption?"

"No. That would have been Joseph McNamara."

"*Would* have been? Did he pass away?"

"Yes. Quite some time ago. He knew he was sick. He told my parents to hire someone he could train and bring up to speed on the company. That someone turned out to be several new attorneys who still couldn't adequately replace Joseph when he passed. Why do you ask? Are you still stuck on the notion of finding some long-lost relative of mine?"

"I'm just exploring possibilities."

He took her hand. "Let go of it, Mikaela. I'll take your prayers and your love and your earnest hope, but no more false hope. Please."

Matt attended church with Mikaela on Sunday, but he spent the rest of the day in bed or in a chair. It caused Mikaela particular worry when she arose on Monday, October 30, to an empty bed. She checked the bathroom and found it empty also. Fear gripped her as she ran into the main living area, expecting to find that Matt fell asleep somewhere, or worse. Instead, she found him trying on his tux.

He turned when he heard the door squeak, his previously confident frame a bit lacking in assurance. "What do you think?" he asked with a one-sided grin.

Mikaela flew to his arms and gathered him close, a sob of relief caught in her throat.

He shushed her concern, placing soft kisses on her salty eyes. With a hand on each of her cheeks, he changed the mood by pulling back to flash her a debonair smile. "I thought I looked a bit scarecrowlike in this monkey suit, but if I still look good enough to drive you to tears, well, then maybe I won't get it taken in after all. What do you say? Feel like going to a ball with me, Princess Mickie?"

His use of her childhood nicknames brought sweet feelings back that eased her stress. "I'll probably come home bruised and battered from fighting off other women, but I'll risk it if you will."

Matt pulled three cards from his pocket. "For you. Hurry and shower."

She chewed on her bottom lip as she read the cards. "Facial and massage at ten. Lunch at one. Nails at two. Hair at four. All at Paradise Spa. Oh, Matt! Thank you!" She hadn't realized how run-down and tired she felt, but the thought of being pampered seemed like life-saving medicine for her.

Matt passed her a glass of sludge as she dashed out the door. "One last surprise," he added before the door closed. "I have dinner reservations at The Blue Duck at seven, so hurry home, Cinderella, so we can make it to the ball."

She ran back to kiss him deep and long, but it was Matt who held on last, ending the kiss with a look that rivaled the excitement of the spa.

"You should go," he said with a melancholy smile. She turned for the door, but when she glanced back, she noticed he was reaching for his laptop, and she couldn't shake the sense that her exquisite day of play was also planned to give Matt time he needed alone.

Matt's leukemia was first diagnosed when he was six, at a time when he was old enough to read the concern and worry on his parents' faces and still enough of a child to be distracted by the allure of surprise. Soon after being told he would need to be hospitalized, he awoke to find a small wooden chest on his bed. Inside was a treasure map of the neighborhood. He remembered the fun of having his busy father stay home from work that day, dressed in a pirate's hat, with one for his mother and one for him. They spent the better part of the day pulling a wagon through the city, following landmarks and counting steps, to this shop and that park, where prepurchased gifts were wrapped and waiting or hidden under a bush or tied to a branch of tree. By the end of the hunt, thirty little gifts were stacked in his wagon. His da carried him home while his mother took charge of the treasure.

Over the next thirty days of treatment, he opened one gift every day—books, puzzles, a compass, crayons and coloring pages, model cars and trains, and an airplane model to build. The suspense of the next surprise lessened the discomfort and fear. He still had many of those toys.

He knew Mikaela wouldn't be as easily distracted, but he hoped she'd enjoy the love behind each surprise, and so he opened his laptop and began designing twelve dreams that either he or his merry men would make come true in the coming year. The pleasure Matt got from the task dwarfed the sadness of the reason for doing it. He felt the giddy rush of love as he saved the file and closed the lid on his computer.

19

The white orchid wrist corsage he ordered from Gino arrived by courier. Matt placed it in the fridge before he left for this treatment. Just enough time remained afterward for a trip to the stylist for a haircut and to have his nails trimmed and buffed. He was fully aware that the adrenaline rush would likely expire in the middle of the gala, but he was also too excited to sleep. After his shower, he was finally able to relax enough to nap.

He taped the central line's tubing to his chest to hide the bulge as best he could. Then he dressed in his now oversized tux, refusing to allow his thinning hair or the blue circles surrounding his eyes to dim his excitement over the evening's plans. He took a deep breath, willing his body to deny his fatigue for six hours so he could be the doting escort Mikaela deserved.

She rushed through the door like an autumn leaf caught

in the wind. Before Matt had a chance to see her, she dashed upstairs where her gown still hung. Thirty minutes later, she truly did descend like a princess, her hair piled high, as if it awaited a tiara, and the diamond and sapphire wedding jewelry serving as the only colors against the black palette of her satin gown. She was tall and slim and regal, sophisticated in dress and bearing.

Her excitement gave her face a natural glow, but her makeup was glamorous, done at the spa, he assumed. He had obviously noticed she was attractive from the first day he saw her, but the beauty he had been drawn to radiated from within her, through those caring eyes, the cheerful smile, the gentle hands intent on providing comfort and healing. Her primary beauty sprang from the selfless way she gave of herself, asking little in return. But tonight, the woman before him was not a nurse or a friend, not a cheerful tomboy/woman patiently waiting on a sickly man. Matt saw Mikaela as she could be, and indeed, as she truly was, an alluring woman who stirred unsettling wants and inadequacies in him. A woman who deserved more. More than he could give her. More than he now was.

His tight throat and rapid, shallow breaths delayed him from responding to her arrival. In truth, he hadn't decided upon an appropriate response when the power to speak returned. Words like *wow* or *beautiful* or *amazing* all felt trite and sophomoric, but the words he wanted to say would confess his want and leave his failings exposed. In his delay, he left Mikaela dangling and hurt.

"I knew it was too much," Mikaela said with rounded shoulders. "The women at the spa said—"

Matt stepped toward her. "No. It's not too much. It's perfect. You . . . are perfect. I . . . I'm awed. I can't find the right words to tell you how beautiful you are."

She remained subdued. "I don't want to embarrass you. I've never been to anything like this before."

"I assure you, every man tonight will wish he was me."

Her red lips twisted into a smirk of disbelief, settling into a quiet smile. "You look very GQ yourself."

Matt crooked his elbow. "Grab your wrap. Shall we go?"

The restaurant was mere blocks from the house. The clientele's attire ranged from men in sports jackets escorting pants-suited women to other couples in formal wear, but he saw every eye shift their way as they entered. Mikaela tightened her hold on his hand.

Matt noticed how the whispers and attention discomfited her. She leaned forward, her eyes downturned and glassy. "I feel foolish, like a girl playing dress-up. Take me home. Please."

In that moment, he wanted nothing more than to return home where the ground rules were established, where sloppy sweaters and evening TV diluted the tug he felt to be a husband in every way. But he was being selfish and unfair to the person he loved most.

He took her hand. "I assure you, everyone here thinks you look sophisticated and lovely."

They picked at dinner and tried to avoid the eyes of

onlookers. Matt felt excruciatingly conspicuous, like "that" guy, the below-average-looking man with the beauty on his arm. The fellow people look at and wonder why *she's* with *him*. In his moment of self-pity, he almost missed that fact that Mikaela was slipping lower in her chair with each course.

"They're still staring at us," she whispered. "We might as well be eating in a Petri dish."

Matt felt a bout of nausea and fatigue pulling on his over-taxed reserves. He checked his watch and called for the check. Mikaela caught the signs.

"We don't have to go to the gala," she said. "Maybe we should just call it a night and go home."

Matt marveled that her instinct was always to put his needs first. He was ashamed that he could not say the same about his motivation this night. He squeezed her hand. "We cannot go home for two reasons. First, I made a pledge to one of the embassy's humanitarian causes for which they are expecting a check, and secondly, I owe you a dance, Mrs. Grayken."

For the first time since her initial descent down the stairs, her smile was bright and genuine. "I will absolutely claim that debt, Mr. Grayken."

The embassy valet took their car when they pulled up. Matt presented the invitation card with their IDs to the security guard at the door. After checking them against a printed list, the guard directed Matt and Mikaela on to security where they and Mikaela's handbag passed through a metal detector. Once they were screened, Matt checked her wrap at the coatroom. He crooked his arm and felt Mikaela slip hers through, even leaning into him. She was quaking like a sapling in the breeze.

"Don't worry. They're going to love you," he whispered.

"I've never even attended a prom. Any last-minute advice?"

"When in doubt, smile. You, Mrs. Grayken, have the best smile on earth."

She flashed him a hundred-watt-er and looked down the hall at the room filled with cocktail-toting guests dressed in elegant attire. "I suppose it's too late to chicken out?"

"It would cause an international incident. World War III – level."

"Oh. No, pressure." She tightened her grip, pythonlike around Matt's arm. "Fine. Just don't leave me. No matter what."

Matt wrapped his hand over hers and was headed down the foyer toward the large open ballroom when a stocky, fiftyish man approached with a warm and welcoming smile. Mikaela assumed he was a member of the embassy staff. Matt handed his invitation card to him, which the man read and responded to with a laugh and a hearty, "Welcome, welcome, Mr. and Mrs. Grayken!"

Matt shook the man's proffered hand.

"Are you the Matt Grayken who used to accompany Donnie and Catherine to our St. Patty's Day party years ago?"

"Guilty as charged." Matt laughed and turned to Mikaela. "Please allow me to introduce my wife, Mikaela."

She timidly extended her hand, which the official cupped within his own bearlike paws. He turned to Matt with widened eyes. "Aye, Matthew, I'd say you've done very well in love and business. Your father has told me about your company. He's very proud of you, and rightly so I'd say."

"Thank you, Mr.—"

"Ah," the man groaned. "Forgive my manners. Of course, you don't remember me. It's Patrick Dunne. Your father and I did a bit o' business together some years ago. I work for the Irish tourism industry. I think there's a lovely collaboration to be had between your Great Expectations and Ireland's castles and wild Atlantic Coast."

"Is the ambassador here tonight?"

"This isn't an official ambassadorial event. I don't believe he's coming. I'm actually the host tonight. But what better backdrop could we have for promoting tourism to Ireland."

He led them into the ballroom and over to a small group of people conversing in a corner. "Trudy, my darling, allow me to introduce you to Matthew and Mikaela Grayken. Be a love and entertain Mikaela while Matthew and I discuss business for a few minutes, would you?"

Mikaela latched on tighter to Matt's arm.

"I promised my wife my complete attention this evening,

Mr. Dunne. I've actually resigned my position as president of the company. I'm acting as CEO now, but I can put you in touch—"

"I'll take a CEO's ear tonight over the hope of a president's call tomorrow. A bird in hand, as they say." He winked at his wife who grabbed Mikaela's arm as Patrick pulled Matt away. Rather than engage in a public game of tug-of-war, Mikaela released her hold on Matt, who looked at her, worriedly.

"It's okay. Come back soon?"

She felt the eyes of other guests on her because of the scene. Trudy Dunne was either completely unaffected by their stares or she enjoyed the attention, but, as requested, she attempted to include Mikaela in her conversation about the current work of some Irish women's association. Mikaela assumed the short older man looking as lost as she felt was the husband of Trudy's friend. He yawned and told his wife, "Why don't I freshen your drink, dear? Perhaps Mrs. Grayken could use a mite to eat."

Mikaela was relieved to leave the center of the room and find a more obscure location, although her knight already seemed to have had a few too many drinks. Undeterred, she followed the gregarious older man to the wall by the buffet table, where a few empty seats remained.

"Allow me to introduce myself, Mrs. Grayken. Morris Kavanagh at your service. May I get you something? A drink? A plate of food?"

"None for me, thank you."

"Very well. I'll just freshen mine a tad and return."

People-watching from the sidelines was entertaining enough for Mikaela. From the chatter going on all around her, she could see that the gathering was an international assembly of politicos and business people. Some chatted with Irish lilts. Others were clearly American, but she could hear a variety of accents.

Matt was still corralled in a corner with his back to her. From the slump in his shoulders, she knew he was fatigued, and she began planning her rescue of him.

Morris returned with two drinks, both for himself, and sat beside her. "I saw your panic when your husband was dragged off, leaving you with two of Ireland's most ardent advocates of meaningless causes."

Mikaela stifled a laugh.

"I figured you could use some rescuing, though I should thank you for giving me an excuse to leave that conversation. I'm afraid I'm still more comfortable on a ship than in a tuxedo."

"Are you a Naval officer?"

He chuckled. "I was a sailor when I was a lad. My father thought it would teach me discipline, and he was right. I should have used that same strategy with my own son rather than throw him into the business world so raw and headstrong."

Mikaela didn't know how to respond to the personal disclosure, so she returned to the topic of work. "What business are you in?"

"Shipping. My father owned several vessels. I captained one of the ships when I left the military, and then he stuck me in an office." He sighed and smiled. "I don't mean to complain. I've been blessed. We're the primary shipper of cargo in Ireland. In fact, now that I think of it, I believe the Graykens use us to move their goods. But I'd still rather be on the deck of a ship than pushing contracts and carrying banners for Delia's social agenda. Unlike my liberal wife, I'm quite content to leave poor, dear Ireland alone."

He downed one drink, set the glass on the floor, and began nursing his other glass along. "Your husband looks so familiar to me."

"He's been coming to embassy functions with his parents for some time."

"It's probably that, but he does remind me of someone back home." He scratched his head. "Ah, yes. Now I remember. I don't suppose he has a brother who's a mechanic back in Galway?"

Mikaela's interest peaked. "In Ireland? No, he doesn't, but are you saying you know someone who looks like Matt?"

"Spitting image. Same build. Same dark hair. Same eyes. A doppelganger, for sure."

Mikaela turned to face Morris. "Do you remember his name?" she blurted out loudly enough to draw attention to herself again.

Morris laughed and patted her hand. "Lovely as you are, isn't one handsome man enough for you?"

She blushed and shrank in her seat.

"I'm just foolin' with you, darlin'.'"

"Matt was adopted from a woman in Ireland. I just wondered if he might have family back there."

"Ah, I see." His face became drawn. "I'll be no help to you then. Poor Hugh." Morris clicked his tongue and shook his head. "Dead in the prime of his life."

"No!" Mikaela felt the news personally. "Do you know how he died?" If leukemia was the cause, it could strengthen the idea that Matt had other family left in Ireland.

"Motorcycle accident, I believe. Killed instantly."

Any remaining hope drained from her. Morris evidently read her disappointment as sorrow. He squeezed her hand. "There, there. Aren't you the dearest thing to grieve the loss of a stranger."

"Do you remember his name? I'd still like to see if he might have been related to Matt."

"Hmm . . . its seems to me it was Hugh. Yes, Hugh Fitzpatrick. A bonnie lad, he was."

Mikaela committed that name to memory. "You seem to have cared for him."

"Oh, I did. He was a dandy fine mechanic."

Mikaela cringed that Morris's grief was so selfish, missing the loss of his mechanic more than grieving that Hugh's life was cut so short. And then she chastened herself, realizing that her grief was just as self-interested.

Morris's wife shot him a look that caused Morris to sit upright. "It appears my break time has expired. I'm remiss in getting my wife a new drink." He stood and latched on to an expressionless, twenty-something who had planted himself near their chairs. "Mrs. Grayken, this is my son Colin." The son swept a blond wave back and barely acknowledged the introduction. "Colin, be a good lad and keep Mrs. Grayken company until her husband returns, will ya?"

Mikaela jumped to her feet. "That's not necessary. Matt and I should be going."

But Morris insisted. "Pishposh. You just arrived, and my poor Colin is as lost and alone as you." With a gentle nudge from Morris Kavanagh, Mikaela found herself face-to-face with the dashing blond who moved into waltz position.

"You'd do well to surrender." The alcohol tainting his breath also caused him to slur. He tightened his arm around Mikaela's waist, raised one eyebrow, and gave her a smile that bordered on a sneer. "My parents have a way of getting what they want."

"Thank you, but I need to get to my husband. I really don't know how to—" She tried to pull away, but his arms tightened even more, proving that this Kavanagh was also accustomed to getting what he wanted.

"Please let me go," she said loudly enough for heads to turn her way. She searched the crowd for Matt, who had now become aware of the attention shifting to her.

She kept her eyes set on Matt as Colin pulled off a three-step drag, forcing her around the room. Matt left his conversation and moved toward her and her dancing kidnapper. Mikaela tried to extricate herself from Colin's hold without creating a scene, but Colin began another round.

Matt finally caught up to him and grabbed his shoulder. Colin stopped and looked from Matt to Mikaela and back to Matt, who he eyed from head to foot. "Mr. Grayken?" His voice dripped with derision.

"Yes. Now get your hands off my wife," Matt said through a steeled smile.

"I owe the lady a final dip." Colin plunged Mikaela back and planted a kiss on her mouth as Matt grabbed his shoulder and yanked. Colin raised her back up, releasing his right hand which he formed into a fist. Mikaela knew he was planning to punch Matt, and she went on the attack with a self-defense trick her brothers taught her. She delivered a kick to the back of his knee, setting him off balance, dropping him to the floor.

Mikaela saw a storm brewing in Matt's eyes, and she wasn't sure if it was anger at Colin or humiliation because she'd intervened. She felt a hundred pairs of eyes on her, and all she wanted was to leave. She pled with Matt. "Please don't make a scene. Let's just go home."

Colin recovered, threatening a second assault, but his father stormed over. "You've embarrassed yourself and our family quite enough for one night. Take your leave now."

Morris blushed crimson and watched his arrogant son's cocky exit. "I apologize, Mikaela. I should never have put you in that position. My apologies to you too, Mr. Grayken. My boy didn't want to be here tonight. I'm trying to bring the little snot along in the company, and I thought he could make some introductions tonight, but he decided to use my request that he dance with your wife as a ploy to get excused. Again, please forgive me for any harm I've caused."

Mikaela latched onto Matt's arm. He spun around and turned for the door with Mikaela nearly tripping along. Nothing was said as he collected Mikaela's wrap from the coatroom and handed the valet the ticket for the car. Once outside, she finally noticed his pale coloring and the shaking of his hands. The car arrived, and the valet jumped out.

She tapped Matt's shoulder. "Would you like me to drive?"

His face remained forward, stern, tight. "I think I'm still man enough to drive my own car."

"I didn't—"

But Matt ignored her, moving to the driver's side as the valet opened her door. They each hugged their own interior door on the quick ride home, and Matt did not attempt to open her door when they reached the house. Instead, he bolted inside, and when she followed him, she found the bedroom door closed and locked. Through the door, she could hear the unsettling sounds of vomiting. Matt had likely been sick all night. He'd sallied forth for her and then things got ugly and uncomfortable, but she was not willing to be blamed for Colin Kavanagh's unwelcome advances.

She waited until the sounds quieted. Fifteen minutes passed as she paced around the living room, returning to Matt's bedroom door and tapping on it, calling for him. When he didn't answer, she did what she promised she'd never do again. She grabbed the steak knife and jimmied the door open, finding Matt sitting on the edge of the bed, his bow tie dangling around his unbuttoned collar. His head was propped in hands, elbows on his knees. He didn't even bother to look up as he asked, "I think it's best if you slept in your own room tonight."

The request pierced her heart like a poison-tipped dagger, delivering hurt and rejection which swirled into an ugly mix of anger and frustration.

"I didn't do anything wrong. That . . . that brute! That arrogant snot—"

"I know."

She almost missed Matt's soft reply.

"What?"

"I'm not angry at you, Mikaela. You didn't cause this. That . . . juvenile swine . . ." His words were forced, ragged, and spoken through gritted teeth.

Her eyes began to sting. She took a step toward him. "Then why are you shutting me out?"

"I need . . . some . . . space." He looked up at her, tears in his own eyes.

"From me?" her voice broke. "Why? All I've ever tried to do is help and support you, and the one time I need your support, you shut me out?"

"You shouldn't even be here. Can't you see that? Can't you see what a joke this is?"

"What's a joke?"

Matt stood on shaky legs and spread his arms. "All of this. You and me and this pseudo marriage. We can pretend we're

198

happy in this little bubble, but it bursts when we step outside into the real world."

"Not for me." She pressed the back of her hand to her trembling mouth. "You once told me this marriage was as real as it gets for you. That this would be the only marriage and I'd be the only wife you would ever have."

"That was before."

Her fighting spirit shoved her patience out of the way. "Before what? Before you broke your stupid rules? Before you admitted you really love me? Why can't that be wonderful? Why are you trying to kill everything good between us?"

Matt stormed up to her. "Did you see how that kid treated you right in front of me?"

"So this is about your pride?"

"This is about my shame. He knew what I am. Half a man. Not even half."

"Stop it."

"It's true. He knew he could lay me out. Take you if you were willing." His voice grew coarse and thready. "He knew you deserved more."

Mikaela moved closer and charged on. "What about what I want? It certainly isn't some Neanderthal."

Matt gripped her shoulders, his face became transformed by his anguish. "I wish we had met a year ago. You'll never know who I used to be. Who I still am inside. I've been pretending I was still that man while we played our game of housekeeping and courtship. But that ended tonight. Seeing you this way. Watching other men admire you . . . You felt it too. I saw it in your eyes when you came down the stairs. The longing to be touched. To be held in arms that could fully love you. And that fire and passion will come to you someday, but not with me. So how can we go on, knowing what you want, what you need? Friendship and respect can never be enough now."

"That's what this is really about?" Her hands cupped his face. "My love for you is real, Matt. Not half-love. Not a game. Do I long for more? Yes, but with you, and if we can't have that, then so be it, because I'd rather wake up next to you than be with anyone else in this world. What are you more afraid of? That you can't make love to me or that you won't make me happy?"

She heard air rush from his lungs as if her words had punctured them. He released her and crossed the room. With his back to her, he said, "I couldn't bear it. To know I . . . was a disappointment to you. That I left you wanting."

Her chest grew tight, and emotion balled up in her throat leaving her unable to offer a verbal rebuttal. She moved to Matt, whose face was torn with grief, as if their fate was already decided. As if he'd already accepted that they were through.

Her hands cupped his face. "You hear me, Matt Grayken. The only way you could disappoint me is if you gave up on us. Do you hear me? Never give up on us. You've already made me the happiest I've been in my life. Whatever we can be together is what's best for me." She pressed her forehead to Matt's. "I promise."

She felt his exhausted body quiver against her. He drew her to him and then pushed her away. "We can't. There's another concern. If we . . . if you were to . . ."

A new, more pressing burden clouded his eyes. "I didn't expect we'd be here, even discussing this. I didn't plan for . . ." He shook his head. "I'm toxic, Mikaela. The doctor warned me about the threat I pose to a baby if you were to get pregnant now, and I haven't made any preparations for . . ."

"I'm a cancer nurse, remember?" She pressed a kiss to his lips. She slowly led him back to the bed as she attempted to ease his concerns. "A married cancer nurse who knew she loved her future husband the first time they met. I willingly accepted whatever limits we faced, but I prepared for this eventuality. I never stopped hoping we'd find our way here." Mikaela smiled as she took the end of his tie. She whispered, "I love you, Mr. Grayken," and slowly pulled it free, gently encouraging Matt to sit.

A hint of a smile tugged at the corners of his mouth. "You amaze me, Mrs. Grayken." His breaths became ragged and deep as his hands slipped to her waist.

The fire she had seen in stolen moments returned to his eyes as he pulled her down beside him. "Oh, Mikaela," he muttered, as she unbuttoned his shirt. He flinched as his taped catheter was revealed.

She pressed her hand over it and said, "I don't even see it," and kissed him again. Together they explored the limits of all love yet offered them.

Mikaela had long since fallen asleep in Matt's arms. They slept side by side like two perfectly fitted spoons. He fought sleep, not wanting to miss a moment of the fresh new wonder of holding his wife, skin to skin, of having fully been one. He threaded strands of her tawny hair through his fingers, taking in the scent of the perfume she wore the previous evening, smiling that she still wore the sapphire and diamond necklace and earrings because the seconds needed to remove them last night could not be spared.

There had been passion and fire, feelings he feared he'd never enjoy with Mikaela, but more incredibly, there was peace. He marveled that serenity and security were his when he now knew exactly what he might lose if he died. Perhaps it was because he now had no regrets. He'd hit the summit of life's experience, loving fully and deeply, and knowing, without any reservations, that he was loved just as deeply in return.

He wrote new memories on his heart—the sound of Mikaela's contented breaths, the excruciating wonder of passion's glow on her face, a new level of human gentleness and understanding that nearly surpassed understanding.

A thought hit him with poignant impact. It was cancer that brought him to the Prospect Cancer Treatment Center. In a roundabout way, cancer brought him Mikaela and made him weak enough to open his heart to her and good enough for her to love. He would fight it with every breath he had, but it was no longer an enemy. Merely an opponent, a challenger that made him change and grow. He was finished bemoaning his situation. He could see a divine hand in everything. Instead of blaming God for his sickness, he thanked Him for bringing him Mikaela. Life was sweet. Beautiful. And he wasn't going to waste a minute of it, however long it lasted.

Mikaela stirred, rolling over within the protective circle of Matt's arms and nestling against his chest. She smiled, and her eyes opened slightly. "I really like marriage."

Matt chuckled and gave her a lingering kiss. "I'm also a huge fan." He wriggled onto his back, leaving Mikaela curled against his right shoulder. His left hand gently traced the curve of her arm as it lay across his chest.

"You're wide awake," she said, half-asleep.

"I'm too happy to sleep."

"Then you're going to die of sleep deprivation, because I think we're going to be ecstatically happy."

"Ahhh . . . what a way to go."

Mikaela leaned up on her elbow, her eyebrows pinched in worry. "Seriously. Why can't you sleep?"

Matt took a finger and pushed her semifrown into a smile. "Because I'm seriously happy. And because my mind is racing with lists of things I want us to do."

"Such as?"

"I have two more days of chemo in this round, and then I get a break while the labs are run. I'd like us to visit my folks this weekend. Eat some great food. Maybe catch a show or two. Doesn't that sound like fun?"

Mikaela settled back against his shoulder with a flirty wiggle. "It sounds wonderful. I love your parents."

"And if the labs look good, I'd like to sail the Atlantic and show you some of my favorite places in the world."

"I've never been on a cruise ship."

"Not one of those floating cities. We'll rent a catamaran and a crew in Greece and sail the coast for a couple of weeks."

"That sounds so romantic." He heard the worry in her reply.

"And if I have another round of chemo ahead, I'll show you my favorite places another way. I have it all planned out, no matter what."

20

Mikaela noticed the positive change in Matt's entire outlook since the last barrier between them had been crossed a week ago. Three days without chemo had already improved his energy level and appetite, but the impact of the treatment was still apparent. His coloring was still wan, his hair was noticeably thinner, and his eyes were still ringed with purple shadows.

Knowing how aware Matt was of the changes to his appearance, she was delighted that he wanted to host the Thursday night poker game again.

"Do they know the leukemia is back?" she asked.

"I told them," he replied simply.

She didn't press for more details about how or when he told them, but she felt relief just knowing that she and Matt were not alone.

Mikaela had grown fond of the group, who welcomed her

into their all-male circle. She received hugs as they entered and more hugs as they exited. In between, she was everyone's favorite hostess. They were astonished by her easygoing manner as they tromped in and set up camp in her living room. She even sat in on a few rounds of cards, but she suspected they threw the game her way whenever she played a hand. She laughed and joked and gave as good as she got, but what she really loved was how pleased Matt was that she loved his friends and how happy he was when the last friend left and they were alone once more.

The planned trip to New York to visit Matt's parents loomed the next day. Mikaela caught Matt studying his appearance in the bathroom mirror when she walked in after five outfit changes. "What do you think about this one?" she asked.

Matt scanned her, from her braided ponytail to her baby blue cowl-necked sweater and skinny jeans. "You look as beautiful as you did the first four times. Why are you so worried? My parents have already met you and they already love you."

"And I want them to keep loving me, but what must they think about us taking a leave from our jobs? That I've ruined their once-responsible son so we can have what must appear to them to be an extended honeymoon? I need to look solid and responsible but not dowdy. I don't want them to think I lie around the house all day draining your savings. What do we say when they ask us when we're returning to work?"

"Those are good questions. I've been thinking that visiting my parents this weekend might not be a good idea."

Panic hit Mikaela. She hadn't given up on finding Matt's birth family, and she needed information only his parents could provide. "What? Our train leaves from Union Station in two hours."

"If you're worried about those questions, consider this. One look at me and they're going to know I'm sick."

Mikaela wrapped her arms around him from behind. "Maybe it's time to tell them."

He leaned his head back against her and met her gaze in the mirror. "When you look at me, I see love and hope. When they know my cancer has returned, they'll look at me with love, but I'll see fear and worry."

"Perhaps at first, because you're the most important person in the world to them next to each other. But they'll see how we're handling things. They'll understand."

"I'm just not sure I'm ready if they don't."

"I still think we should go." She moved beside him and looked at him in the mirror. "I was wrong when I said this is *our* fight. It affects them too. They're going to hurt whether you tell them today or in a month, but the longer you delay, the worse it will hurt because they'll know you didn't trust them."

Seconds ticked by as Mikaela watched Matt stare into the mirror. He reached his arm around her and pulled her against him. "I'll tell them right away if I have to face another round of chemo, but not this trip, okay?"

"Okay. I can put a little concealer under your eyes to hide the shadows. And we can buy some spray color at the pharmacy to make your hair look thicker."

"Thanks. And we'll plan our evasive answers to all potentially awkward questions on the ride up."

"Sounds like a good strategy."

"I never thought I'd ask my wife this question."

"What question is that?"

"Give me a makeover, please."

Matt gave his Yankees baseball cap a tug over his thinning hair before sweeping his mother up in a hug.

"You look thin," she said, her worry evident.

"Don't let Mikaela hear you say that. She's the cook in our house."

Mikaela rushed in with a prepared diversion. "Can I copy some more recipes from your cookbook this weekend?"

The request clearly pleased Catherine Grayken, and the first hurdle was crossed. Donovan Grayken had a few concerns of his own before they reached the house.

"I called over to your office the other day, and they said you hadn't been to work in weeks. The last time we talked, you said you were planning to head to Europe and look for opportunities there. When is that happening? I understand the need to pull back a bit and settle into your marriage,

Matthew, but you can't be hands-off if you want your business to thrive."

"Did I mention that Mikaela and I attended a party at the Irish embassy a week ago? I met with an old friend of yours, Patrick Dunne, who's involved in tourism now. He wants Great Expectations to book excursions to Ireland's coast."

"I think that's a great idea. I've been telling you to do that for years."

Mikaela took a deep breath as another large hurdle was crossed. The men talked shop for hours while the women cooked and looked at photo albums. Catherine willingly brought out Matt's baby album, where his earliest photos were displayed. Against Matt's wishes, Mikaela broached the topic of Joseph McNamara with Catherine.

"Matt told me about the attorney who arranged the adoption. He said Joseph McNamara was one in a million. He wished he had someone like him in his company."

"There'll never be another Joseph. He was as loyal as a Labrador. The dear man worked himself into an early grave watching over the company and protecting our interests."

"He must have loved you both very much."

"Indeed he did. And we love his family too. There's old history there. You see, Joseph was employed by the law firm that handled the Grayken family whiskey business back in Ireland. One day, out of the blue, his wife ran off and left him with three children. Well, between unreliable nannies and sick little ones, Joseph's billable hours suffered, and he was fired, but Donnie convinced his brothers that it would be cheaper to drop that law firm and hire their own corporate attorneys. When they agreed, Joseph was Donnie's first hire."

"So Donovan saved Joseph's career and his family."

"I suppose so. And Joseph dedicated himself to repaying that gift. He was a legal marvel for the company and for us personally. He worked tirelessly to find Matthew for us, and he handled all the legal work, for which we'll always be grateful. When we left the whiskey business and moved to New York, Joseph and his family moved with us. Joseph remained our lead attorney until the day he died. He and his children were like family to us. They're grown now, but we still hear from them from time to time."

Mikaela wondered how far this indebted, loyal attorney had been willing to go to find the Graykens a child. Could he truly not find the mother, or did he prefer not to have his employers know the details behind the adoption? Mikaela still had nothing but hunches and suppositions. And the name of a dead mechanic, Hugh Fitzpatrick, from Galway, Ireland.

The foursome found plenty to fill the two days. They crossed off every item on Matt's wish list, but Mikaela's greatest enjoyment came from watching Matt look and act more like himself. He stood erect instead of defaulting into a hunch when relaxing as he had for the past few weeks. She couldn't tell if he truly felt as well as he appeared, but it cheered her heart to see a ready smile on his face and to hear his laughter fill the room.

They navigated uncomfortable questions artfully, but there had also been several tense moments when Catherine or Donovan studied their son so intently that either Matt or Mikaela scrambled to divert their attention elsewhere. This constant game of evasion was exhausting, making Matt's cancer ever present and consuming. As much as they loved Matt's parents, they longed for home, where no secrets remained, where they could push the reality of Matt's cancer away for hours, and sometimes days, and pretend their wishes and prayers were guaranteed.

At the train drop-off, Catherine held on to Matt for what seemed like minutes. When she released her son, she turned to Mikaela and wrapped her in a warm embrace saying, "Please get Matt to a doctor, Mikaela. He's been dodging our concerns all weekend. I think something's wrong, but you're the only one he'll listen to."

Mikaela didn't know how to respond. She looked at Matt who was engaged in an equally harrowing goodbye with his father. She deadened her emotions, grabbed her bag, and turned for the door to the station.

A silent pall fell over them as they waited on the platform. Fatigue, both physical and emotional, had taken its toll. Once they boarded the train and found their seats, Matt leaned against the window and fell into blessed sleep, but Mikaela's mind fast-forwarded, to next week's lab results, the possibility of more chemo, the need to tell Matt's parents the truth, and the battle that might ensue over Matt's treatment. She was caught in the middle between her promise to Matt and the request of his worried parents. The weight of all these concerns was crushing.

The comforter needed comfort. She longed for her parents' shoulders to slump into and for their ears to just listen while she ranted and cried her way back to peace and hope. She suddenly missed George's sideways glances and open arms. She needed her brothers.

With a quick check of her watch and some calculations for the time difference, she took a chance on catching her oldest brother awake. He picked up on the second ring.

"Mickie? Is everything all right?"

"I'm sorry. Did I wake you?"

"No, no. I'm just lying here, buying a few minutes before I have to get moving. What's up?"

"I just needed to talk to my big brother." Her voice broke, and she could hear the rustle of the bed. She knew George was now sitting up, giving her his full attention.

"Are you crying? Did that husband do something to make you cry?"

She cupped her hand by her phone to keep her conversation as private as possible while she rushed to assure her overprotective brother. "Matt's wonderful." She took Matt's hand. "I'm not hurt. I'm just a little sad. I needed Mom and Dad today, and then I just wanted to talk to you."

"And why are you whispering? I can barely understand what you're saying."

"I'm on a train. Matt's asleep and I don't want to wake him."

"What are you not telling me, Mickie? You know you can tell me anything."

"Matt's sick. Very sick."

She heard George's deep, slow sigh. "That's why you two rushed into getting married, isn't it?"

"Sort of."

"What's he got?"

"Leukemia. AML. It's bad."

"Uh, I'm sorry, baby. How can I help you? Does he need a donor? Do you need us to get tested?"

"He needs a close family match, but he was adopted. The only lead I have on a family member is remote, and even if he was related to Matt, he's dead."

"Oh, Mickie. I'm sorry. You've hit a wall."

"I have his name. Hugh Fitzpatrick, from Galway, Ireland."

"But you don't even know for sure if they're related."

"I've prayed harder for this than anything in my life, George, and I just have a feeling that he was Matt's brother."

"You mean you hope. And even if he is, what good will it do you if he's dead?"

"It's more than just hope. The adoption was arranged privately by an attorney who felt indebted to Matt's parents. No one can find any record of the mother, so there's no proof that there aren't more family members over there."

"You're grasping at straws, Princess, and I get it. If I were in your shoes, I'd try to find hope anywhere I could, but please don't see facts where there aren't any. Don't set yourself up for a fall."

A fall was inevitable. She'd been dangling by a rope over a cliff since she heard about Hugh Fitzpatrick, and George was sawing away at it.

"Do you need me there? I can hitch a ride on a transport plane. I could be there within a few days."

"Thanks, but . . . now is not a good time."

"I understand. I love you, Mickie. I'm always here for you. All of us are."

She moved the phone away from her face and sniffed. "I know."

"I'm telling the rest of the family. From now on, send a video message to the whole clan. I want you to remember that you're never alone."

21

Matt gave Mikaela an obscure reason for his early-morning errand. He wanted to speak confidentially to the doctor about the recent lab report. For that reason, the day felt more like a quest than a medical appointment because the results would determine the course of many lives.

The strain of the New York trip and of avoiding his parents' questions had shaken him, but the minute he and Mikaela crossed into the safe zone of their home, he felt the return of the heaven-sent calm and peace he'd found the night he lay awake watching Mikaela sleep beside him.

His hands were steady and his steps strong, as he was led down a sterile hall to the doctor's personal office. He offered a continuous prayer for good news as his footsteps echoed down the hall. He thought of the places he hoped to share with Mikaela, and the twelve trips he planned for her to take if he couldn't. They had been printed and bound into a book by an office store and hidden back at the house. He was prepared, whatever the outcome, and that outcome would determine which of his plans to set in motion.

Dr. Gorman welcomed him at the door, and with a minimum of small talk, they got to the point of the meeting.

"Matt, I wish I had better news, but I'm afraid that nothing we've tried thus far has given us the results we were hoping for."

The news hit Matt with a dull thud. "Which means?"

"I'd like to hit this hard, with everything in our arsenal. More red cell and platelet transfusions, immunotherapy, some new chemo drugs."

Matt tried to make light of the news. "That sounds unpleasant."

"It would be very intense, and, honestly, you could feel considerably worse before you feel any improvement. We'll want to monitor you carefully. I've made arrangements for you to be admitted to St. George University Hospital."

Those were the words he most dreaded. "St. George? For how long?"

Dr. Gorman hedged before answering. "Three to four weeks at least."

A calendar appeared in Matt's mind with blackness erasing the November memories he hoped to make with Mikaela. Every nerve in his body fired randomly, hot and cold, pain and shock. He sat back in his chair and grabbed the back of his head. He thought of being separated from Mikaela when they'd just barely found one another. He thought of the home she'd made for them, with the tree and the twinkle lights and their love story told in ornaments. He thought of his parents.

"Can't I go home at night? I'll return every morning, bright and early, but I want to sleep in my own house, in my own bed."

Dr. Gorman shook his head with finality. "I've spoken to a colleague there. They'll want to run IVs day and night."

Matt found the courage to voice his ultimate fear. "I don't want to die in a sterile hospital."

"I'm not going to let that happen, Matt, but don't let your mind go to the darkest outcome. We have a lot of fight left. I'll stay in touch, but I'm passing your care off to a colleague at St. George. He's had success with stubborn cases."

Matt could only see the ultimate end of his life, and he wanted a timeframe so he could plan. "Will I make it to Christmas?"

"Just focus on following the treatment plan."

The doctor's refusal to answer left Matt simultaneously raw and numb. An overwhelming weight fell upon him at the thought that he would need to deliver this news to Mikaela and his parents. "I need time—"

"Listen to me. You've got to give your body its best chance of getting that miracle Mikaela's been praying for. And this is your best chance."

Matt felt his head nod in involuntary agreement. "How soon?"

"I wanted to start this weekend, but you left town. We need to get on this immediately."

"One more day. Please."

"It's a bad gamble, Matt."

"One day. I'll check in tomorrow evening. I promise."

Hope and faith felt like hummingbirds. Visible and within reach, but elusive and hard to catch. He decided that the best way to handle these fragile gifts was to simply let them come to him, so he proceeded to deal with the things within his control, and leave the rest to Providence.

He called Daniel. "Hey, man. I'm going to need to convene a private DPS meeting in a few days."

He heard Daniel groan. "I'm sorry, brother. How are you holding up?"

"Okay right now, but I'm being admitted to the hospital tomorrow, and I'm going to need a big favor from you, my friend."

"Just say it and it's as good as done."

Matt ended that call and dialed Mikaela. He needed to get her out of the house for a little while, and shopping seemed an easy distraction. "I feel like bangers and mash for lunch. What do you say?"

"Okay."

He sensed wariness in her tone.

"And maybe something decadent for dessert. I'm going to be tied up for another hour or so. If you shop, I'll cook."

He counted the silent seconds, knowing they reflected the degree of her growing worry.

"Sounds like a plan. Where have you been this morning?"

It was a question for which he had prepared. "Just doing what I do best, Mrs. Grayken. Dreaming and scheming."

"So, you'll be home soon?" She didn't sound reassured.

"In about an hour or so. See you soon, Mrs. Grayken. I love you."

He ended the call quickly before his rising emotions tinged his voice. The next stop was Gino's flower shop for two dozen cut and trimmed roses, which he laid in a trail from Mikaela's parking spot, into the house, and to the bedroom. Overwhelmed by the sense that this could be the last night he and Mikaela would share this bed, he pulled the duvet back, and scattered the petals of the last four roses across the pristine white sheets.

He pulled the book of adventures from the bottom of his closet and turned pages filled with photos he had taken over the years at each location. He included a letter corresponding to each location, telling her why he wanted her to go there. Matt had set aside the funds to cover each adventure and he filed a document for Ben with his attorney, asking Great Expectations' new president to personally arrange each trip for Mikaela if things didn't end well for Matt.

He bit his lip to quell the emotions rising inside him at the thought that he might not be able to share his favorite places on earth with the person he loved most in the world. A thought pulled him to the living room where the tree stood. Seeing it dressed for Christmas was a reminder of what he was fighting for, and the fight meant there was hope. Cheered somewhat by that prompt, he placed the album on the bookshelf, where Mikaela would be sure to find it if he didn't make it home to share it with her.

He changed into his tux and searched the CD rack for the soulful album that broke him the first week of their marriage—Amos Lee's *Arms of a Woman*—when the agonizing nearness of Mikaela was torturous. He set it up in the player, then lit a pumpkin-scented candle and lowered the rest of the lights, leaving only the Christmas tree's tender glow to illuminate the rose trail. With the CD player's remote in hand, he waited for Mikaela to open the door.

His smile reflected the effusive joy and relief he felt at seeing Mikaela enter. Uncertainty pulled at her mouth when he walked to her, his tux's tie dangling loose, his shirt collar opened to the top of his vest. He took the grocery bag and collected flowers from her and set them on the island. "These can wait," he said as he clicked the remote, releasing the folksy hunger expressed in the queued song. His arms slipped around Mikaela's wary form. "I still owe you a dance, Mrs. Grayken."

She offered no playful return. Instead she searched his face, her suspicion evident and unrelenting, even as her arms gingerly encircled him.

His lips brushed along her forehead. "Do you know you smile in your sleep?"

"You saw Dr. Gorman today, didn't you?" She buried her face in the crook of his neck.

He smiled down on her and nodded against her cheek.

"Round three?" The words were muffled against his chest.

"Yes." He tipped her face up to receive a kiss. He recorded the taste of her mouth, the soft feel of her against him, the way she leaned into him, needing his strength.

"When?"

"I check into St. George tomorrow night."

She lifted her head and gazed up at him with shining eyes. "That's exactly what you didn't want."

"Now I want something else even more." He ran his thumb along her cheek. "I want to do everything I can to have more time with you."

He slipped his hand down her back, and she shivered. He pulled his tie loose and wrapped it around her. With a gentle tug toward the bedroom he said, "Take me home, Mrs. Grayken. Take me home."

22

Matt was affected more deeply and quickly by this round than by either of the previous rounds of treatment. A sleeping chair was arranged for Mikaela, and she spent nearly every hour by his side, leaving only to shower, change, and eat.

Since her Sunday call to George, she and her large family of brothers and sisters-in-law video chatted daily. She introduced Matt to Team Compton, and they refused to allow chemo to excuse Matt from their raucous humor.

"Don't think faking cancer will get you out of the Compton brother beat down for running off with our sister," Abe joked.

Thomas asked, "Did she tell you we were her only dowry?"

And so it went as Mikaela remembered how good it felt to laugh again.

She slipped down to the hospital lobby Wednesday morning and found it elegantly decorated for Thanksgiving. She hadn't even given the holiday a thought, but the turkeys and Pilgrims brought back loving reminders of the laughter-filled holidays from her childhood. She longed to make similar, simple memories with Matt, to know times when their biggest worry would be whether or not the table was set for enough people.

She strolled into the gift shop searching for snacks and noticed a tree decorated with Christmas ornaments. A little red train engine dangled from a golden thread. It reminded Mikaela of the bedtime story, *The Little Engine That Could*. The train, and its motto, "I think I can," seemed to be a perfect mission statement to inspire Matt.

She purchased the glass train, and when she handed it to Matt, she said, "I think you can," earning a smile from her very sick patient. He fingered the ornament thoughtfully, replying, "I know I can, with you by my side." He wrapped it in a napkin and handed it back to her. "Take it home for me, will you? I'd like to imagine it hanging from our tree."

She stuffed it into her purse and settled on the chair in his room, to watch Matt sleep as IVs dripped into his veins. She thought of Hugh Fitzpatrick. His name continually nagged at her as did George's call for her to be logical. Finally, she argued back to the heavens, *What good is it to pray and plead for a miracle and then ignore what could be the answer?*

With no real idea how to proceed, she Googled "Irish Death Records" and was sent to a genealogy site that only allowed access to records from 1958 and before. Her only remaining hunch was to find the giver of the lead—Morris Kavanagh—and her only lead to him was the gala's host, Patrick Dunne. Now, how to find Mr. Dunne?

She figured the Irish embassy was the best place to start, so she Googled that and found a number. Step two was perfecting a professional but truthful excuse for the information she needed. The next morning, she placed the call. A woman answered in a polished, polite voice, asking if she could be of service. Mikaela swallowed, remembered the stakes, and ploughed on.

"Hello. I certainly hope so. I'm Mrs. Matthew Grayken. My husband and I attended the gala at the embassy on October thirtieth, hosted by Patrick Dunne. Mr. Dunne proposed some joint business ventures with my husband's company, Great Expectations. I'm afraid I can't find his contact info. I was hoping you could give me his number."

"I'm sorry, Mrs. Grayken. We have a policy of not releasing private information. It's a reflection of the times we live in."

"I understand. Could you possibly give my contact information to him?"

"Yes. I could do that. What is that number?"

Gratitude zipped through Mikaela, and then she realized her chances of receiving a return call would increase exponentially if it appeared the request was from Matt, so she gave the woman Matt's name and number and asked, "The matter I need to discuss with Mr. Dunne is time sensitive. Would you ask him to return my call today, please?"

"I'll place my call to him right away. I have no control over when he'll call you back."

"I understand. Thank you so much for your help."

The call ended, and she grabbed Matt's phone off the utility table, turning the ringer down to buzz. She felt she had scored one small victory.

Matt stirred and half opened his eyes. "Who were you talking to?"

Mikaela changed the topic quickly by scooting over and placing her free hand on his cheek.

"That feels nice," he said with a smile. "I love you, Mrs. Grayken."

"I love you, Mr. Grayken. More than you can imagine. How are you feeling?"

Mikaela noticed that he also adeptly changed the subject. He took her hand. "I haven't handled things very well, Mikaela, and I'm sorry."

"What do you mean? You're doing all you can do."

"I think it's time for me to tell my parents everything. They deserved to know from the beginning. I've been selfish, and I've placed you in a very uncomfortable position. I'm releasing you as my medical officer. I'm going to handle this myself so they know all my choices were mine."

Mikaela had a few patients who had similar wrestles over when and how to tell their loved ones about their diagnoses. She squeezed Matt's hand and smiled sadly. "Tell them all your choices *are* yours. We've still got a lot of fight ahead."

Matt closed his eyes and nodded. "You're a good soldier. Your brothers taught you well."

His eyes drifted closed. She placed her head into the curve of his neck and laid one arm across his wired chest, listening to him breath.

The phone buzzed in her hand, and she gently lifted her head away from Matt's and walked into the hallway to answer it.

"Hello. Mikaela Grayken."

"Mrs. Grayken. So nice to hear from you. I'm returning your husband's call. I was just leaving my office, but I definitely wanted to respond as quickly as possible to Matthew."

She recognized Patrick Dunne's voice as soon as he replied.

"Mr. Dunne, I actually placed that call. I hope you'll be able to help me. I need to get in contact with one of your guests from the party—Mr. Morris Kavanagh."

Mr. Dunne immediately began apologizing for Colin Kavanagh's unseemly behavior, which prompted the Graykens' hasty exit from the event. "I can't begin to tell you how upset we all were, Mrs. Grayken. Especially Morris Kavanagh. I've known the man for years, and I can assure you that he has severely censured his son."

Mikaela didn't mention the conspicuous absence of any apology from Colin or the failure of his father to follow-up with her since the encounter. She did notice that Dunne seemed nervous about her response to the assault she suffered, which meant that Morris Kavanagh might likewise be worried.

"I'd like Morris Kavanagh's phone number, Mr. Dunne. I believe he owes me a conversation."

"Of course. Of course, but I hope you don't hold me or my government responsible for his son's dreadful behavior. Is there something I can tell him for you?"

"No. As you can imagine, this will be a personal call. I'll handle it myself."

"Of course. Of course. I have it right here . . ."

Mikaela copied the number, thanked Mr. Dunne, and planned her next move, which, judging from Mr. Dunne's reaction, would be even trickier.

Deciding that the straightforward approach was best, she dialed the number, but there was no answer. She left a brief message asking Mr. Kavanagh to return her call, and she hurried to Matt's bedside, to await the call from Ireland.

Bag after bag of fluid was emptied into Matt, who threw up nearly an equal volume. He looked terrible, and Mikaela knew he felt worse than he looked. They quickly ran out of small talk to fill the never-ending hours, and TV became an almost painful reminder that they were avoiding the topic on both of their minds.

"When do you want to tell them?" Mikaela asked.

"Friday," Matt said. "They'll want to rush right down here, and the weekend is easiest for them."

Aside from the anger and hurt she anticipated from them, she also feared something else. She felt a dread she couldn't put into words, as if the fragile world she fought so hard to hold together was about to shatter or be taken from her. The thought made her hands shake.

"You need to go home," Matt said. "You're so exhausted that you're shaking."

"I'm just a little cold."

"Take one of my blankets." He tried to lift one that covered him, and the effort showed on his face. Mikaela stilled his hands and reassured him. "I'm fine, Matt. I'm fine."

He slumped back into the bed, a look of frustration on his face. "You're single-handedly the greatest thing in my life, Mikaela. I'm aware of that every second. As sick as I look, I really am a very happy man." He brought her hand to his lips.

Mikaela's eyes teared. "We are everything my parents told me love would be. Thank you for loving me like that."

She gently moved the leads and wires enough to lay her head back near his neck and they fell asleep that way.

More quiet hours passed as nurses and techs slipped in and out of the room, changing IV bags, taking specimens for tests, and checking vitals. The mood lifted when the poker group arrived. Matt laughed and Mikaela squealed with happiness as she rushed to each of them. "I can't believe you brought the game to Matt."

"Of course we did," Daniel said with a wink. "He won my Han Solo last week. It's worth a thousand dollars. You don't think I'm going to let him get away with that, do you?"

Mikaela wrapped her arms around Daniel and whispered, "You can't know how much I love you for doing this."

Daniel pulled back, his own eyes moist as he softly replied, "For him and for you, Mikaela. Remember that. We're all here for you too."

"Let go of my wife, Casanova!" Matt called out comically from his bed. With her back to Matt, she grabbed her phone, wiped her eyes, and said, "I'll leave you Jedi to your battle."

She barely made it to stairwell before the flood of pent-up emotion roared from her—love, relief, terror, worry, and grief. She hated the sense of helplessness that consumed her. It took her back to her parents' last days when despite all her care and love and faith, they still passed away. She was terrified about tomorrow. She had been Matt's coconspirator in hiding the truth from his parents. It had been easier before she met them. Before she loved them and they loved her back. They would forgive Matt because he was their son, and the one in need of their compassion. But her? She wrapped her arms around her torso as the shivers overtook her.

The door opened, and she moved to the corner to allow the arriving person to pass without having to meet their eyes.

"Matt sent me, Mikaela."

It was Daniel's voice, but soft and caring, and absent his usual humor and sarcasm. She kept her back to him and tried to fold further into herself. Gentle hands grasped her shoulders. He turned her and drew her against himself, but she kept her arms wrapped around her own body, as if they alone were holding her together.

"Somehow, it'll be all right. If anyone deserves a miracle, it's you and Matt. What you have is so far beyond what most people think love is."

Her shaking slowly eased, and she found the strength to stand unsupported again.

"He's telling his parents tomorrow."

"I know. I know everything, how he asked you to marry him so you could be his caregiver, but you fell in love instead. You were supporting his choices. That's what I'm going to tell the Graykens too. I'm your backup, Mikaela."

She didn't understand what he meant, but she appreciated the thought. "Thank you. My heart aches for them. There's no way we can explain this without hurting them even more."

"The whole situation is awful. For everyone. You included."

"I knew what I was getting into."

"But you thought it was going to be a job. You didn't know you were going to fall in love with your patient."

"Yes, I did. From that very first day."

Wonder crossed Daniel's face. "That's what Matt said about you. It sounds as if you two were meant to meet. Hang on to that tomorrow."

The thought revived her hope. "Thank you for checking

on me. I just need another minute or two. Tell Matt I'm okay, will you?"

"Sure." Daniel gave her an understanding smile before leaving.

Mikaela checked her phone. Morris Kavanagh had not returned her call. She called again and left another message, intent on doing everything she could to move Providence along.

The call to Matt's parents was as gut-wrenching as she expected it to be. Matt's voice broke, and she could do nothing to relieve his guilt and sorrow. He started at the beginning with the June diagnosis and choosing an alternative cancer center and treatment program. He told them it was where he first saw Mikaela. He fell apart when he explained why he asked a total stranger to marry him, and their response summed up the pain that disclosure caused them.

"Are you saying your choice was to die with a stranger's help rather than give your parents a chance to save you?"

Mikaela could tell from Matt's responses that the Graykens now doubted everything about their marriage and even whether Mikaela really loved their son at all. She mouthed, *Do you want me to talk to them?* and was grateful when Matt shook his head no and pled on with his folks.

Nurses came in and out, concerned by the toll the conversation was taking on Matt. One of them stood there, ready to take the phone away, but Mikaela walked her out, promising she'd end the call in a minute if Matt didn't. She gave him a look conveying that information, and he nodded his understanding.

"I've got to go. Please understand that *I* did this. These were my choices, and I made them long before I ever spoke to Mikaela."

Their response caused the color to drain from Matt's already pale face.

"No. I didn't do it to hurt you. I never wanted to hurt you. I did it to ease my fears. but Mikaela helped me realize how wrong I've been, and I'm sorry."

Mikaela guessed what the Graykens' were suggesting by Matt's response.

"No. I won't consent to being transferred to New York. We'd love you to come here and support us, but don't blame this on Mikaela."

His jaws bulged in anger and he said, "She's not a stranger. Don't ever call her that. She's my wife in every way. I love her, and I love you. We both do. Text your arrival information. Daniel will pick you up, but if you come, please come accepting all I've told you."

He clicked the call off and clenched his jaws tight. "If I could have foreseen how hurt they'd be . . ."

She had tried to tell him so many times, but there was no victory in reminding him now. A gulf seemed to have opened between them, with each of them needing some space. "Are they coming?"

"I think so." He laid his arm across his eyes. A tear slid into his hairline. "I want them to come, and I almost dread it. That's a terrible thing to say at a time like this."

Mikaela reached a hand out and rubbed his arm.

"I've made such a mess of things."

She kept rubbing.

"I've hurt them. We've all hurt you. I'm so sorry."

She drew near him and kissed his forehead. "Maybe things will be better when you speak to each other in person."

He turned his head away from her. "When they see me like this? I already look like death."

"Stop it." She sat back, reeling from the hopelessness in his voice. "It was a phone call, Matt. A terrible phone call, but it didn't change your diagnosis one bit from what it was this morning or yesterday. We're still in this fight."

"I don't think you should be here when they come."

A cold chill snaked along her spine. "I'm not hiding from them. Seeing them won't be any easier the next day or the next."

He turned her way. "I'm trying to protect you."

"I don't need protecting. I need you to not shut me out."

His volume raised. "You ran out of this room yesterday. Tell me you're not scared."

Her lips began to tremble. "Why are you doing this?"

"Because we're not in our protective little bubble

anymore, Mikaela. When they arrive, reality is going to hit us both. We might as well prepare now."

She set her hands on either side of his head and leaned down to look directly into his eyes. "Nothing is going to change. I'm still going to be here, and we will still love each other. Nothing is going to change anything that matters."

23

Each ticking second of the clock felt like the countdown on a bomb as Matt and Mikaela awaited the Graykens' arrival. Everything either of them had said in the past few hours seemed to irritate the other, so Mikaela stepped into the bathroom several times, presumably to fix her snarled bun and wash her face. Matt drifted in and out of sleep over the next hour, and they relied on the TV's curtain of background noise to fill the vacuum left by their uncomfortable silence. Mikaela began to think she'd been wrong about their marriage's ability to withstand any blow the Graykens' visit might level. Things were already changing.

Daniel texted Matt from the lobby. "They're here," Matt said with a sober tone. "Help me sit up, will you? Make me look as healthy as possible."

Mikaela was on the window side of his bed, smoothing his blankets, when Matt's parents opened the door. They appeared to have aged years since she saw them a week ago. Their faces were drawn, their eyes lined, their mouths down-turned, even when they tried to smile at their son. Mikaela noticed the conspicuous effort they made to make no eye contact with her at all.

Matt reached a hand to her. She glanced at him to check on his reaction and saw him lock eyes with his parents. Contrition etched his face.

"Thanks for coming," he said, his voice faltering.

No one moved. Mikaela released Matt's hand and stepped toward them with her arms opening in welcome, but Catherine hugged her purse tightly against her coat, and Donovan Grayken kept his gloved hands clasped before him, offering her no reciprocation of warmth or love, so she stepped back and retook Matt's hand.

Daniel appeared from behind the Graykens and said, "I'm starved." His eyebrows raised in Mikaela's direction. "Mikaela, how about joining me?"

She caught his obvious effort to give her an excuse to leave the silent tribunal, but she'd done nothing wrong. She had honored her husband's wishes, and now she preferred to stand her ground. Matt squeezed her hand.

"You deserve a break. You've been here by my side for days." He smiled reassuringly. She knew Matt had planned for Daniel to be there as her "backup." He was still trying to protect her.

Her eyes pled with Matt to let her stay and keep her promise, to be his advocate, his voice, his wife, but his love-filled expression and the warm squeeze of his hand pled back, asking her to allow him to be her husband, her defender. She relented. The muscles in her face were drawn so tight she could barely smile back. She offered a meager nod.

As she moved toward the door, the Graykens stepped into the room and out of her way, as if she were toxic to them. Tears burned her eyes as she moved to the hall. Daniel welcomed her with a sympathetic smile.

The click of the door shut her fully out. Fifteen steps down the hall, she lost it. "They treated me like an enemy. I thought they loved me."

Daniel raised his arm and drew her against him as they continued down the hall to the elevator.

"I forgot to grab my phone." She broke free of Daniel and turned for the room, but he swept her back into a full embrace. "What if he needs me? How will I know when it's safe to return?" she cried against him.

"He'll call me."

She looked back at the door.

"They're terrified. And hurt. And angry at Matt, but they can't be angry at their son, who is possibly dying, so you're the easy scapegoat."

"Is that what they told you?"

"More or less. Come on. I really am hungry, and you need a change of scenery."

Against Mikaela's objections, Daniel bought soup for each of them and found a table by the windows, overlooking nearly bare autumn trees. "What else did they say?"

"It doesn't matter, Mikaela. If Matt gets well, things will smooth over."

Her eyes fixed on his as the obvious response to that question, *and what if he doesn't?* hung unspoken between them. She watched the color drain from his face and return in a blush of color as worry lines etched his brow.

"Just eat your soup, okay?"

She took one spoonful and stared out the window, forgetting Daniel and the food.

Daniel relented. "If you had it all to do again, would you have done things differently and gone against Matt's wishes, or would you have made the same choices?"

"Of course I'd make the same choices to support Matt."

"Then how much does what the Graykens think really matter?"

She gave her soup a random stir. "I guess not much."

He covered her hand with his. "I know how loyal your love is, Mikaela. I promise you that Matt is up there, defending you just as loyally, while also trying to comfort his parents. It'll work out. You'll see."

A text came through Daniel's phone.

"Is it Matt?"

Daniel nodded. "Yeah."

"Is he ready for me to come back up?"

"I don't think it's going well. He asked me to take you home. He said he'll see you in the morning."

She was sure her heart stopped beating or her lungs

refused to draw air, because for a moment, everything froze in her. "He's pushing me out."

"No," Daniel insisted. "He just needs more time with his parents."

She wondered if he'd even feel comfortable calling her, and then she remembered, "My phone. I need to get it."

At that moment, a nurse Mikaela recognized came by the table. "I mentioned I was leaving on my dinner break, and your husband asked me to drop this off to you."

She gave a parting smile, completely unaware that by offering to run that errand, she had inadvertently destroyed any excuse Mikaela might have had to reclaim her spot by Matt's side. She couldn't find the will to utter thank you, so Daniel did instead.

Mikaela barely remembered the drive home, and when she arrived, the house that had been their fortress against the reality of their situation now felt devoid of comfort. She passed the bulletin board, where their embassy gala tickets hung, and the blender she used to whip up Matt's nutritional drink she had lovingly titled "sludge." She touched the calendar created online using photos of the two of them on their various outings. The squares now read like a medical journal of appointments and tests, sprinkled with hopeful words and bright stickers to camouflage the weight of their fight.

Needing something to salvage the happiness they'd known and hoped to reclaim, she moved to the great room to plug in their tree. Its soft glow felt like a warm hug, and the ornaments provided a tangible reminder of all she and Matt had done, and were, together.

She reached into her purse and found the little train ornament. After gently unwrapping it, she hung it from the tree saying, "We can get through this, Matt. I know we can. I know we can."

Mikaela touched the few dried rose petals Matt had collected and placed in a bowl on the end table. She followed their pull back to the bedroom where she remembered Matt's drawn expression as he packed an overnight bag for this hospital stay. It was hard to believe they'd been so ecstatically happy just a week before.

A brief apology text came through from Matt, asking for her patience, and promising a call as soon as his parents left his room. The call never came, so she assumed they stayed until he had fallen asleep. As angry and sad as she was about being dismissed from Matt's room, she admitted that she was exhausted, physically and emotionally. She made little effort to disguise her mood on the evening video message to her brothers. As expected, replies chimed in all night from worried faces with offers to come to her. As badly as she wanted to accept, she held her brothers off, admitting to herself that there was a chance she might truly need them later on.

She slept hard, but not soundly, falling asleep quickly and awakening several times. Up, showered, and dressed by seven, she was determined to reclaim her spot before the Graykens arrived.

Matt's pale and tired appearance was always more shocking to her when she returned to his room after a visit home than when she stayed straight through with him for days. A small panic gripped her heart when she first entered. Matt's expression assured her he was equally dismayed by their separation.

"I've watched that doorway since six, praying you'd walk through any minute. I'm so sorry about last night."

She rushed over to him, tossed her coat off, and wrapped her arms gingerly around him with a hug and a kiss. "I admit I was angry. Not at you, or your parents necessarily, but at the situation."

"I created that situation."

"Did you make any progress with your parents, or should I prepare for the cold treatment again?"

"They're hurt. They feel we both lied to them. I told them you were only doing what I asked, but that made matters worse. Knowing that I deceived them and avoided them was even harder for them to swallow."

His fingers rubbed his temples. "I don't know if they'll ever forgive me."

Mikaela rubbed his arm. "Are they coming back today?"

"They're here for the weekend. I'm sure they'll be in soon."

Panic rose again in Mikaela. "What should I do? Do you think I should stay?"

"I wish I had something better to tell you." Sorrow filled his face. "You're caught in a vice I created. I can't ask them to go, and I don't want you to go. I think it'll be a tense and painful day."

She watched how the stress in his face and voice also showed up on the monitors. That development worried her more than her feelings. She took his hand in hers and pressed it to her lips and lied. "I'll be fine."

The Graykens arrived soon after. Again, she watched the expressions on their faces transform from stressed, to fearful, to forced calm, and on to disdain when their attention moved to Mikaela. She needed to at least attempt a repair, so she stood and moved toward them, but Catherine put her hand up and held her back. "I'm sorry, but I'm not ready to talk to you yet."

Matt strained to sit up, calling out, "Don't speak to Mikaela that way, Mother,"

Mikaela felt herself shrink inside, but rather than risk a further breach between Matt and his family, she returned to her spot by his side where she found his hand outstretched and waiting for her.

The silent standoff in the room continued so Mikaela turned the TV on. No one spoke, except for a few moments when a play in a football game warranted a cheer, or when a nurse entered. Relief finally came Sunday evening when the Graykens kissed their son goodbye and left for New York with a promise to return the following weekend. And so, she feared a pattern was being established, with Mikaela claiming the weekdays and nights by Matt's side, enjoying the respite of new voices and conversation on Thursday when the poker group arrived, and then relegating herself back into the shadows on the weekends.

She was fairly certain Matt had again texted Daniel, asking his raven-haired friend to run interference between Mikaela and his parents the next two Saturdays when Daniel swept Mikaela away to a movie or a walk or to a restaurant to eat. Mikaela kept herself occupied during the Graykens' Sunday visits by sleeping in and heading to her place of solace, the stone church, for its late-morning service. Matt was clearly the one paying the price for the tension in the room, but short of disappearing all weekend, she didn't know how else to manage things.

Mikaela had secured permission to use a family waiting room to serve a modest Thanksgiving dinner on Thursday. She hoped the offer of a family meal would ease the tension between the Graykens and her. Matt extended the invitation, but they declined, explaining that though they intended to travel to D.C. to see Matt early that day, they would be dining with friends in the evening.

Matt punched the end-call button and slammed the phone on his bed table. "I'm telling them not to come at all. I don't want to see them if they can't apologize to you."

Mikaela appreciated the gesture, but she knew Matt loved her. Causing his parents further hurt wouldn't solve anything, so she pasted on a reassuring smile.

"Don't do that. Let's just look at this as a romantic first Thanksgiving for two."

Thursday came, and while the Graykens spent the

morning with Matt, Mikaela roasted a small turkey and made the sides. By afternoon, she loaded a basket with sliced turkey, stuffing, and gravy, all in a microwaveable dish. Three small containers held relish, potatoes, and green beans almandine. Two slices of pie sat in a small plastic square. She hefted the basket to Matt's room and found three nurses surrounding his bed. She dropped the basket to the floor and rushed to his bedside.

"Matt? What's happening?"

A nurse pulled her away while the other two changed bags of IV fluid and checked Matt's vitals. "He spiked a fever about an hour ago. We think he picked up an infection."

Mikaela lurched forward. "What kind of infection?"

"The labs aren't back yet, but we're starting him on a broad-spectrum antibiotic to get ahead of this. He's already more lucid."

"Why didn't someone call me?" Mikaela heard the frustration in her voice, and she cringed when she saw the nurse stiffen.

"We were just about to. We've been busy trying to get on top of this."

"I'm sorry. I understand. I'm just . . . It's different when the patient is someone you love."

Mikaela sat by Matt's bedside all night, monitoring his vitals and checking his temperature until his numbers normalized. Sometime around midnight, she ate some cold turkey and a piece of pie.

Friday through Saturday was extremely uncomfortable.

Mikaela's attention remained riveted on Matt, who looked more pale than usual, ramping up his parents' worry. His fever returned late Friday night, accompanied by sweats. Quick response from the nursing staff brought it down once again, and this time, Matt seemed to be himself once more.

On Saturday, November twenty-fifth, an angel dressed in desert khakis appeared in the doorway. Mikaela felt her body go limp with relief. A moment later, a rush of joy swept through her, energizing her. She jumped from her chair and hurried to her brother George, sweeping him out into the hallway where she could greet him beyond the Graykens' scrutiny.

He held her close, and she squeezed him tight. "What are you doing here?"

"We had a transport headed for Andrews. I caught a lift."

"Oh, you don't know how much this means to me. I didn't realize how alone I felt until I saw you standing there."

"I should have followed my gut and come sooner. How's Matt doing? I guess I should meet the guy."

"He's . . . tired. He's . . ." She couldn't find the words, and George pulled her against him.

"I'm so sorry, Mickie. You chose a hard road, Princess."

She pushed back and smiled up at him, noting the wrinkles appearing at the corners of his eyes. "Just like my brothers." Since her father's illness and passing, George took on the role of family rock and Compton Clan leader, but today she realized he too was a man with many burdens. "How're Jeannette and the kids?"

"All good. Busy. They miss you."

"I'm trying to do better about calling."

"It's okay. We all know you've had a lot on you." He glanced at the doorway and Mikaela started to cry.

They walked down the hall and back until Mikaela's emotions were in check again. After a slow, deep breath, she led George into Matt's room and over to his bed to introduce him to her husband. She noticed that Matt had prepared for their return by raising his bed forward, and pushing the blankets away, making himself appear less like an invalid.

"Matt . . ." she turned to the Graykens, "Mr. and Mrs. Grayken, this is my oldest brother, U.S. Army Captain George Compton."

Matt extended his hand. All Mikaela saw was how small and frail his hand seemed in George's. George laid his other hand on Matt's shoulder and leaned in, but when he spoke, his voice was conspicuously loud enough for the Graykens to hear.

"My six brothers and I weren't too pleased about you sneaking Mikaela off to get married without asking us first. Lucky for you, she clearly loves you, and she says you make her happy, so that's good enough for us. But if that changes for any reason . . ."

Matt leaned his head back and smiled. "I know. Mikaela already explained the penalty. Something about becoming a martial-arts dummy."

"That's it. Glad we understand each other." He laughed and stood. "Just kidding. We're family now." He turned to face the Graykens. "Our parents are gone. Mikaela was the valiant one who stayed home and took care of them until they passed away. That's the kind of person your son married. And considering the hard things he's facing, I'd say he chose pretty darn well, wouldn't you?"

Their heads dipped slightly, but they didn't reply. Mikaela noticed that Matt's eyes were glassy when he said, "I'm very aware of how amazing she is."

"Glad to hear it." He turned back to the Graykens, completely unaffected by the silence of the two stoic seniors, and gave them a wink. "But I'll check in from time to time just to make sure."

George turned back to Matt. "Mikaela is strong because she knows she has seven linebacker-sized soldiers, seven equally loyal sisters-in-law, plus nineteen nieces and nephews behind her. Family is our treasure. It's your treasure too now, Matt."

Matt eked out a thank you.

"And now, if you don't mind, I'm going to steal my sister away for a few hours." He placed his arm behind her, to lead her out of the room, and made her feel that she was as strong as he'd said.

She drove him to their home and showed them their Christmas tree.

"That's beautiful, Mickie. Really beautiful, yet somehow it reminds me of the tree at home, when Mom hung all the crazy-looking macaroni and tissue-paper ornaments we made over the years. It was like a time capsule, reminding us of our childhoods. Only our family understood all the memories on that ugly tree."

She studied the tree before her, recognizing for the first time that their childhood tree, filled with ragged, priceless ornaments, had been the inspiration behind this project.

George fingered the red heart ornament. "Mom would be so pleased to see this tree."

"She is. She tells me all the time, in my heart."

"I'm glad you feel them close. I'm sorry about the Graykens. I know you loved them."

They headed out the door and into the neighborhood for a short stroll, but Mikaela couldn't shake her frustration over her in-laws' coldness toward her. "I understand that they can't be angry at Matt right now, but why do they need to shut me out?"

George ran a rough hand over his face. "I think it has more to do with the Graykens than with you. I've seen my share of loss and grief, Princess, and it changes you, carves you into someone new. Sometimes you're better, stronger for it. Sometimes it cuts too deep, and you break. It's not right or wrong, and it's not fair. We do our best, and the rest just is what it is."

Her emotions ran close to the surface again, and she steered the conversation on to topics beyond Matt and his parents. They passed Gino's flower shop, and the florist rolled out to greet Mikaela.

"Matt hasn't been here for Friday flowers in a few weeks. Is everything okay?"

Tears welled in her eyes and Gino raised a hand, letting her know she need not reply. He pulled a bouquet of roses from a bucket inside and handed them to her.

"Since Matt can't buy you flowers today, let me be his proxy."

She thanked him and carried the bouquet in her arms as they strolled to a café known for their Philly cheesesteaks. George finished swooning over his first bite but Mikaela had only torn away a piece of roll. "You told us about that Irish guy who knew someone who looked like Matt's double. Have you heard back from him?"

She placed her elbows on the table and leaned her chin into her hands. "I've called him three times, but he never calls me back."

"I ought to fly up there and bang on his door."

Mikaela laughed. "Oh, I'm sure the Army would love that."

"But seriously. Wasn't his son the one who manhandled you and embarrassed Matt at that party? He should be bending over backward out of fear that you'll sue his cocky little snot-of-a-son for sexual assault. I'd seriously like to fly over there and shake the address you need out of his father."

He had given Mikaela an idea.

They drove to D.C. and walked along the Tidal Basin for an hour, their arms linked.

"I think this is the first time I've felt like an adult with you. You've always treated me like a kid."

He pressed his hand over hers. "You'll always be my kid sister."

"But something's changed between us."

"You've taken on a lion-sized fight, Mickie, and you're handling it like a champ. I'm proud of you." He shook his head. "It's pretty humbling to see what you're up against, and yet you head back into that room, day after day. It would crush some people, but not you. That's courage. That's incredible love. Matt really is a lucky man, but he's also been good for you. No matter what happens, I'm glad you found each other."

Mikaela checked her watch and felt an urgency to return to Matt. They reached her car and drove back to the hospital's parking garage, where George's rental was parked. She found a slot a few cars away and pulled in.

She walked George to his car, and stepped into his arms. "Thanks so much for coming. You don't know how badly I needed you today."

"The brothers have all been talking. Most of us can take emergency leave. We're just a phone call away. Are you making plans for Christmas?"

"Matt will still be in treatment at least until December fifth."

"And then?"

She pressed her lips together, and she shrugged. "I guess we'll see."

"Apply for a passport quickly. Jeanette is holding two

places for you guys for Christmas dinner. Come if you can, okay?"

Mikaela let the image of her and Matt seated at a family table for Christmas settle over her. "I'll hold on to that."

George pressed a kiss to her forehead. "If you need me . . . for . . . you know . . ." He swallowed hard. "I'll be here for you. We all will be."

She tightened her arms around him and cried into his jacket before pulling away and wiping her eyes. "So where are you off to?"

"Meetings at Langley."

"On a Sunday?"

"We work 24/7. The world's a little crazy right now, in case you haven't heard."

"I'm proud of you. Thanks for saving the world."

"Just like you, Mickie. You're one of the brave now too."

With a final smile, George entered his car and drove off, and Mikaela headed for the hospital room, not feeling very brave at all, but with a plan to get Morris Kavanagh's attention.

The ease and pleasantness of George's company made the painful return to Matt's room almost stifling, but as soon as Mikaela's gaze fell on his love-filled eyes, she saw relief and gratitude, and she remembered that regardless of the

Graykens or machines or medical traffic in and out of the room, her home was wherever Matt was.

She carried the bouquet in and replaced the week-old withering blooms Matt had ordered for her last Friday from the hospital florist. She leaned over him and kissed him, lingering an inch above his face. "Love you. I missed you," she whispered.

"I was afraid George came to carry you away from this place and me."

The tension around his eyes told her there was truth to his fear. "Not a chance," she assured him, sealing her words with another kiss. She thought she saw a softening in Donovan Grayken's expression.

Scooting a chair close, she wrapped her arm around Matt's and took his hand. "George agrees that you're a keeper."

Matt's free hand pressed comically to his chest in exaggerated relief. "I like your brother, but . . . he's a little scary. I hope this means I'm off the hook as a practice dummy."

Matt laughed, and her own laughter followed freely. It sounded like music to Mikaela's ears. "I think so."

He tightened his hold on her hand. "I love you, Mrs. Grayken."

What Mikaela loved most was that he said it unabashedly, in full voice, loud enough for his parents to hear. She replied back with equal volume, "I love you too, Mr. Grayken."

His parents rose soon after the exchange. Catherine stood

first. "I'm tired, Donovan. Call for a taxi. I'm ready to return to our hotel."

Donovan stood and helped her with her coat. They both moved to Matt and said goodbye, but Donovan also looked up at Mikaela and offered her a little smile.

As she sat in her pew at the stone church the next day, she gave thanks that perhaps some of the Grayken chill was thawing.

24

The worrisome fever and sweats returned Tuesday along with bruises in various places on Matt's body. The doctor ordered more labs, and more meds to be administered over the next few days as the staff battled the symptoms. Mikaela knew what the doctors were looking for before they said anything, and she also knew the frightening complications that could develop if Matt's white blood cell count continued to rise unabated, and if the abnormally formed leukemia cells began to clump and occlude or clog the vessels. The mortality rates for patients with these complications was high, and things went south very fast.

On Thursday, she had the nurses bring her a basin and wash cloth, and she bathed the sweat from Matt's exhausted body. Each time she laid the cloth against his pale skin, she felt an overwhelming rush of love and protectiveness for this man. A battle was raging inside her. She hated seeing him languish this way, his body assaulted by chemicals and foreign materials jutting from his arms and chest. But she also couldn't bear the thought of losing him, of not exploring every single option that could, if only with the smallest chance, extend their life together. In that moment, she understood the Graykens' agony. She too was torn between her love for Matt, and loyalty to her promise to spare him from these very outcomes.

She paced the hall while the lab techs drew more blood from a man who already seemed as pale as parchment. Desperate, and feeling powerless, she remembered George's pep talk about her being brave, and she remembered the long-shot-card Morris Kavanagh held. She called his number again. When the voicemail picked up the call, she left a message that shocked even her.

"Mr. Kavanagh, since you have refused to show me the courtesy of a reply, I'm left with no choice except to resort to the bully tactics your family seems to understand. My next call will be to our company's attorney—"

She heard a muffled click and some background noise, followed by the clearing of a throat which she guessed was Morris Kavanagh's.

"Mrs. Grayken," he began in a sober tone. "Please forgive my delay in returning your call."

"*Calls*, Mr. Kavanagh. Six to be exact."

"My apologies. How can I help you?"

She had felt much braver when she was speaking to a voicemail recorder, but her courage returned with one look through the open doorway at Matt. "If you thought ignoring me would make me forget your son's behavior at the gala, you're sorely mistaken. One phone call to our attorneys and Colin's life could get quite litigious. You have information I need. I'd prefer to reach a solution that satisfies both of us."

"I hardly think a rousing dance and a stolen kiss will raise much attention in court."

Mikaela felt even more dismissed, and she wished she could reach through the phone and throttle the man. Instead, she upped the ante using chips she was pretending to own. "My husband is very sick, Mr. Kavanagh, and you have Hugh Fitzpatrick's contact information, the very information I need to possibly locate his next of kin. I know I'm going out on a limb with this, looking for a miracle, but if there's any chance he was a blood relative of my husband's, I want to meet his family, so listen closely. How would you like to lose all the Grayken family shipping business? Not only Grayken Industries out of New York, but also the family's whiskey exports? And if that's not enough, perhaps seeing the future head of your company's picture splashed across the media as a sexual predator will get your attention. I imagine that could be bad for business."

She heard a tired groan and the squeak of a chair. "For what it's worth, my wife and I have already insisted that Colin see someone professionally. You were the first woman to suffer because of one of his tantrums, and I'm dreadfully sorry, both for his actions and for ignoring your calls."

"I doubt I'm the first, Mr. Kavanagh, but I hope to be the

last. You told me you wished you'd given your son the same bottom-up start your father gave you. It's not too late. I'd prefer not to ruin his life, so I'm offering Colin a chance to redeem himself, but I'll need some proof that he has changed after this therapy. And I think some restitution is in order. Not for me, but for people in general. So arrange some community service. Something meaningful and a bit uncomfortable. I'll trust you with the details, but I'm not going to let this go until I'm satisfied that he understands he owes people, particularly women, some respect. In return for my offer, I want something in exchange—contact information for Hugh Fitzpatrick's next of kin."

"Mrs. Grayken—"

"Mr. Kavanagh, if there is the slightest chance of a familial connection, I want that chance. My husband's health has deteriorated during the weeks you've ignored me. I'm a desperate woman now, and I want the information on his next of kin soon, or my own patience will wear out, and I will contact our corporate lawyers."

"Very well. All I can do is try, Mrs. Grayken. I'll call the garage where he worked and make some excuse for contacting his family. I'll be in touch."

"Today, Mr. Kavanagh. Today."

Her hands were shaking when she hung up the call. If all went well, she'd soon have the means to test her theory about whether or not Matt had living relatives. A new worry struck her. What if the only information Morris Kavanagh was able to get was an address? Would she risk leaving Matt's side to fly to Ireland, even for a few days? And once she found them, what if they denied any knowledge of Matt or an adopted child? The thought was too bleak to consider, but the opposite was little better. Even if they were related, would they be interested in saving a long-lost brother or son? Would they agree to be tested, and be willing to endure the donor process? And even if all the stars aligned and there was a living relative who matched Matt's markers and was willing to fly across the Atlantic to save the day, could a transplant happen in time? The shaking in her hands swept to her torso.

She wrapped her arms around her middle and paced to an empty waiting area where she slumped into a chair. This theory had been her magic bullet, a Hail Mary pass, her desperation play. Its likelihood of success was statistically zero, but it was all she had left in her arsenal if Matt's leukemia was shifting into leukostasis, greatly increasing his risk of stroke or death.

Her love of medicine, and of the patients she worked with, had nudged her to read everything she could on all facets of leukemia and related disorders. Her broader knowledge had helped her explain complicated lab results to Matt. Now frightening symptoms, statistics, and grim prognoses haunted her. She expected the leukostasis diagnosis any time, and she knew she needed to make a plan before it came, when Matt's prognosis would be grim and she might falter in making the needed hard choice.

She leaned over her knees and prayed silently for a final confirmation of what she should do. Matt's original request had been for her to simply ease his passing and be by his side, but now she had a stake in this fight. She thought of all the prayers she'd offered and all the other loved ones already lost to her. She had her answer, and she prayed Matt would understand.

When she returned to Matt's room, she found his eyes pinched closed and his brows furrowed. She leaned over him and brushed damp hair away from his face. "What's wrong, Matt? Are you in pain?"

He winced and nodded. "My head is pounding. It hurts so bad I can hardly focus."

Headaches and blurred vision were symptoms of leukostasis. She swallowed her fear, leaned into her training, and pushed the call button to report the symptoms.

Matt's nurse arrived quickly with news of her own. "The labs are in. The doctor is coming up to discuss them with you. I'll make him aware of these new symptoms."

Mikaela pulled out her cell phone and checked for missed calls, though she knew there had been none. She called Daniel next. "Are you available? I need your help."

"Give me an hour. Should I call the others?"

"No. I'm also calling Matt's parents. I'll need you to pick them up later tonight."

"I'll tie up some loose ends and be in the car in ten minutes."

"Thank you, Daniel."

The next call would be the hardest, but she held off until the doctor's official confirmation. He entered, his eyes down and fixed on his tablet. He clicked a few links and pressed a crooked index finger to his lips as he thought. Mikaela held her breath, waiting for him to speak.

"I believe you're a nurse, am I right?"

"Yes."

"Then I know you'll understand the gravity of what I'm about to say."

"Is Matt in leukostasis?"

The doctor nodded slowly. "I'm afraid so. We'll begin leukapheresis right away. You should call his parents."

Her legs shook as she stepped back into the hall, and her hands would not obey her attempts to punch the correct buttons. After three attempts, she dialed Donovan Grayken's number. She could hear the wary tone in his voice as he said, "Yes, Mikaela?"

"Mr. Grayken, Matt's white blood cell count is further elevated. It's very high. He's in a condition called leukostasis."

"What does that mean?"

"His risk has greatly increased. The doctor is doing an intervention treatment, but I think you and Mrs. Grayken should come down."

"What are you saying? Are you telling me my son might die tonight?" She heard his voice break.

"No. No." But she knew she didn't sound convincing.

"We'll check the train schedule and call you back."

She stepped back into the room to Matt's bedside and laid her head on his shoulder. Her phone buzzed, and she jerked away from Matt to be sure to catch the call.

"Hello?" she frantically blurted into the phone.

"I have an address, Mrs. Grayken. I'm texting it to you now. I had to fabricate a tale just to get that. It's for Hugh's sister Kate. She's all the family he had. I hope it helps your husband. I truly do, but in either case, I'll set my Colin straight and assume we're square once I do?"

"Yes. Yes." She ended the call with little regard for Colin Kavanagh's future as she waited for the text to arrive. She heard the anticipated ding and saw the blessed information for Kate Fitzpatrick. She placed her cheek beside her husband's and called his name. "Matt, I need to talk to you. Please wake up."

His eyes fluttered and reclosed. "I can hear you. It's bad, isn't it?"

She kissed his temple and whispered, "It's more complicated. You know I love you. Please tell me you know that."

"I know." He raised a faltering hand, and she pressed it to her cheek.

"I can't sit here and watch you die, Matt. I told you I could, but I can't anymore. Not if there's even the smallest chance that you have a family member in Ireland. Someone who could possibly save you. I'll second-guess myself for the rest of my life if I don't try."

Worry lines stretched across his forehead. "Mikaela—"

"Please, Matt." She pressed her forehead to his and fought to stave the threatening tears. "You told me you wanted to do everything to give us all the time we could possibly have. That's what I want, too."

"Perhaps this is all we get."

"No. I don't believe that." She pulled back and framed his face in her hands. "You're fighting by submitting to all these procedures. Let me fight, too. I want to go to Ireland to see if you have family there. Tell me it's okay for me to go." When he didn't answer her, she again brought her brow to his. "Please tell me I have your support."

She heard the swish as the door opened wider. Daniel cleared his voice and halted in the doorway until Mikaela collected herself and motioned for him to meet her in the hall.

His dress shirt was unbuttoned at the collar, and panic fired in his eyes. "What's happening?" he asked. "Did the fever return?"

"He's so sick, Daniel. It's hard to explain, but it's like his blood is clotting in his veins. He's high risk right now."

Daniel rubbed his large hand over his face. "What can I do? How can I help?"

"I have reason to believe Matt might have family in Ireland. I have an address. I want to go there and see if they'll donate bone marrow to Matt."

"Mikaela, do you hear yourself? That's as wild a goose chase as there is."

"I know. I'm way out on a limb here, but it might be his only hope. Just tell me I'm not crazy for considering it."

"Does Matt know?"

"I was telling him when you came in."

"What if he . . . what if you're gone when . . ."

Tears welled in her eyes. "I know. That's my one argument for not going. I've called his parents. I'm waiting to hear from them."

Daniel became sheepish. "They're already here. They called me to pick them up. They're speaking to the doctor now."

Mikaela's face flushed with humiliation. "They don't think enough of me to tell me they've arrived. What will they think when they hear I'm leaving for Ireland?"

Daniel's gaze dropped to the floor, avoiding any reply to the question. "Did you buy a ticket?"

"Not yet. I'll do that next."

He laid a hand on her shoulder. "Let me book it for you." He shut down her argument as soon as she began. "Mikaela, no offense, but Matt is family to me too. I was tested during the last relapse, and I failed as a donor. Since I can't give him my marrow, let me at least buy you a ticket to find someone who can."

She relented when she saw the Graykens' haggard forms heading her way. She breathed to calm her racing heart and walked to meet them saying, "I'm so glad you're here."

Fire flew from Catherine's Irish eyes as she laid into Mikaela. "I hold you responsible for this. I told you Matt would neglect his healthcare. I trusted you. I asked you to be our eyes and make sure he got the care he needed, but instead of persuading him to seek proper attention, you encouraged his reckless choices for weeks. You delayed getting him here, to a proper hospital. And you call yourself a nurse. I hold you responsible if he dies."

Donovan took her by the arm and muttered sternly, "That'll be enough, Catherine."

But Mikaela sucked in a pained gasp at the accusations Catherine Grayken hurled at her. Her only defense was offered softly. "I love Matt."

Her confession of love had no apparent impact on the woman, who thrust a shoulder back and said, "What good has come from your love?" With that final barb, Catherine turned away, leaving Mikaela feeling hollow and condemned.

Donovan Grayken stood in the doorway, watching her wither, but she was powerless to propel herself away from his view. She saw him approach her, and steeled herself for what she assumed was his own barrage, but instead she felt his arm slide across her shoulder and his other hand take hers as he led her down the hall.

"I know it sounds like Catherine is blaming you, but the truth is, she's angry at herself."

Mikaela's head spun around to face him.

"It started after the first bout of leukemia. Once we got Matt well, we hovered and smothered him, treated him like a piece of china, as if he were sick even when he was well, and he rebelled. He's been rebelling ever since. He tried to make the same choices during the second round of cancer that he made this time. We forced our will upon him, and once he was well, he took off for about a year. We feared we'd never see him again. When he did return, Catherine tried to subdue him with guilt over her stroke. And it worked for a time, but we always knew if the leukemia returned again, he'd run and hide it from us."

The news stunned her. "He always speaks very highly of you both."

"He's a good son. Better and kinder to us than we deserve, but it hurts to know how much we missed with him."

"I'm sorry."

Donovan shrugged. "All love is not the same. We sensed something odd about your relationship, a tension and unease between you. Now we understand that you were his nurse and friend first, but we hoped . . . well . . . Catherine placed all her bets on you to save our boy."

Mikaela stopped walking and faced Donovan. "I understand what you're going through. I promised to see his wishes through, but I can't now. I do love your son, Mr. Grayken. I love him too much to just let him die without trying everything I can." She drew a deep breath. "I'm going to Ireland. I may have found a blood relative of Matt's there. I want to verify their relationship and try to get them to donate marrow to Matt."

Donovan's face contorted, and he shook his head in dismissal. "That's a fool's errand, child. Don't you think we tried that? I spent thousands of dollars and sent my attorney to scour the nation of Ireland, and he could find no such relation, and yet you think you have?"

She had no will to argue on. "I have to at least try."

She turned for Matt's room and found Catherine seated

in Mikaela's spot, holding his hand. It was clear Mikaela could do nothing more for Matt here without engaging his parents in a fight she knew Matt didn't want. Her decision was made. She moved to the other side of Matt's bed, bent low over him, and whispered. "Matt, I'm going to Ireland. I'll be back within three days. Do you hear me?"

He forced one eye open and touched her cheek. With a smile, he said, "Remember the Amish inn? What I told you?"

She reran her memory back to that trip and Matt's conversation about how the faith of the Amish made heaven seem so close and sweet that it removed the fear of death for him. Recounting that, and seeing how frail Matt was, filled her with foreboding, She pressed her cheek to his, placing her lips by his ear. "No, Matt. Don't say it."

"But it's true. I'm not afraid of death, Mikaela."

"It's not time yet." She nuzzled his cheek and found his lips, placing a trembling kiss there, filled with every hope and promise left tucked in her heart. Her hands framed his jaw as she said her final goodbye. "Three days, Matt. You be here when I get back. Promise me."

The right side of his mouth lifted into a half-smile. "Then bring us back a shamrock for our tree."

"I will. I promise."

She looked at Daniel who was already on his feet, with keys in his hand. Catherine's eyes bored holes into him, and Mikaela watched him head for Donovan instead. "I'll be back by eight to take you to your hotel."

"Where are you taking Mikaela?" Catherine called out.

But Daniel didn't answer, and Mikaela kept equally silent as they headed for the door.

"There's no need for you to return for us, Daniel. It's clear where your loyalties lie. We'll call for a car on our own."

Daniel touched his head and gave her a salute of sorts and left the room.

She heard Catherine say, "She's leaving, Donovan. She's leaving our son."

Mikaela braced for such a response, but she didn't try to defend her decision. Kate would be her vindication if she found her and convinced her to return. And if she failed . . . well . . . She refused to consider that option.

25

During the entire ride to the airport, Mikaela second-guessed her decision to leave Matt. Once she passed through security, she saw a kiosk bedecked in full Christmas regalia, and there in the front was a tree laden with hand-made, clay Christmas ornaments. The owner was busy adding calligraphy to customize pieces for other customers while they waited. Mikaela's eyes fixed on one ornament as a wave of melancholy washed over her. It was a fireplace with a Christmas list trimmed in tiny hearts, pinned to the mantel. The list had only one request, and it read, "All I want for Christmas is you." All she could think of was Matt.

"I see that one of my pieces is bringing something or someone to your mind."

Mikaela's throat was thick, and so she simply nodded.

He came to stand beside her, and following her gaze, he pointed to the scroll. "You're missing someone."

She nodded again.

"What's their name?"

She swallowed past the lump in her throat. "Matt. Matt Grayken."

"A good Irish lad."

She smiled and nodded again. "Yes."

"And your name?"

"Mikaela." She held out her hand. "Nice to meet you."

"And you too," he said as he took her hand for a brief shake. "How do you spell Mikaela? I hear all sorts of names each year, but that is a rare one for me."

Mikaela spelled it out for him, and as she did so the artist lifted the ornament from the tree and carried it to his station. A few seconds later he held it up for her to see. Matt's name was written at the top, and Mikaela's was written at the bottom. "My creations rarely leave people speechless as this one made you today. It's yours as my gift."

Mikaela protested, but he carried on, wrapping it in tissue paper.

"I want to pay you. I insist."

He dug around in a box under his table and pulled something out. When he held it up, Mikaela nearly gasped. Dangling from his fingers on a red velvet cord was a lovely little green shamrock with a red velvet bow tied to its stem.

Her mouth hung open and her eyes burned as she stared at it. "How did you . . . how could you . . . ?"

"An Irish Shamrock for an Irish lad who's clearly loved. I'll let you buy this one. Deal?"

A new wave of confidence warmed her heart. "Deal."

The wonder of the coincidence, that he should offer her the very thing Matt requested she bring home, made her think of miracles and Christmas magic. She paid for the shamrock and hurried for her gate with the good luck totems tucked into her purse.

Daniel had her booked on the next direct flight to Ireland's Dublin airport. He also arranged a hotel room for the night and a bus ticket to carry her on to Galway the next day. It was eight p.m. when the plane pulled from the gate. Mikaela slept during most of the seven-hour flight, and checked her phone when she landed. It was three a.m. back in D.C. so she dared not call Matt, but she found a text message from Daniel.

I returned to the hospital to offer Matt's parents a ride. They were gone, but Matt told me they're moving him to New York. He doesn't want to worry you, but he also doesn't have the will to fight them. Maybe you should come home.

. . . he doesn't have the will to fight them . . .

. . . he doesn't have the will . . .

. . . will you marry me and be my legal voice when I can't speak for myself?

Her body felt as if it were liquefying, as if her chin, shoulders, arms, and even her torso, were sliding, dripping toward the floor. She had failed in her primary purpose. To be Matt's voice. To prevent exactly what was happening right now, with Matt lying in pain, in a sterile place, while his parents overruled his wishes. He hadn't filled out a living will because Mikaela was going to be there to speak for him. The promise, made when they were only patient and nurse and that should have been strengthened by the blossoming of love, was now as useless as if it had been written on water.

She tried arguing that she was attempting to save his life. But taking extraordinary measures had not been part of their agreement. Then again, neither had love been. But love had changed everything, including the contract. *She* wanted more time with him. It was what she hoped for and prayed for, but it was also what Matt wanted too . . . wasn't it? But at any cost? At *this* cost?

Will you be my legal voice when I can't speak for myself?

Matt was in this position only because of his love for her.

She dropped heavily onto a bench, feeling guilty for not wanting him to die. The absurdity of the argument left her doubting everything she had done and been to Matt. And then George's voice came to her.

> *. . . loss and grief changes you, carves you into someone new. Sometimes you're better, stronger for it. Sometimes it cuts too deep and you break. It's not right or wrong, and it's not fair. We do our best, and the rest just is what it is."*

She wiped her nose and gathered her things. She was doing her best. Now everything depended on finding Kate Fitzpatrick.

It was eight a.m. in Ireland, and she gave thanks for the sleep she got on the plane. She grabbed a quick breakfast at an airport café, longing to call Matt, but she did the math and realized it was three a.m. in D.C. She sent a text instead and quickly received a reply. Emboldened, she called, and a weak voice answered, "Good morning, Mrs. Grayken."

Tears sprang to her eyes at the ragged sound of his speech. "I love you."

"I want to assure you that I know that. I love you too, Mikaela."

The frailty of his voice frightened her. "I'll be home soon."

"Call before you book your return. Okay?"

"Is it true your parents are moving you to New York?"

She heard his long, deliberate sigh. "Daniel must have told you. Yes. I've been loopy." His slurred speech proved that point. "They're pushing hard."

"Oh, Matt, I'm so sorry. I've failed you. I could—"

"No. I trust your instincts. I'm throwing Han Solo in . . ."

She could barely decipher his words. "What? Hans Solo? I don't understand."

"Remember poker? When I beat Daniel? I still have one hand to play. Trust me."

———

Matt kept his eyes closed as his mother pulled the blanket up around his chin.

"We've made the arrangements. You'll be moved by special medical flight tomorrow morning." She tucked the blanket in around his shoulders.

"That's not what I want."

She leaned over him and placed her cheek against his. "You're saying that because you think there's no hope, but we're taking you to the doctors who helped you before. Please trust us."

He heard a rustle from the direction of the chair. "Da," he called out, hoping to find an ally in his father.

"I agree with your mother. I think this is best. We love you, Matthew."

He knew they loved him. Their pain was evident, and though he didn't cause their pain, he exacerbated it through his deception, and he wouldn't add further to their agony by fighting them now. He pushed through the pounding in his head and tried another tactic.

"I want my wedding photo. I'm not going without it."

"Wedding photo? That business contract is over. You need to let go of—"

"Don't." The pain added a finality to his voice. "I love my wife."

Through lids barely opened a micron, he observed the shock and dismay on his mother's face. "Very well," she said through her iron-set mouth. "Where is this photo?"

"On the TV stand. The house keys are in my bedside table's drawer. Da, I think you should go with her."

They both began putting on their coats. All he could do now was wait.

———————

Catherine knew the silence in the car was sure proof that Donovan was angry with her. He hadn't helped her with her coat or taken her arm as they walked to the car or asked her if she was warm enough when he adjusted the temperature in the frigid vehicle—the first time in nearly fifty years of marriage.

She held her purse against her chest like a shield, defending her position for when the dreaded confrontation began. Donovan's eyes remained straight ahead, focused on the road, but she knew his mind was back in Matt's room, replaying her last words with their son. As they turned onto Matthew's street, he began.

"Why did you have to push so hard?"

She bit her knuckle and stared out the window, hoping she could wait out his anger.

"Even if, by some miracle, we're able to save Matt, we'll likely lose him again anyway. He's going to push us away, like the last time."

More angry silence passed between them as they sped past storefronts. Catherine pressed her knuckle harder against her lips. She had a few bones to pick with Donovan too.

"Woman, I wish you were as skilled at holding your tongue back there as you are now."

She spun on him. "I could say the same, Donovan. You humiliated me this afternoon, scolding me in front of Mikaela. Taking her side over mine."

"Whatever those two began as—a business contract or a friendship—he clearly loves her now."

"And she left!"

"To try and save him. As foolish as it sounds, did we not try to do the same?"

She heard the thickness of his brogue and the Irish cadence to his words, and knew his emotions were being drawn from a deep, primitive love to save his family. She harrumphed but could mount no defense, but Donovan continued to double down.

"And you've arranged to separate them by flying him to New York without consulting her or even telling her where he'll be. He might not see her again. How cruel is that? Do you think he'll forgive you for that?"

"She caused this! Instead of being a proper advocate for sound medical care, she encouraged his foolhardy decisions."

"Our son is not a sheep, Catherine. He's a headstrong man who knows his own mind. And perhaps you forget what happened eleven years ago. We haven't had much contact with Matthew in the past few years. I believe it was Mikaela who brought him back to us."

Catherine turned back to her window and hugged her door as Matt's house came into view. Donovan exited the car without opening her door, though she didn't expect his characteristic manners to benefit her at this moment. Instead, he headed straight for the back door of the house and entered.

She was torn between going in to find evidence of their sham marriage, and risking the pain of finding evidence of a happy life her son lived apart from them. She remained in the car with her hand on the door handle, until Donovan came back to the door, his face drawn, his eyes pained, calling for her.

She stayed in her place for several seconds, fearing to see what had upset Donovan, until curiosity overtook her. With slow, deliberate steps, she climbed the five stairs and entered Matt's kitchen.

A flood of warmth hit her like tear gas, bringing her emotions forward. Multicolored love notes from Mr. Grayken to Mrs. Grayken were stuck to the fridge alongside photos of the two, showing happy faces doing simple things—planting flowers, cooking dinner, and lounging at home.

Dried rose petals sat in a dish on the counter, and Matt's tie lay strewn along the floor. Mikaela had been home some during the four weeks of chemo and had likely tidied up around the house, but Catherine knew she was seeing images from their last day at home together, before heading to the hospital.

She found Donovan standing in the great room, staring at the far wall. When she turned the corner, heat from shame and guilt burned through her as she gazed upon a fully decorated and lit Christmas tree.

Donovan extended his hand to her. "Come. See."

His voice was soft and emotion-filled. His eyes glistened with a mixture of joy and sorrow as he took her hand and led her to the tree.

"Look at the ornaments." He picked a star from the tree and turned it over. "See? Each one has a little sticker with a date and note. *September 11, High Rock.* Look here. . . a bride and groom from their wedding, an airplane from their flight to New York the first time they visited us. It's all here. We're here too." His voice was filled with wonder. "It's the story of their life together. There's love on every limb."

"This is why he sent us here. He wanted me to see this." Catherine stood ramrod straight, as she compared her show of love, dragging Matt away from his home and wife, to this. "Oh, Donovan. I wouldn't listen. What have I done? What have I done?"

26

A local woman riding in the bus seat beside Mikaela attempted to start a conversation with the American tourist. Mikaela answered her questions in short phrases to quickly return to her thoughts, but from time to time, her companion would point out sites and castles in the distance. Mikaela came to appreciate the impromptu tour, recognizing the diverse landscape, with modern cities and ancient ruins, as Matt's native land. She imagined him as a child, living here for a time, and wondered if Ireland was on the list of places he wanted to take her. She also wondered if he'd live long enough to ever return again.

The bus lumbered over country bridges that covered endless streams running through pristine pastureland and past quaint villages. Within miles, a new town or city emerged until the vehicle pulled in Galway's Bus Eireann Bus Station.

An attendant assured her that her destination on St. Dominick's Road in Claddagh was within a good walk. Mikaela opted for a taxi, which drove her along the rocky edge of a waterway that spread to an endless sea. For a moment, the beauty of the place calmed her roaring nerves.

The taxi stopped before a white stucco house trimmed in wood painted a pretty maple color. It was attached to a similar house that sat to the left and painted a light coral. She checked the address, paid the driver, and gathered her things, standing on legs that barely supported her small frame.

She walked to the door, rehearsing her opening line again, as she had a hundred times before. Resolved, she rapped soundly on the door, behind which every hope lay, and said a little prayer. When no one answered, she knocked again with the same result. It was nearly lunchtime, she figured, and likely the worst time to try to reach someone who might be working. Disappointed but undeterred, she knocked on the door of the coral house.

A round, elderly woman answered in a wary brogue. "I saw you pull up and figured you'd be coming my way when I saw your taxi drive off."

"I'm looking for Kate Fitzpatrick. I was told she lives next door."

"You're American. How do you know Kate?"

Mikaela didn't want to admit she was a stranger. "I think she's related to my husband. I wanted to meet her while I was here in Ireland."

"I'm afraid she's gone."

Mikaela felt her heart slam to the floor. "Gone? To work? For the day?"

The woman began to close her door. "I don't know when she's due back. She paid me next month's rent, asked me to collect her mail, and left last evening, lickety-split."

A cold chill of defeat flooded through Mikaela. Desperate, she placed her foot in the doorway and threw more questions at the woman. "Do you know where she went? Does she have family in the area?"

The woman backed up and closed the door against Mikaela's foot, but Mikaela didn't withdraw it. "I'm sorry," she pled. "It's just . . . it's critical that I reach her. It literally is a matter of life and death."

The woman seemed unfazed, and if any emotion registered at all, it was annoyance. "Yeah, the people at Hugh's work gave her a warning that a crazy American woman might show up, asking around about Hugh, God rest his soul. Kate's been through enough. She don't need people dredging up her pain. Now get on with you."

Tears filled Mikaela's eyes. "Please. I'm not crazy. I'm desperate to save my husband. I've come all this way. Give me something. Please. A phone number. The place where she works. Anything."

The woman's expression softened. "Your husband's sick too, is he?"

"Yes," Mikaela answered as chills coursed up her arms. "Was Hugh sick when he died?"

The woman pressed her lips into a tight line and nodded.

"He and Kate were private folks. Just moved here a few months before Hugh died, to save money. It was clear he was ailing. I didn't ask Kate about the details, but I read in the paper that he was riding his motorcycle when he slipped on the gravel and into the path of an oncoming car. Died instantly. Kate hasn't been the same since losing him. He was all the family she had, far as I know."

"I think my husband may be another brother. Do you have a number for her?"

"Just the house phone, which won't do you any good."

Mikaela was running out of options. No family. No phone. "How about work?"

"She's a house painter. Works for herself."

Mikaela's lips trembled, and her voice broke, making speech difficult. "A priest? A friend?"

The woman reached a hand to Mikaela's shoulder. "I'm sorry I'm no help. Maybe try Father Murphy at the parish down the street. He conducted Hugh's funeral."

Mikaela thanked the woman and raced to the weathered stone church. Inside she found a priest talking to a man. She waited until the two concluded their conversation, and the priest made his way to Mikaela.

"May I help you?"

"Are you Father Murphy?"

"I am."

"Father, I'm Mikaela Grayken. I arrived here this morning, hoping to find Kate Fitzpatrick, but her landlady says she's left for at least a month. It's urgent that I find her. Do you know where she's gone or how I can reach her? Please, Father. I need a miracle."

He pointed to a pew, and the two sat.

"I wish I had the answers you're seeking, Mrs. Grayken. Neither Hugh nor Kate were actively part of our congregation. The first time I met them was when I was making visits to the University Hospital. One of my parishioners was being treated in the oncology center there."

"Are you saying Hugh had cancer?"

"Yes. Leukemia, I believe. Hugh was quite sick, and Kate was his devoted caregiver."

The news both bolstered and destroyed Mikaela. She had been right. There was hope for Matt, if only she could find Kate. "I need to find her, Father."

"I'm afraid I don't have any answers for you, Mrs. Grayken. Kate was devastated by Hugh's untimely death. I don't know where she might have gone. I believe they were all the family either of them had."

Mikaela knew that wasn't true, but being right meant nothing if she couldn't find Kate, and soon. The futility of her quest burned in her. Failure made her painfully aware that she'd sacrificed precious time with Matt for nothing. All that mattered now was getting home to him. The only hope remaining literally would require a miracle.

Her distress must have shown on her face. The priest cupped his hands over hers. "Your burden is heavy, child. I can't give you what you seek, but I offer you what I have. I'll add my faith to yours in prayer."

Without the will to stand or speak, Mikaela nodded, and the priest prayed aloud. Her mind raced ahead to the obstacles that still lay ahead of her—to finding where the Graykens had taken Matt and facing their judgment as she fought for time with him. She did hear the kind priest's petition for peace, and for God's mercy, two things she ached for, and when the amen was said, her face was wet with tears.

"Where will you go?"

She pulled a tissue from her pocket and wiped her eyes. "Home. I'll head home as soon as I can get a flight."

"Sit here as long as you need. I'll call a taxi for you."

"Thank you. Ask them to come now. There's nothing left for me here."

She wondered how she would find Matt and, worse, how she would face him and admit that she'd failed. The news was too devastating to share over the phone, but she needed to connect with him, and tell him she was coming home.

She pulled out her phone and found a text waiting for her there. It was from Matt's number and it read, *I'm in DC. Is deas liom bualadh leat. Hurry home, Mikaela.*

It didn't sound like Matt or feel like a message from him. *Is deas liom bualadh leat?* She wondered what message had been altered by her phone's auto correct feature. Panic seized her at the thought that someone else contacted her for him. Was he not able to do it himself? She called the number but there was no answer. Next she called Daniel, who also knew nothing, but he booked her flight once again, and promised to pick her up when she landed at five a.m.

She cancelled her hotel reservations in Dublin and bought a bus ticket there instead. A taxi took her straight to the airport. She bought a quick bite before boarding. She was grateful Daniel bought her a window seat. She curled into a ball against the side of the plane, wanting to be invisible on the flight home, as her thoughts raced on to dark possibilities. At some point, drained and wrung out, she thought of the priest's prayer, adding her own prayer to the faithful father's petition. Having exhausted every effort available to her, she did feel some peace, or perhaps it was merely complete fatigue from having her failed quest end so quickly. She had crossed the Atlantic twice in thirty-six hours with no time to check into a hotel, catching her only sleep midair. The next thing she remembered was being awakened when the flight attendant gave her shoulder a gentle shake to remind her to position her seat for landing.

True to his word, Daniel was waiting for her at the closest available spot. She clung to him, and he to her, as she asked, "Have you heard anything?"

"No. But I haven't tried calling them. I figured they're asleep. We'll head straight to the hospital."

As she and Daniel approached the hospital's front desk and signed in, Mikaela's thoughts were stuck on the anonymous text sent from Matt's phone.

"Patient's name?"

"Matthew Grayken." She waited for their visitors' passes to be completed with Matthew's room number—202 in the Bartholomew Cancer Center—but the woman did a double take at her screen and held up a finger, indicating for Mikaela to wait.

"Are you Mrs. Grayken?"

"Yes."

"There's a note here." She scribbled something on a scrap of paper and handed the message to the volunteer at her left. "Melissa, will you escort Mrs. Grayken and her guest to the visitors' lounge on three?"

Mikaela looked at Daniel, whose face showed the same concern she was feeling. "Why are we being directed there? Matt's room is on two. What does the note say?"

The woman looked at her screen again. "Just that we're to direct Mrs. Mikaela Grayken to the visitors' lounge on three when she arrives. I'll alert Dr. Marcosky that you're here."

Mikaela leaned over the counter and grilled the volunteer. "Is my husband all right?"

"I'm sorry. I don't have that information, Mrs. Grayken. Dr. Marcosky will answer all your questions."

Mikaela grabbed the front of her blouse and took two deep breaths, as if holding the fabric would steady her racing heart.

Daniel reached for her other hand. "Don't panic. There could be any number of reasons why the doctor wants to see you."

"Name one that isn't bad."

Instead, he pointed to the volunteer leading the way to the appointed room. They exited onto the third floor, which appeared to be office and clinical space rather than cart and computer-lined hallways bustling with nurses and IV-pole-bound patients. The volunteer opened a door marked visitors' lounge and motioned for them to enter. Mikaela's first sight of anyone familiar was of the Graykens who were leaning upon one another, asleep.

She leaned against Daniel, confused and frightened as she wondered what scenario would cause them to be here and not in Matt's room. Catherine awoke and nudged Donovan. Mikaela braced for the dreaded news and the indictment naming her as the cause of Matt's decline or passing. "Where's Matt?" she asked, her voice faltering, her eyes on fire with welling tears.

The pair hurried to their feet and rushed to her. She stepped back defensively, but Catherine scooped Mikaela against her and held her tight. "Oh, Mikaela. Can you forgive me? I've been so awful to you." She opened her arms and wiped at her tears, making room for Donovan, who also waited to embrace Mikaela.

"Forgive us both, Mikaela. We've been selfish, frightened old fools. We are so grateful for you. For all you've done. It truly is a miracle."

Mikaela was reeling. She still had no information about Matt, and she was so exhausted that none of this was making any sense to her.

Utter penitence transformed Catherine's once angry face.

"Matt sent us to your home. There's such a spirit of love there. And we saw the tree. I realized how good you've been for Matt, and how wrong I've been for blaming you for things that were our doing and Matt's."

Mikaela was exhausted and confused, unable process what was being said. All she wanted was to see Matt. "Where is he?" she asked Donovan. "Why isn't he in his regular room? I thought . . . I thought . . ." She drew a shuddering breath.

Catherine took her by the shoulders and looked to Donovan, who answered. "This is the transplant floor. They're getting his room ready while he's in radiation, but he'll be out soon."

"The transplant floor? No. I need to talk to Matt." She shook her head as she tried to make them understand that she'd failed to find Matt's sister.

"Our current worry is Matt. They don't know if he's strong enough to handle the preparation his body needs before the transplant can occur." Donovan swallowed and continued on with an artificially positive tone. "But if you could just see the change in his attitude since Kate arrived."

"Wait. What?" said Mikaela. "Kate? Kate Fitzpatrick is here?"

Puzzled looks appeared on both of the Donovan's faces. "Yes. That's what we've been saying. You did it, Mikaela. You gave Matt a fighting chance. Kate arrived late last night. Didn't you receive her text?"

She felt as if she were lost in a fog.

"Now that I think about it, her battery was dead after her

long flight," said Catherine. "She used Matt's phone to text you."

"Kate is here," she repeated numbly. Mikaela's voice broke as the magnitude of that truth hit her. "I thought I failed. I went to her house, but she'd left town, and no one knew where she'd gone." Her hand covered her trembling mouth. In a broken cadence, she said, "I thought I'd left Matt's side for nothing."

Donovan took her into his arms again. "We're so grateful you followed your instincts instead of allowing us to dissuade you."

Whatever hurt or anger she had felt toward the Graykens slipped away. She hugged Donovan back, relishing the feel of strong arms around her.

He released her and smiled. "I believe we had a bit of divine intervention as well. Kate saw that YouTube video of Matt saving that little girl at the airport. She caught the resemblance to Hugh immediately and remembered Matt's name. Then Morris Kavanagh called Hugh's former employer to get the contact information for Hugh's next of kin. The owner walked in on the conversation, and was none too happy that Kate's private information had been shared. Kavanagh explained why it was needed, but the owner was so worried for Kate that he called her to apologize for the breach of trust, and told her the whole story, to warn her to be prepared if a crazy woman named Grayken came with a story about her dying husband being a relative. Well, Kate put two and two together and contacted

Kavanagh to get Matt's number. They had a first reunion over the phone."

Fatigue and relief suddenly flooded over Mikaela like a tsunami. Matt and Kate had found each other, and now Matt had a chance. Mikaela dropped into a chair as she remembered the strange text from the previous night and her cold reception by Kate's landlady.

"And guess what, Mikaela," added Catherine. "There's more good news. Kate had been approved to be a donor for her brother, Hugh, before he died, and the doctors in Galway are sending all her files here to expedite clearing her as Matt's donor."

She needed to see her husband. "How is he? He sounded so weak on the phone."

Donovan slid his arm across her shoulder and pulled her close. "I think you're the medicine he needs most right now."

Dr. Marcosky arrived to bring everyone up to date on the progress being made. Matt's new room was finally ready, and the family piled in to await his arrival. Faithful Daniel said goodbye and left the family to reconnect. A dark-haired woman appeared in the doorway. Mikaela recognized her resemblance to Matt immediately. She rose from her chair and met Kate's outstretched arms midway across the room. The two women hugged and thanked one another as they cried together and laughed.

"Matt and I are getting along well. And I'm so sorry for that text mix-up. I was tired, and I forgot that Matt's phone wouldn't identify me."

"What does *Is deas liom bualadh leat* mean?" She butchered the sentence, and both women laughed.

It sounded like music when Kate repeated it. "It's Irish for 'nice to meet you.'"

Mikaela sat on Matt's bed and patted it, inviting Kate to join her. "Does Matt look exactly like Hugh?"

"It's uncanny. I've had a longing to find my other baby brother since my mother told me about him. More so since Hugh took sick. We didn't have anyone else. My mother's fancy family kicked her out when she came home pregnant her first semester of college. She didn't love my father, but she was desperate, and he was all too willing to have a wife who could work while he played and drank. I was five when she delivered Hugh. It was years later, and over her third pint of stout, when she confessed that Hugh was a twin."

She looked at Donovan Grayken. "I hope you won't mind if I tell the story as I know it."

Donovan pressed his lips tightly and nodded for her to continue.

"Mom cried to the midwife handling her pregnancy that she could barely keep her daughter fed and that she mourned the poverty awaiting these new babes. It was then that the midwife told her about a lawyer with wealthy clients who wanted to adopt a child privately. She said his offer included paying all the mother's medical expenses and a stipend for her sacrifice and recovery."

Donovan shook his head in shame. "I did send him to make inquiries about available children, but I never authorized such an arrangement, Kate. It's illegal and immoral."

"They knew that, but things were bad at home, and Mom started considering the option of offering up one of the babes in order to give them each a fair start at life. Her mistake was in telling our father. He met with the attorney and Father upped the ante, and, to their surprise, the attorney agreed to his terms. Arrangements were made for Mom to deliver in Cork under an assumed name, with the midwife attending. When the babies were born, the midwife handed one off to a private nurse who carried him out of our lives."

"How long have you known?" asked Mikaela.

"Twelve or thirteen years now. Soon after our father died. That's when I finally understood why Mom was such a miserable, tortured soul. Her guilt tore at her for selling her baby. She passed away a year later, when Hugh was seventeen. I became mother and sister to him."

"I'm so sorry for all you've lost, Kate."

She shrugged and smiled. "Matt tells me you know a thing or two about loss as well."

"I think we're both due for a sister."

Kate extended her hand. "You took the words right from my mouth."

Matt's gurney arrived. Mikaela jumped from the bed and to his side. "Hello, Mr. Grayken."

Joy, like that known on Christmas morning, showed on Matt's face upon seeing her. "Ah, Mrs. Grayken. You're the best thing I've seen all day." As she kissed him, his IV-tubed arms wrapped over her in a hug.

"You have a sister."

"Because of you." He closed his eyes and smiled. "Kate's great. Thank you for being stubborn and for never giving up."

She took his hand in hers. "We still have a long road to claim that miracle."

"You are my miracle."

"I'm also obedient." She reached into her purse and pulled out the ornaments from the airport. "You asked for a shamrock for our tree? Well, here you go." She also handed him the second one.

Matt squinted but couldn't read the tiny print, so Mikaela read it for him. "It says, 'All I want for Christmas is you.'"

"Me too, but you." He kissed her hand. "We're not quite out of the woods yet."

"My money is always on you, Mr. Grayken."

"I'm going to give it my best, Mrs. Grayken."

The skies were gray, a perfect canvas for the expected snow. The doorbell rang, and Mikaela called out, "Come in, Kate," welcoming her sister-in-law's expected arrival. Kate struggled under the burden of a large shopping bag. "This is my first family Christmas in a long time. I may have overdone it."

"Impossible," said Mikaela. "It's Christmas!"

She picked up a red box trimmed with a green bow and handed it to Kate. "First family Christmas? First tradition."

Kate pulled the ribbon and dug through the tissue paper, pulling out a three-inch pig-tailed imp dressed in a sweater set and skates. Across the sweater was the word, "Big Sister."

"Merry Christmas, Kate," said Mikaela, handing her an ornament hanger. "Choose a place of honor on the tree."

Kate made her way past boxes and bags and over to the tree, admiring the carefully chosen decorations while Mikaela looked on. She found a spot and hung her ornament near the little red train.

"Now you're an officially adopted Grayken," said Mikaela through moist eyes.

"Just like you."

Donovan and Catherine had become such regulars that they arrived, dressed in their Christmas finest, through the kitchen door without ringing the bell, as per Mikaela's invitation. "How are our two best girls?" called Donovan as he set down his own bag of gifts to sweep them each up in a hug.

Catherine set a loaded pie keeper on the counter and joined in the love fest. "The turkey smells divine, but you're not ready."

"It'll only take me a minute." She handed each of the Graykens a small box tied with a bow. "It's our first Christmas together. I have personalized ornaments for each person to commemorate the occasion. Here's what I chose for you two."

Donovan pulled out a chubby Santa, and Catherine found a Mrs. Claus in her box. Each ornament had the recipients' names, and the year, painted along the backs.

"Now every year, when I pull these ornaments out of the box, I'll remember my first Christmas as a Grayken." She handed them hangers, and they too added theirs to the tree.

The doorbell rang once again, and Daniel entered before Mikaela could reach the door. "Mind if I let myself in? It's cold out there."

Catherine pointed at Daniel and said, "There's snow on your hat!"

"It just started," said Daniel as he hugged Mikaela and placed a kiss on her cheek. "Merry Christmas, Mrs. Grayken."

"Merry Christmas, Daniel. You look very handsome. Thank you for coming today. You were there when it all began. By the way, I believe you remenber Matt's sister, Kate Fitzpatrick?"

He stared across the room at the dark-haired beauty dressed in red, joining her in three long steps. "Oh, we've shared a call or two in the interim." He winked at Kate. "But in case you've forgotten me, I'm Daniel Lebed, best man at Matt and Mikaela's wedding. We go way back, to the day we hijacked a bald nun's wig and spent three weeks in detention. I had no idea how fortunate that friendship would prove to be."

Kate giggled softly. "I hope this hijacking occurred in grade school and not in college."

"It did, but I can assure you, things only escalated after that."

All right, you two." Mikaela handed Daniel a box. "Everyone gets an ornament to hang on the tree. I selected this one especially for you, Daniel."

Daniel wore an expression of great expectation as he rooted in the box. His smile faded into shock. "You wouldn't? You didn't?"

Mikaela struggled to maintain a straight face. "I would, and I did."

"What? What?" asked Kate. "Now I'm feeling a bit let down about my skater girl."

Daniel frowned and said, "Your skater girl probably isn't worth a thousand dollars on eBay." He pulled the Han Solo figure from the box. It hung from a silver cord.

"Mikaela . . . "

"Matt won that fair and square, DPS rules. Besides, that's one ornament that will always remind me of your devoted friendship to Matt."

"And to you. Just as steadfast."

She gave him a kiss on his cheek and he added the figure to the tree.

She checked the wall clock. "Give me ten minutes to get dressed. You can start loading the bags into the car."

Ten minutes later, she descended the stairs to an empty house, wearing the white dress she wore to her wedding. She looked at the tree and said, "I love you, Mr. Grayken." She turned and surveyed the home where she became a wife. A smile graced her lips and a tear glistened in her eye as she left the house, locked the door, and entered the backseat of the packed car.

"Are we ready?" asked Donovan, who was serving as chauffeur.

Mikaela looked at every face in the vehicle and smiled at these people she loved. "Very ready," she answered as the car pulled out of the driveway and onto the street.

As they drove, she rehearsed and rehearsed her part, until she felt certain she could get through it without crying,

Once inside, Donovan crooked his arm and smiled into her eyes.

"Thank you for arranging all of this. It's the greatest Christmas gift you could have given us."

"We needed it too. Our courthouse wedding was about friendship. Today's gathering is all about love. I'm sorry it's so private and small. None of your friends are here."

"Neither are your brothers."

She returned his compassion-filled expression with a bright smile and a squeeze on his arm. "It's the best we could do under the circumstances, but Daniel is streaming it live, so it's as if they're here."

A few of Matt's nurses slipped into the room, dressed in their scrubs, and Dr. Marcosky's intern popped in from rounds. At ten o'clock, on the dot, the chaplain looked to Mikaela, who nodded to him that it was all right to begin, and he in turn nodded to the organist, who brought the hospital chapel's organ to life. The small assembly stood, and Donovan held on tight saying, "Are you ready?"

"My knees are shaking, so no matter what, even if you have to throw me over your shoulder and carry me all the way," she pointed straight ahead, "get me down the aisle to that handsome man."

With a hearty chuckle, Donovan replied, "Will do," and with a side whisper, he added, "Even though he's adopted, I still think he gets his good looks from me."

"Definitely," Mikaela replied. "Without a doubt."

Donovan led out, and Mikaela matched him step for step,

but her eyes were set on the thin, pale man whose eyes were likewise, fixed only on her. Weak and unsteady, Matt still radiated a calm assurance as he stood by the chaplain in his rented tux. Perhaps it was in part because, for the short hour the doctor allowed, his body was free from IVs and monitors, giving him a glimpse of the future Dr. Marcosky now felt confident he would get to enjoy following next week's marrow transplant. With God's help, and Kate's gift, they were beating the odds.

And so, today, they prepared to give his parents the two gifts they most wanted—to see their son and Mikaela take their vows and to spend the first of hopefully many more Christmases together.

Unable to resist the urge to feel Matt's arms around her for the first time in many weeks, Mikaela didn't wait for Donovan to release her. She slipped from his arm two steps out, and melted against Matt, who seemed prepared for her. The guests wiped their eyes, as did the chaplain, who provided a caption to the unscripted moment.

"I think we can all understand that this moment is the fulfillment of many answered prayers for love and for health, prayers offered by parents, by family members not present today, by friends and medical staff, and of course, the many prayers raised by Matt and Mikaela."

Matt pressed his forehead to hers and said, "Thanks for sticking around and marrying me twice."

Mikaela's voice quivered as she replied, "Thank you just for sticking around."

They each understood the depth of her meaning, and with a deep breath, Mikaela stepped back, clasping his hands.

The music stopped, and the chaplain continued. "Before we begin the ceremony, Mikaela and Matt have asked me to invite you all back to Matt's room at noon for a small Christmas buffet. That will give the staff time to get Matt settled and the caterer time to set things up. And now, please bow your heads in prayer."

Mikaela grasped Matt's hands and listened intently. She had prayed for a miracle, and she counted it answered, by the wonders of medicine, by getting information to Kate, and by simply helping her and Matt hang on. She credited it all to the love and mercy of God.

When the amen sounded in the chapel, the chaplain called for everyone to be seated, and he began.

"This ceremony is a celebration of love and a recommitment to the vows Matt and Mikaela took in August. But they wanted to express them again, before all of you, because the challenging journey they've been on has changed and strengthened the bond they made, and brought a new understanding of love into their marriage.

"What is love? To the old, it is companionship, loyalty, and memories. To the young, it is excitement and physical attraction. Many liken love to a fire. It begins with kindling that ignites quickly with sparks and brightness, but a fire made of kindling requires one to constantly search for more fuel. Some couples tire of the effort, and the fire dies. But wise couples know that adding a log will make the fire endure. It may not have the same spark of kindling, but it provides warmth and light that will see them through the long nights ahead."

He picked up his Bible. "Matt and Mikaela understand this. I've looked in on them over the past four weeks, and I've seen them display the purest kind of love—service, sacrifice, patience, comfort, a willingness to submit their own will for the good of the other. In them, I see wisdom expressed in 1 Corinthians 13:

Charity suffereth long, and is kind;
Charity envieth not; charity vaunteth not itself, is not
puffed up.
Beareth all things, believeth all things, hopeth all things,
endureth all things.
Charity never faileth:

"Charity is the pure love of Christ. That's what I see in this couple. Now, Matt and Mikaela will share the vows they expressed to one another in August."

Matt and Mikaela shared their respective verses from Percy Shelley's *Love's Philosophy*, uttered only four short months ago, when they were awkward with one another, and unsure about their relationship's duration or direction. So much had changed in those months. They had suffered and triumphed enough for two lifetimes, and they were beating the odds.

At the conclusion, when their guests expected a kiss,

Catherine came forward holding two gold boxes. She handed one to Matt. He opened one, revealing a glass ornament—a decorated Christmas Tree—which he held out to her for all to see.

"Mikaela, my wedding gift to you is this little Christmas tree, representing our tree at home. For those who don't know, our Christmas tree has been up since September." The audience gave a little giggle that matched Matt's. His voice sobered once again. "You chose ornaments that inspired me to go out and live my life, and others that celebrated small victories and moments shared. You helped me see that life, no matter how long or short, is worth celebrating, and you gave me the will to fight for more. And for that, I will love you forever."

With glassy eyes, Mikaela turned to receive the other gold box from Catherine, which she opened, revealing a car ornament. She held it out and smiled at Matt.

"My wedding gift to you is a car and the promise that I'm in this journey with you for the long ride, because there's no one else in the world I want to share this life with but you."

Matt enfolded Mikaela in his arms. While his lips hovered a thread's width above hers, he pulled her close and looked into her eyes, whispering, "The road ahead could still be bumpy."

"Then you'll need a good partner, and you're in luck. I just happen to be available."

"For a hundred years or so?"

"At least, Mr. Grayken. At the very least."

"I'm going to show you the world. I love you, Mrs. Grayken."

She placed her hand along his cheek and, without a note of glibness said, "You are my world, Mr. Grayken."

He gave her a long gentle kiss that offered the promise of many more to come. Their kiss was kindling and logs, sparks and warmth, filled with light they would need for the long road ahead, but they were not fearful or wary. They had been out on a limb before, and their forever love had pulled them back.

And they trusted it would always see them through.

– THE END –

BOOKS WRITTEN AS L.C. LEWIS
Free Men and Dreamers
A sweeping series capturing the triumphs
and struggles of the first American-born
generation, and America's second
war of independence

Volume 1: *Dark Sky at Dawn*
(Best Books Finalist, USA Book News)
Volume 2: *Twilight's Last Gleaming*
(Best Books Finalist, USA Book News)
Volume 3: *Dawn's Early Light*
Volume 4: *Oh, Say Can You See?*
(2010 Whitney Award Finalist)
Volume 5: *In God is Our Trust*

BOOKS WRITTEN AS LAURIE LEWIS
Unspoken
Awakening Avery
The Dragons of Alsace Farm
(2017 RONE Award Winner, 2016 Whitney Award Finalist, 2017 New Apple Medallion Winner, BRAGG medallion
Winner.)

Sweet Water
(2017 Readers' Favorite Award)

ACKNOWLEDGMENTS

Each book is a destination on a writer's journey, and so I owe thanks to many people who've supported my personal writer's journey, leading me to *Love on a Limb*.

My husband Tom is a wonderful, patient support. Thank you, honey. I can write with some expertise on the subject of love because of you.

I have the greatest, most talented critique group. Writing, sharing, celebrating, and commiserating with them has made me a far better writer. Thank you, Beth, Lisa, Sarah, and Lisa.

Talented author, editor, and publisher, Elizabeth Petty Bentley, performed the grammatical gymnastics required to edit this book during NaNoWriMo. Beth, you amaze me. Thank you for teaching me. No more autonomous body parts. LOL.

Pam Dove is another hero for answering a panicked 911 call for an additional edit. Pam, thank you so much!

The beautiful cover was created by dear friend and talented artist Keslie Houser who labored through at least fifty mockups and changes. Thank you, Keslie!

Dr. Wayne Allgaier and his brilliant wife Vicki have beta-read nearly every one of my books. Two of the busiest people I know, they still found time to read the manuscript, do some editing, and provide feedback on the storyline. Wayne also served as the medical advisor on *Love on a Limb*. I am indebted to them for their ongoing support.

Many thanks to the LDS Beta Readers Group for allowing me to tap into their extraordinarily generous brain collective. Their feedback on the cover and blurb was so helpful!

I also am blessed with a spectacular street team, The Willowsport Crew. These ladies beta read manuscripts, provide incredible feedback on titles and covers, and they help with social media marketing. Many thanks to Laura Lewis, (not a relation except by love), Shauna Joesten, Christine Clark, Khadra Michaelsen, Pam Dove, Connie Gilbert, Michelle Mebius, Debi Paisie, Cyndy Packer, Heather Watson, Babs Hightower, and Jacklyn Good.

My greatest thanks so to you, the reader, for putting life on hold for a while, and allowing me to take you out on a limb for love.

– Laurie Lewis

ABOUT THE AUTHOR

Laurie (L.C.) Lewis is a Marylander—a weather-whining lover of crabs, American history, and the sea. She is a proud LDS wife, mother, and grandmother, and she admits to being craft-challenged, particularly lethal with a glue gun, and a devotee of sappy movies.

Love on a Limb (2017), is her tenth published novel. Laurie's other women's fiction novels include Sweet Water (2017), The Dragons of Alsace Farm (2016), Awakening Avery (2010), and Unspoken (2004), written as Laurie Lewis. Using the pen name L.C. Lewis, she wrote the five volumes of her award-winning FREE MEN and DREAMERS historical fiction series, set against the backdrop of the War of 1812: Dark Sky at Dawn (2007), Twilight's Last Gleaming (2008), Dawn's Early Light (2009), Oh, Say Can You See? (2010), and In God is Our Trust, (2011).

Her romantic suspense novel, *Leverage*, launches in February 2018. She loves to hear from readers, and she can be contacted at any of these locations.

Website: www.laurielclewis.com
VIP Readers' Club:
https://www.laurielclewis.com/newsletter
Twitter:
https://twitter.com/laurielclewis
Goodreads:
https://www.goodreads.com/author/show
1743696.Laurie_L_C_Lewis
Facebook:
https://www.facebook.com/LaurieLCLewis/
Instagram:
https://www.instagram.com/laurielclewis/
Amazon:
https://www.amazon.com/-/e/B001JPC6XY

Join my VIP Readers' Club and get
get my award-winning
The Dragons of Alsace Farm.

AN EXCERPT FROM LEVERAGE

SCHEDULED FOR FEBRUARY 2018 RELEASE

LEVERAGE

By
L. C. Lewis

The Morning of
Wednesday, June 4, 2014
Gifford Pinchot National Forest,
Washington State

Dying had been the easy part.

That truth had been proven many times over the past twenty-two years, but never clearer than today. The battle-fields and combatants had changed over the years, but Julia knew she was still very much at war. Few knew the truth about the Mogadishu incident, but while her colleagues enjoyed the privilege of rank, she had gone dark, living as a chameleon, exchanging personas and cities nearly as frequently as some replaced their toothbrush. A botanist in Jakarta. A biologist in Darfur. An American teacher in Laos. Or was it Banjar, or Riyadh? She couldn't keep the details straight anymore.

Google alerts appeared in her inbox on topics Julia Brown was monitoring, striking dagger-like fear into her heart. Her elbows fell onto the lab table and her head dropped into her hands. She was tired on a day when a lapse in vigilance could be deadly. In response, she returned to her old crutch, popping two ancient Xanax from a prescription filled twenty years ago. They were far less effective at quieting the voices, but today she needed the help, whatever help she could get.

The fatigue of the never-ending war, fought with unseen enemies around every turn, left her whiplashed from glancing over her shoulder at every twig snap or footfall from behind. She set her attention on the one constant in her life—Tallie— and the unnerving little ditty she sang to the child night after night in one third-world bed after another.

Tallie and Julia two-by-two, we've got a secret known by few.

If you come for me, we'll tell on you. If they catch us, they'll get you too.

But at twenty-two, Tallie was no longer a child amused by the ditty. Julia has also placed her in danger.

For fifteen nomadic years, Julia dragged Tallie from one forgotten corner of the world to another. Seventeen moves appeared to have rendered the weary pair untraceable, and Julia's handler eventually permitted the Browns to return to the United States and take a job as off-the-grid park rangers. They manned one of several mountain-top ecological stations situated throughout the 1.3 million forested acres of the Gifford Pinchot National Forest in Washington State. The remote location, paired with the handler's rigid cyber security perimeter of alerts and strict protocols, insulated the pair from those searching for them, so when seven years passed without incident, Julia thought they had beaten the odds. That they were safe.

And they were, until the alerts began arriving in her inbox.

Fear snaked down her spine anew as she read today's alert details. Her name had surfaced twice in the past twenty-four hours—in an USFS publication, *The Sentinel Magazine* —and in an online name database search. *Coincidence?*

Just then, as three more alerts popped up in her inbox related to the events and colleagues from that hellish 1993 day, the Spokane station's hourly news report crackled over the old radio with a mention of the most celebrated member of their military group.

"Breathe. Breathe," she ordered her body, but neither her heart nor her lungs obeyed, each going rogue, thundering like horses within her chest. In a dual assault, her eyes were glued to the word *Mogadishu* on the computer screen while her ears were attuned to the radio station's sanitized bio of her former military colleague. The knot in her throat grew with each mention of his name until she could scarcely pull a ragged breath. A third volley came when her cell phone buzzed across the lab table, flashing a name of another member of the "team." The shock zipped down her limbs and jerked through her hands, sending glass test tubes tumbling to the floor to shatter.

A pretty, tanned face poked around the edge of the doorway. Deep furrows ran between Tallie's pinched brows as her green eyes darted between the unanswered phone and the broken glass on the floor. Silently, she twisted her waist-length hair into a tan rope, tying it into a knot at the base of her neck before reaching for a dust pan and broom to sweep the shards of glass off the wooden floor. She moved with conspicuous quietness, and when the last shattered bit was in the pan, she stood to exit just as discreetly.

Julia forced a strained "thank you" through tight lips. They were the first words the pair had spoken to one another that day. Tallie stalled and glanced back over her shoulder, visibly affected by the rare courtesy. Unnerved by Tallie's study of her, Julia segued into, "Clumsy me."

There was much about Tallie that Julia didn't understand, but from childhood, she could read the girl's expressions as easily as she could read the trail of a mountain lion in the woods. Tallie was no pushover or easy sell, and her head cocked a degree to the left as she weighed her mother's comment. After several unanswered seconds, Tallie's delicate head offered a submissive nod and she returned to her own space.

Julia stared at the empty doorframe as failure picked apart her one perceived success. Try as she had, she had been a fool to believe she could raise a normal child as a fugitive.

Her self-analysis was disrupted by another call, this time from the Browns' supervisor, whose calls to her personal cell phone, enhanced by a satellite hot spot, meant it was a personal call. She had no time for this right now. Sputtering out a string of expletives, she grabbed the phone and growled, "What do you need, Louis?"

"Whoa. Never mind. It can wait. Get back to me when you can."

The worry tingeing his southern drawl brought his lean, caring face to Julia's mind. Ever since he found out she had a satellite hot spot and could receive private calls on the mountain, as opposed to the network-wide calls on the Forest Service radio, Louis's conversations had taken a more personal turn. He'd asked her out a dozen times but she had never allowed things to progress. Still, he had been the closest thing to a friend she and Tallie had. Julia knew he would be there for Tallie if the need arose.

She took a deep, calming breath. "I'm sorry. I'm kind of swamped over here."

The tension eased in his voice. "I understand, but most people would be happy to hear they're getting a departmental award."

In an instant, all the random alerts clicked into place like tumblers in a lock. The shaking in Julia's hands commenced again. "What's this about?"

"Don't make my agony worse by telling me you've already forgotten how you slaughtered all comers at the USFS picnic," teased Louis. "A man can only eat so much humble pie."

A sheen of sweat broke over Julia's body, turning to an icy chill. She caused this. All of it. At forty-six, and after decades of laying low, the pint-sized warrior saw the annual ranger games as a chance to measure the deterioration in her skills. Instead, she had won six of the ten events outright, and with the adjustments for gender, she had blown all contenders away. In a moment of pride, she had lowered her guard and led the enemy directly to her door.

"Anyway, one of the rangers told some writer for the U.S. Forest Service Bulletin and he wanted to include a piece about you for an article he was writing about diversity in the USFS."

Julia felt her heart stop and then slam against her chest. How could she have been so stupid? Every muscle and sinew in her body tensed and she raked one hand through her shortly-cropped curls as she paced. Someone had surely found her. How much time did she and Tallie have? Days? Hours? There was no way of knowing.

She nearly growled, "What did you tell him?"

Louis's voice became instantly commanding. "Wanna tell me what's really going on?"

With an ability perfected during years of practiced deception, Julia injected a forced calm, and even a touch of embarrassment into her voice. "I don't like people talking about me this way. It sounds as if my colleagues think I'm some sort of oddball or freak."

The ruse worked so well that Louis rushed in to comfort her. "No, no, no. They're proud of you, Julia. You're the best ranger we've got."

Just then, his other line rang and Louis placed her on hold to take the call. When he resumed their conversation, Julia sensed the change in his tone.

"We'll have to talk about this later. A camper called in a smoke sighting in your sector—maybe a campfire left unattended—near the barricade by the old swinging footbridge. It's nothing big yet, but that means someone purposely breached the barricade, and it could spread fast with these weather conditions. If you're too busy, I could take a run up there."

Julia feared Louis could hear the pounding of her heart through the phone. "No, it's my area. I'll take it."

"And while you're at it, could you check the old bridge and make sure the warning sign is still up? The last thing we need is some fool hiker or camper falling to his death today."

"I'll check it out and radio you when I get there."

"Roger that." His voice softened, his affection for her evident. "I worry about you, Julia. You don't seem like yourself. Let's pick up this conversation later, okay?"

The nervous chill returned as she ended the call. Instinct told her the timing and location of the fire was no coincidence. Was it all a set-up to lure her out into the open? Were they already here? So close to her home? So close to Tallie?

Her mind spun as she calculated their financial reserves. If they managed to get away undetected they would have to live cash-only for a number of years. Was there enough for that? She had managed to save some of the initial front money given her when this ruse began back in 1993, adding as much of their salaries as she could over the years. It would be tight, but doable.

She was tired of reinventing her life, a survival tactic that began the day she peered through the darkened window of the black SUV that rolled past the pitifully small funeral cadre marking her death as Lieutenant Diana Howard. The grievers were comprised of the political elite—her father's faithful cohorts. They stood like macabre columns in their black cashmere overcoats, supporting the man at the graveside of his only child. Her reported suicide seemed to have been an unbearable finale for proud Joseph Rutherford Howard. He remained just long enough after the hired preacher's remarks to cast an unceremonious handful of dirt on the coffin assigned to hold Diana's mortal remains.

Her disappointed father was her only personal mourner. No friends. No other family. No brothers-in-arms who had watched Diana's transformation from a paranoid youth, self-destructively following in her dead mother's footsteps, to a stable, decorated Army officer. Frightened little Tallie was all she had then, strapped in a car seat beside her, the evidence of her other great sin. Twenty-one lonely years passed for the lonely pair.

Julia knew she would finally have to end the charade and

tell Tallie everything. There were so many secrets, so many . . . Julia felt a dry heave rise in her throat. She knew it was time to let Tallie choose whether to run or not. It was time to finally set her free.

Julia's thinking took an immediate shift. That formidable look-the-Devil-in-the-eye expression spread over her face. Before she could think twice, her Glock 21 with a thirteen-round magazine lay in her palm—soothing, powerful, and, she hoped, dispelling any glimmer of fear or doubt. She grabbed more clips, her cell phone and satellite hot spot, her Forest Service radio, and Bluetooth earpiece. With a Kevlar vest zipped under her USFS shirt, she turned to her computer, setting the timer to initiate a total cleanse in an hour. If she was lucky, she could disarm it remotely.

If she wasn't, a flimsy lock box in the bottom drawer of her lab table held a manila envelope with five thousand dollars and banking information to a secret account. What to do about Tallie? Julia hated flying blind like this. She quickly drafted a message to Tallie and placed it in the manila envelope. Tallie was thorough. She'd break into the box and find the note—not much comfort in the timid girl's hour of need, but she doubted the girl would expect anything more.

She moved to the cabin door, intending to slip away, but the scrape and squeak of the old wood drew Tallie's attention.

"Do you need my help?" Tallie asked timidly.

Julia kept her face forward toward the aerial panorama that hovered above the forest, refusing to risk her intuitive daughter's scrutiny at this moment. Instead, she delivered her questions with Oscar-worthy detachment. "Did you finish running your half of the samples?"

"Yes."

She recognized that defensive tone in Tallie's voice, as if her very worth was being measured. "And the chromatography report? Is that finished and ready to submit?"

"I submitted it two days ago."

A wellspring of pride filled Julia's bosom. "Then take the truck and run over to the main station. Tell Louis the generator at station three is acting up. Ask him to order another."

"I could take some tools and head over there on the four-wheeler to check it out."

Julia should have anticipated that this would be her response. She needed to get Tallie where Louis could protect her. He'd be the first person to know if something went wrong today.

Julia closed her eyes and breathed in slowly to calm her voice. "No. Report the problem to Louis and let him earn his paycheck this month. Then relax by the falls for an hour." She paused and heard the silent shock over the invitation. She couldn't resist a last glimpse of her life's work, if this was to be her last. Turning, she studied the perplexed young woman standing before her in a pair of jeans, a t-shirt, and a lab coat. Even with her lightly-colored hair tumbling out of its knot, Tallie was as lovely as a shock of fresh wheat—tall, naturally beautiful, fresh, and innocent. Tallie's face and frame resembled her father's, but Julia had muscled that frame, and trained Tallie's razor-quick reflexes and mind. If she was all Julia would leave behind to mark her time upon the earth, she had done well.

"Enjoy a day off, Tallie. You've earned it. You're . . . you're a good girl."

That meager offering of affection caused tears to sting Julia's eyes at a time when she could ill afford such weakness. With an aggravated slam of the door she shut herself off from Tallie and the emotion she felt, knowing she had, in all likelihood, ruined the rare compliment for the girl.

Julia pulled the binoculars from the nail on the porch beam and surveyed the terrain, looking for any glint of reflected light, signaling that someone was doing the same in her direction. Seeing nothing, she climbed down the stairs and threw off the tarp that covered the four-wheeler before mounting the all-terrain beast. It roared as she increased the fuel feed and backed it into the clearing. Just as she headed down the mountain path she saw Tallie exit the cabin with keys dangling from her fingers. *Good girl,* she thought, as she began her descent, carefully watching the truck in her side mirrors to be sure it took the path to the main road. An uncharacteristic vulnerability washed over Julia as the distance between mother and daughter increased. She felt for her gun once more, clicked her radio on, and called Louis.

"I wasn't sure you were still talking to me."

"I'm just having a bad day, Louis. I'm sorry. Forgive me?"

She heard his chair scoot forward and envisioned him

placing his elbows on the desk, taking this request dead seriously.

"You know I'd do anything for you, Julia. Are you on the four-wheeler? Is this fire spooking you? Just hold up. I'll come right over and meet you at the site."

She heard another scoot and knew he was reaching for his hat and keys.

"No. No, Louis! Listen to me. It's nothing, just mother/daughter stuff. I've sent Tallie your way in the truck. We've both been holed up together too long and we needed a break. Look after her for me, will you? I mean, say something nice to her today, okay?"

His voice relaxed like the winding down of a toy. "Oh, I get it. Sure, sure. I don't have much parenting advice to offer, but Tallie's an adult now. You've got to expect she'll want to try her wings a bit. I'm actually happy to finally hear it."

Julia enjoyed the white noise of Louis's awkward advice as she approached the designated site. A fire was blazing in the ring with fresh logs, a sign that it was recently set. No campers or equipment were evident, bringing every hair on her neck to attention.

Julia fingered her Glock and broke Louis's conversation stream. "I'm here, Louis. This fire's fresh. I'll extinguish it and then recon the area to find the idiots who set it and left."

"Maybe I'd better head over there."

His voice was tense and protective, and once again Julia wished she had opened her life a crack to let this good man in. "Don't worry, Louis. I've got this."

"All right. Man alive, Julia, I sure hope they didn't try to cross that swinging bridge. Good grief." He groaned. "I should have been shaking someone's chain in Washington to make sure that decrepit old thing was removed by now. Check it out, will you? Let me know if the darned thing is even still hanging—"

She could imagine his elbows back on the desk and his forehead falling into his open palm, waiting to rub the frustration from his brow. She wished she were there, in his office, right now, but she had work to do.

"—on second thought, maybe I should come after all."

Julia knew if someone was waiting for her they'd remain hidden until her conversation ended, and she saw no point in delaying destiny. Not wanting to alarm Louis further, she brightened her voice and answered with assurance. "No, no. No need. These idiots are probably just looking for more wood. I'll check back in a few, okay? And remember to be extra nice to Tallie today. It's her birthday."

"It is? I thought it was in the spring."

She heard the incredulity in his voice. *Another gaffe. She couldn't keep the details straight.* She ended the call and dismounted the rig with her Glock raised.

Less than a minute passed before two men exited the brush with their hands in the air. The younger and smaller of the two eyed the gun and stopped cold, but an appreciative smile broke across the face of the larger, sixty-ish man when Julia's Glock angled his way.

He maintained steady eye-contact with her and slowly lowered his hands. "Just as formidable as ever, I see."

Though age had altered his appearance somewhat, the flat, red scar that marred the entire left side of his face made his identity unmistakable. It was a symbol of their shared past and it caused every nerve in Julia's body to twitch in preparation for a fight.

"Why are you here?" she challenged. "I've kept my side of our agreement."

"It's good to hear you're still a team player."

The indignity of the comment left her weak-kneed and dazed. "How dare you suggest otherwise after all I've sacrificed?"

"We've both suffered because of your choices. I just needed to be sure where you stand. You've gotten sloppy . . . drawn too much attention to yourself. It's time to move you again."

Her jaw tightened. "It's not just me. Our high-profile friend deserves a portion of the blame." Julia's head jerked in the direction of the other man. "And who's your flunky?"

"He knows only what he needs to know. He's here to clean up your mistakes, so how about cutting him a break? Put the gun down."

The silent air echoed with snap of twigs as her feet shifted. *Think, think, think, Julia!* She held her gun steady as her eyes darted between the men. "What about Tallie? I can't just pick up and move her like before. She's not a child anymore, Major. She'll have questions."

The man's face softened at the mention of Tallie. "How much does she know?"

Julia wanted to laugh out loud, but a sarcastic snicker was all that escaped her disciplined lips. "She knows nothing. We've done a fine job of seeing to that, now haven't we?"

The man's hands curled into fists and then his finger jutted forward as he glared. "I'm the closest thing you've got to a knight in shining armor, remember? And let's not forget who started this mess."

The pounding in her temples returned at the reminder of her part in the cover up. But the retired officer had his own secrets—secrets Julia could expose. He had also as much as admitted he believed Tallie knew nothing and posed no threat. It was Julia they feared—Julia, and what she could reveal to the world.

"Don't worry about Tallie," the scarred man said. "It's all been arranged. She'll be told that you two were referred for a special environmental program for the Department of Defense . . . one that requires a transfer to the DOD with sensitive clearances. We'll explain that she needs to work undercover with a new identity."

Julia noted the concern that tinged his voice at the mention of Tallie. "*Undercover?* She'll never buy that. She's a savvy twenty-two-year-old who works for the U. S. Park Service. Forest Rangers don't go *undercover!*"

"You'd better hope she buys it," he growled back. "We're thinking of her."

"You don't know anything about *her*. *I* hardly know her. What if she chooses not to go?"

Julia was just as concerned about her own ability to switch lives again. The strain of the intrigue, bearable in her younger years, now seemed too onerous. She was tired, no longer possessing the wherewithal to fabricate and maintain a new identity, and she didn't want to face Tallie's questions. Julia knew it was time for an exit plan.

The note to Tallie, left in the lab table drawer, was a vague enough goodbye to cover even this eventuality, and convinced that Tallie would be all right, Julia focused on her own escape and survival. She'd hidden away a little escape fund, buried in a secret cache on the mountain. It wasn't much, but enough to get her to somewhere secluded and buried deep. Now to slip away before Scarface saw her as a threat to be eliminated.

She almost wished this pair had come armed so she could shoot them and call it self-defense. If she were unscrupulous, two bullets would still end her problems, but her conscience required better of her. "Daughter of a murderer" was not a title she would also brand onto Tallie. The girl would have enough to deal with if everything came out.

While her old "friend" gestured impatiently for her to follow him, she discretely scanned the periphery for some advantage she could exploit.

"Hurry up. You've been a pain in my neck for over twenty years. We've got a lot of work to do and very little time to accomplish it. I need you and Tallie on a plane in four hours."

Julia feigned cooperation by lowering her gun, hanging her head, and nodding her agreement. The smaller man slumped in relief, and then turned back towards the trail, but he was not her problem—Scarface was, and he was unwilling to move until Julia closed the gap.

"Move it, Julia," he said, gesturing for her to hurry to him.

She backed up, wanting more than anything to slap the sly grin off her nemesis's scarred cheek. Clearly aggravated, he headed her way with his hand outstretched like a claw as Julia's phone began to ring. She looked at the screen and hid the relief unleashed within her when Louis's number appeared there.

"It's my supervisor. I'm late reporting to him. He might already be on his way here."

Scarface blew out an aggravated rush of air. "Get rid of him and make it quick."

Julia knew these would likely be the last words she'd ever say to Louis, and likely the last chance to get a message to Tallie. "Hey," she answered cheerily, rushing on before he could say a word. "Everything's under control here. The fire's out. I'll be heading down soon."

She started to cut the call off when Louis's voice replied, "Glad to hear it. Tallie's here. She says you weren't yourself today."

Scarface slid his hand across his throat and pointed to his watch. Julia was tired of threats and bullying. She raised an eyebrow at Scarface and muted the call. "I'm being ripped away from the only friend I've had in twenty years. Give me a minute, or with one word I'll have this area crawling with rangers. You choose."

She drilled a glare into Scarface, doubling down on her bluff to bring in witnesses. Panic and fury crossed his face as he turned around and backed up a few steps. Julia had won the point, but she had not been a team player. She could see it in his eyes. She was now a nuisance. Perhaps a liability. She couldn't think clearly, but escape appeared to be her only option, and she had a plan.

Louis was repeatedly calling Julia's name when she turned off the mute. She slipped the keys from her pocket and concluded the call. "Trust me, Louis. I know what I'm doing. Give Tallie a big hug for me. Let's meet at the Trappers' Shack Café in fifteen. I'm suddenly hungry for something decadent." *Click.*

As she pushed the phone deep into her pocket, she knew the affection in the message would send up a host of red flags to love-starved Tallie. Louis and Tallie would dissect the rest of her message and see the oddities the rendezvous at a place she detested ... the suggestion that a health food devotee like she was ever hungry for something decadent. When she proved to be late, they'd rush here where, if all went well, they'd find nothing but her keys which they'd eventually use to open the drawer that would explain things to Tallie. If the situation went awry, they'd at least find her body quickly.

Scarface turned his back to shield his burning match from

the mountain breeze as he lit his cigarette. In that moment, Julia raised her gun and blasted repeatedly into a large dead limb spread above his head. He jerked and crouched as leaves and wood chips rained down upon him, and before he could escape, the limb fell, knocking him to the ground.

Julia dropped her keys, turned, and sprinted two hundred yards towards the old hanging bridge. The span was fairly short, only forty feet or so, strung over the deep gorge decades previous. After Mount St. Helens erupted, the number of guests visiting the area increased substantially, warranting the construction of a new metal bridge a few hundred yards down the path. For safety reasons, the old span had been closed to the public, but she felt confident the weakened ropes and slats would bear her tiny frame while completely preventing Scarface from following.

To Julia's shock and surprise, the retired officer recovered quickly, though he was checking his head for blood as he chased after her. Julia reached the bridge before he had even cleared the tree line, stopping short as she reached the warning sign posting the danger of crossing at this point. The dilapidated condition of the ropes caused her to rethink her plan, but Scarface emerged from the tree line, and she darted midway onto the bridge.

Her pursuer read the sign and called out to her as he extended his hand her way. "Why did you attack me? I'm just playing by the rules you set in motion years ago."

"Why should I trust you?"

"Julia, remember who you're talking to. We've both had

the power to destroy one another for years. If I wanted you dead, we wouldn't be having this conversation."

Her paranoia eased enough to accept that he had come to honor an old promise. Nothing more. Julia met his gaze for several long seconds. "I'm sorry. I can't do it anymore. I want out."

He rubbed his fingers deep into his eyes and sighed long and low. "You know as well as I that there is no complete out now. Diana is dead. Tallie will need some explanation. The secret controls all of us to some extent, I'm afraid, but we'll find a way to make it bearable. Just come back in. Please." He stretched further in her direction.

She felt a shake, and then a rapid jerk as the brittle left upper line attached to the rock wall broke, leaving only one other upper and two lower lines remaining. Scarface shouted and drew up close, reaching as far as he could for her. "Hurry, Julia. Hurry!"

She barely weighed one hundred and twenty pounds, though the bridge groaned under her feet as if she were double that. Julia quickly scanned the lines to see where the next breach was likely to occur, and she saw the spot. It was the right lower line, three feet from land. The ancient, decayed rope was so frayed it looked like a brush, and she stood spellbound, as piece after piece flayed loose from the connected line.

She inched forward and the pieces broke faster with each shift of a foot, then she looked at Scarface and shook her head. "I'm not going to make it."

"Don't say that. You *can* do it! Just try. Please . . . just try."

Julia heard the pleading in his voice, and finally she understood what her choices had cost this man. As the casualties had mounted over the years, she had wondered if protecting these secrets would all be worth the cost. Now, she would never know. She took a deep breath in preparation for another step, feeling another violent lurch as the frayed lower rope broke free. Julia clenched the remaining upper rope, determined to hold on, while dancing her feet along the remaining lower line in the hopes of finding some support there. There was a momentary calm as she hung by a literal thread above the jagged trees in the gorge. Looking at her horrified former colleague, she quietly said, "Go. There's nothing you can do. If you get caught here it will all have been for nothing."

She watched a sorrowful acceptance slacken his face. His outstretched hand lowered as he offered a few words of comfort. "I'll watch out for Tallie."

She still wasn't sure she could trust him, but there was nothing more she could do now. The die was cast. But she could still influence the way the game would play out.

Julia jerked her head right, gesturing for him to go and leave her alone. With a final nod, he turned and walked away without looking back. She knew one more detail needed to be attended to, and closing her eyes, she prayed for time enough to complete the task. She looped her left arm over the rope, nestling it under her armpit while her right hand fished in her pocket for her phone. She shoved it back into her pocket when the last lower rope broke, gasping in pain as the lifeline cut into her armpit, dangling her one hundred fifty feet above the toothpicked terrain. Once again, she fished the mobile device out. This time she managed to bring up the contact screen. Another lurch told her the threads of this final line were ripping apart, and mere seconds remained. Clenching the phone in her right hand, her left sorted through the short list to a contact designated by the initials E. N. D. where a drafted message was saved and ready to be sent. Her right index finger was poised above the send button as the last line broke. Clenching her arm to her body like a vice, she pushed the button, then dropped the phone.

Like Tarzan on a vine, she swung forward, slamming into the gorge wall where she began to slide down the rope, its fibers slashing through the fabric of her shirt, biting into her armpit as her hands grasped to get a hold and stop her descent. Bloodied hands, bloodied arm, then searing, tearing muscle. She wanted the pain to stop, so she kicked away from the earthen wall, spread her arms wide, and let her battered body free fall towards the greenery and rocks far below.

– *Scheduled for February 2018 release*

www.ingramcontent.com/pod-product-compliance
Lightning Source LLC
Chambersburg PA
CBHW070534260626
47161CB00002B/385